ALSO BY ANN BEATTIE

ONLOOKERS

Stories

ANN BEATTIE

SCRIBNER

New York   London   Toronto   Sydney   New Delhi

Scribner
An Imprint of Simon & Schuster, Inc.
1230 Avenue of the Americas
New York, NY 10020

First Scribner hardcover edition July 2023

SCRIBNER and design are registered trademarks of The Gale Group, Inc.,
used under license by Simon & Schuster, Inc., the publisher of this work.

For information about special discounts for bulk purchases,
please contact Simon & Schuster Special Sales at 1-866-506-1949
or business@simonandschuster.com.

The Simon & Schuster Speakers Bureau can bring authors to your
live event. For more information or to book an event,
contact the Simon & Schuster Speakers Bureau at 1-866-248-3049
or visit our website at www.simonspeakers.com.

Interior design by Kyle Kabel

Manufactured in the United States of America

1   3   5   7   9   10   8   6   4   2

Library of Congress Cataloging-in-Publication Data

Names: Beattie, Ann, author. Title: Onlookers : stories / Ann Beattie.
Description: First Scribner hardcover edition. | New York : Scribner, 2023. |
Summary: "Onlookers is a story collection about people living in the same Southern
town whose lives intersect in surprising ways"—Provided by publisher.
Identifiers: LCCN 2022061603 | ISBN 9781668013656 (hardcover) | ISBN 9781668013670 (ebook)
Subjects: LCSH: Southern States—Fiction. | LCGFT: Short stories.
Classification: LCC PS3552.E177 O55 2023 | DDC 813/.54—dc23/eng/20230105
LC record available at https://lccn.loc.gov/2022061603

ISBN 978-1-6680-1365-6
ISBN 978-1-6680-1367-0 (ebook)

For Jay and Devon

CONTENTS

PEGASUS

Definitely not the strangest situation, but somewhat unusual. Since February, Ginny has lived with her fiancé Darcy's father, a lovely man, retired, a doctor. His profession alone didn't explain how he'd assembled (as he put it) his "kingdom." During Bill Clinton's presidency, he began investing in real estate, as well as the stock market. He knew Clinton. Slightly. He still donated generously to the Democratic Party. He'd once held a fundraiser in support of Hillary at his home on Rugby Avenue. Actually, that was his former home. After his wife's death he moved to Ivy, into a smaller, still rather grand house with a Juliet balcony off his bedroom and stained glass panels depicting the seasons hung in the den's windows. Ginny didn't know the doctor when he was more politically active, but he'd shown her photographs taken the day of the fundraiser for Hillary. At the last minute, though, Hillary had sent one of her personable assistants, so no one could be too cross with her. Ginny had scrutinized the photographs. The brass, oval ice bucket (no longer on display) was large enough to bathe the dog; that day, it was filled with champagne bottles ("Prosecco," the doctor always corrected her). There'd apparently been two drink coolers, though one had been ruined when the doctor's wife threw it at a possum nosing through their trash.

Ginny now knew many things about the couple's life, because any question about where something came from turned into an occasion for the doctor to reminisce. ("She always reached for whatever was handy. One time she banged a picture hanger into the living room wall with a Le Creuset pan.")

Of course, when Ginny met the doctor, she had no idea she'd ever live with him. They were introduced pre-Covid, after her third date with Darcy (though that date lasted for two days). Afterwards, she'd decided to leave Brooklyn and move to Charlottesville, into the apartment Darcy rented on Altamont Street. She'd questioned whether it was wise to start living together so soon, though she justified it by telling herself that she'd liked the town a lot, during the time she'd lived there previously (she agreed with Darcy that it was much changed), and she had a good friend in town. Darcy had convinced her the move wasn't crazy because they'd had such an immediate connection, and (she had to agree) everything they did was fun. He'd persuaded her by doing a great imitation of Christopher Walken (he knew it was good, though in his opinion, everyone could do him). His impersonation had Walken saying things like "Young love was meant to be." So they'd put her possessions in a van (they were now being stored in her friend Jeanette's basement); she'd sold her books to the Strand; she'd donated most of her clothes to an organization one of her roommates worked for, which sent them to Haiti. The other roommate had called her selfish for walking out on them with no notice. The last few minutes in the living room, with one roommate crying and the other cursing her, as Darcy lowered his eyes and carried out her two suitcases, had been traumatic.

Then (sprinkle of Tinker Bell's wand), she was elsewhere.

Darcy's apartment occupied half a floor of a two-story 1920s house. The owner's son and his teenage son lived on the ground floor; Mildred and her daughter lived next door on the second floor, on the flip side of the kitchen wall. Mil's daughter, painfully shy, thin, with unruly hair no product could subdue, went out only to go to church. Soon after meeting Ginny, Mil hinted, more than once, that they should invite her daughter over for "sweet tea." (They had. Once.) Mil's age—her daughter must have been at least fifty—reinforced Ginny's sense that she was living in a time warp. It didn't seem like she was in the real world: no one rushed around; if anyone laid on their car horn, it was because they were dead; neighbors paused to talk to each other every time they met. Norman Rockwell couldn't have invented a more neighborly place. On their street, there was even a special greeting: Instead of raising a hand, both men and women flapped one hand animatedly. She'd never seen anything like it. Her first day there, she'd discovered rosemary growing as a hedge! It was the scent that drew her attention. Soon afterwards, she'd stopped abruptly when she saw the size of the mint field that spread, untended (mint liked that), amid another neighbor's scraggly rhododendrons and azaleas. Even Mil's daughter hadn't known it grew wild there (she liked mint, but rosemary "stank"). Ginny tried to remember to make excessive hand movements when she encountered someone.

But what paradise, however odd, lasts? Soon thereafter, Darcy decided not to renew his lease at the much higher rent. They should have known something was up when two men with ladders arrived early one morning and shutters were put on the house. Their parting gesture had been to sand, then paint the front door pale yellow, adding a pineapple-shaped brass knocker. Darcy's mouth twisted as he read the letter from the landlord (he lived in Norfolk, but the son and his son had both averted their eyes when they encountered Ginny and Darcy, as soon as the renovations began). The neighborhood had become too noisy, Darcy complained. He no longer liked living downtown—and what was with raising the rent? What was Mil going to do? The whole area too often reminded him of the 2017 Unite the Right rally in what was then called Lee Park, just blocks away. Heather Heyer had died when a car driven by a twenty-year-old from Ohio plowed into the crowd of counterprotestors. Darcy hadn't been there, but he spoke as if he had. He was a Yale graduate who'd majored in acting. When he returned from Japan—assuming the virus was ever brought under control—the two of them intended to go house hunting. Charlottesville real estate prices were rocketing skyward, with buyers bidding above asking price for houses in Belmont the day they were listed. Darcy and Ginny were considering Staunton, or perhaps Lexington. Meanwhile—though she still felt the loss of it—other people lived in the sunny, lovely old apartment, while she'd moved in with the doctor, and Darcy remained in Tokyo, acting the part of Brutus on YouTube, hoping the American Shakespeare Theater of Tokyo would reopen before he left the country, so that just once he could perform in front of a live audience.

Ginny hadn't protested when Darcy was invited to become part of the just-assembled troupe, largely American, with one actor from Denmark and another from Berlin (the son of one of Darcy's teachers at Yale, who'd helped get the whole thing going), as well as several Japanese actors—one of whom was featured in a full-page Bottega Veneta ad in the *New York Times* fashion magazine. Initially, the plan had been for Darcy to go to Tokyo and get settled ("What did he think that meant, buy two tatami mats?" the doctor asked Ginny); then she could sublet the apartment and join him. In that time before everyone began to sequester—now it seemed either like yesterday, or like long-ago life in a vanished world—Ginny had felt she couldn't object, because they were both committed to working at things they loved. This was something the doctor grudgingly agreed with—grudging only in the sense that he thought inherited money rotted people's souls, but there it was. His own father's second wife had surprised the whole family: Though the old man had excluded all of them from inheriting anything in his will, opting instead to support his wife and his stepchildren, she'd nevertheless slipped Darcy fifty thousand dollars—and what a miracle it was that none of the doctor's other children knew it. So, yes, okay, try out whatever it is that you love, but don't overindulge just because you've got the means to do so, was the doctor's attitude. ("My god, my father remarried at eighty-one—that's unusual enough—but he found himself a woman with scruples. Maybe not a sense of fairness and equality, no, but it seemed she'd passed up a chance to go to the Royal Academy of Dramatic Arts herself, so she did make a generous gesture to *one* of her stepgrandsons.")

Dr. Robert Boyd Anderson (Robbie, to friends) was nearly seventy, and had not practiced medicine for the last three years. He had one daughter, Cassie, a BoA bank officer in Memphis, who lived with her husband, a CPA. Cassie had been an only child until she was five, when the twins (whom she still resented) were born: red-haired, round-faced boys with a permanent blush. Next came handsome Darcy (yes, as in Mr. Darcy). Their mother had been a much beloved teacher of English at Tandem, though she left when she became pregnant with Darcy. Her final child, Dante (yes), was born two years, two months after Darcy. She'd nearly died when she developed gestational diabetes during the pregnancy, but she'd died instead from a heart attack during a game of croquet the summer before Dante entered fourth grade.

When Ginny first fell in love with Darcy, she'd been delighted to learn he had a sister. She'd always wanted a sister—though, as Darcy had warned her, "You might not want this one." Cassie was as he'd described her: beautiful; energetic (a euphemism for manic, in the doctor's opinion); self-assured; willful. She now kept a shrine to her mother in her guest bedroom where Darcy and Ginny had stayed on their Meet the Family visit to Memphis. (The tour had also ended there, as the twins were too busy to fly in, and Dante never answered his phone or returned messages.) It was during this time ("It's our courtship!" Darcy said, channeling Christopher Walken) that Ginny learned of the doctor's wife's diary (on its cover, she'd neatly filled in her name: Anita Elizabeth Granger Anderson) which, when Cassie discovered it after her mother's death, she had photocopied in its entirety, highlighting passages that she insisted made clear her mother's love for other women before giving a copy to everyone in the family, including the doctor.

Ginny hadn't known what to make of it when she'd seen Darcy's copy: Anita had written such things as *Shopping with Edith, such joy!* or mentioned her first-ever dip in a hot tub, *Naked, no doubt with more female observers than on the day I was born!* This diary was one of the things Cassie was still discussing with her therapist. At her home in Memphis, her mother's vanity table sat inside a shallow closet ("What about the significance of putting it in there, huh?" Ginny had asked Darcy). Anita's Chanel No. 5 had been placed atop a white doily; the ebony-handled brush, bristles up, was thick with wisps of Anita's dark hair. Cassie said she sniffed the brush before going to bed. Apparently, she ignored the perfume. Her mother's wedding portrait, framed in cardboard, had been added to the display, as had her knitting needles, splayed in a vase like flowers—though it seemed likely those would have been kept elsewhere. Robbie very much hoped one of his children would bestow his late wife's name on a child. So far his daughter had produced none. Neither had the others, with the exception of two girls sired by Dante, the first conceived during his third year of high school, the other by a flight attendant with whom he'd had a one-night stand in a Holiday Inn near Logan Airport, where he'd been bitten by bedbugs. He'd been given no say in the naming of either child, and his father had paid the flight attendant a lot of money to go away, as well as giving her his year-old BMW ("The better to make her exit").

Topics always to be avoided with Robbie were: Dante's first shrink, who'd temporarily converted him to the Bahá'i Faith, before he himself had a breakdown; Dante's debts; Anita's diary ("No respect for privacy! The children set upon those photocopies like they'd found the Holy Grail"); the beagle mix's age; Cassie's husband's regrettable interest in illegal big-game hunting ("Covid put an end to that, since the Africans couldn't"), and in paintball.

Some days, Robbie pretended Ginny was Anita. He liked to call her by his late wife's name. He used her given name in public. He'd say, "Allow me to introduce Ginger Katherine 'Ginny' Worth, my lovely daughter-in-law"—he was rushing that, though it was only a technicality. He'd said this during the winter to old ladies in leggings, North Face fleece jackets in solemn shades of green or blue, and ballet flats, running, masked, in or out of Foods of All Nations. No doubt some of these women had been his wife's friends. Anita might have sat among them at St. Paul's on Sundays, or golfed with them at the country club, or—if you believed Cassie—had affairs with them. Ginny often asked about the things in the doctor's house, but rarely inquired how he knew someone, though sometimes a woman would linger long enough for her to find out: "When Anita and I were at Hollins," or, "Did you know my sister's moving back to town, Dr. Anderson, and she's missed your book group all these years, so you might ought expect a call!" ("I'm not much of a reader anymore, as my short-term memory isn't what it used to be," he'd replied, averting his eyes in that recognizable way, as if the prettiest girl had asked him to dance when he had a sprained ankle.)

With one notable exception, Ginny didn't think his short-term memory was worse than anyone else's his age, though he disagreed: "I'll be lucky if I remember to come to your wedding."

But he had gotten lost recently, just days before. Robbie had driven off to rendezvous with an intern at the hospital, but had gotten the day wrong. He'd driven to the parking lot of Foods— their café was serving takeout coffee, but metal tables were set up outside, now that the weather was mild, and they were very popular—then he must have walked out of the parking lot. He became confused because new, tall buildings near the underpass obscured familiar landmarks. He'd eventually gone inside one and found a Coke machine. He had enough change to buy a can, after which, refreshed, he'd asked someone for directions to the old hospital on Jefferson Park Avenue. Outside, he'd turned in the wrong direction again, then had no idea where to go, "other than avoiding the ramp to Route 250, which apparently has become a rocket launch." A friend of Cassie's who recognized him pulled to the side of Old Ivy Road to see if he was okay ("There are great advantages to small-town life, though this is hardly that, any longer"). Since he had no memory of where he'd left his car—that was bad—Cassie's friend had driven him home and stayed until

Ginny opened the door. She'd been painting her toenails. She'd hobbled to the peephole with cotton balls separating her toes. There she'd stood, at noon, wearing the sweatsuit she'd slept in, topped by her favorite sweater from Orvis, her drying hair coiled into two big waves, fastened with long bobby pins. She'd been aware that her present look conjured up Princess Leia.

"Anita," he'd said contritely, "I've been away too long."

TODAY SHE WAS INDULGING Robbie by helping him strategize about keeping his failing memory secret from the family. The family was extensive (at first he'd said "expensive," which had made perfect sense to Ginny, before he corrected himself), though Ginny and he agreed that he needed only one slightly philosophical, bemused little set speech, that he should keep it simple. It was his opinion that all his children were perceptive, though otherwise lackadaisical. Dante was the only exception to his children's being "tightly wound." In no way could Robbie benefit from their worry, only suffer it.

She assured him she wouldn't say anything to Darcy. She reminded him of what a helpful clue he'd provided, remembering that he'd parked just past "the lampshade store." She'd gotten a ride to the Foods of All Nations parking lot when her friend Jeanette got off work. They'd ridden there, both double-masked, windows down. His Saab had been parked just about where she expected to find it, not easy to see at first, wedged between SUVs. What she'd taken to be a ticket clamped under the windshield wiper turned out to be a flyer advertising a "Carries Out Only" restaurant. (Later, she and Robbie had had a laugh about that.) She'd returned home, as proud to be returning his car as a child holding up her drawing. Ginny made light of his mistake by telling him that she'd once borrowed a car and gone grocery shopping and driven back to her Brooklyn apartment without putting the bag in the trunk. It had still been in the parking lot when she returned. A pigeon had pecked open a bag of beet chips ("Never heard of them. I'd like to give them a try"). The bird had almost been brave enough to continue eating when she coasted to a stop, but when she opened the car door it had flown off with a great beating of wings. She'd felt sure that if the pigeon had been dexterous enough, it would have flashed her the evil eye over its shoulder. ("A *shoulder*? I'm not an ornithologist, but I remember a bit about bird anatomy!")

She liked talking to Robbie. She felt she could tell him almost anything. If she found something confusing, he enjoyed agreeing vociferously, before providing a reasonable, reassuring answer. Also, they often ended up laughing. She confessed to him that when she was a teenager, she'd shoplifted. ("Books about vengeful birds, was it?") He said he routinely doubled the amount he actually dropped in the church collection plate when providing figures to his accountant. She told him that as a six-year-old, she'd discovered her Christmas present in November, then faked surprise on Christmas Day. He said he'd knowingly accepted another man's raincoat from the coat check person at the Boar's Head Inn on a windy, rainy night (two days later, "not the next day, mind you," suffering remorse, he'd returned it). So many days, there was worrisome news about Covid. Winter dragged on. After dinner, it became their routine to watch Gabriel Byrne in *In Treatment* on the television in the den, with a screen no larger than the small antique mirror in the guest bathroom. Other times they watched *Poirot*, whose solutions she often had trouble understanding; afterwards, Robbie would patiently explain who'd killed whom and why. Her real interest was in hearing the theme song and seeing the same opening, night after night: David Suchet, one arm bent behind his back, walking mincingly in his dandyish shoes.

The twins, who worked for Microsoft in Seattle, were busy and rarely in touch with their father, though at Christmas one had sent a small LED light on an adjustable headband from Amazon, and the other had sent an arrangement from a local florist that consisted primarily of red anthurium and pinecones. His daughter sometimes typed brief letters and included photographs of her flowering trees and bushes, but rarely called. Darcy sent separate messages to his father and to Ginny (hers often included naked, priapic men he'd drawn with the help of some app—surely there weren't emojis for *that*). To both Ginny and his father he embedded links showing the various approaches he took when enacting the role of Brutus. He had so many followers on YouTube! If Dante phoned at all, it was at odd hours. He tended to call his father Bobby (Robbie had summoned Ginny to the landline and handed her the phone, saying afterwards, "There's nothing wrong with my hearing, do you believe me now?").

Once—to be honest, twice—Robbie had told Ginny he'd received calls from his wife; naturally, she assumed he must have been dreaming, but he insisted that they'd been actual calls. Robbie felt sure that eventually she'd be able to listen in, since they were filled with long pauses on the other end; so far, no calls had come in when she was home ("She's got good instincts about when you're gone"). He swore her to silence because he knew his children would pity him for not accepting that their mother was gone. Ginny had tried to remain noncommittal ("I know what you're thinking—that I've watched too much Alfred Hitchcock"). The doctor did not much like telling other people what was obvious, especially because he believed he was more intelligent than most. "Does Anita know about Covid?" Ginny had managed, after he mentioned the second call. She hadn't exactly been kidding—she meant to imply that his anxiety might have led him to misinterpret whatever the calls were—but he'd taken her to task for joking. In the first call, Anita had spoken to him from a garden. Her voice had been faint, but insistent. "A request?" Ginny asked. He'd pondered: well, Anita had discussed the advantages of annuals versus perennials in a way that made him sure she was speaking, if not in code, metaphorically. Her wispy voice faded in and out, though he'd instantly understood that she could do no better. But, oh yes: she'd wanted to know who Ginny was. She'd also said—as she had when she was alive—that they should have stopped after having Cassie and the twins. ("I'm sorry if that's distressing, Ginny; I realize that would mean you couldn't be affianced to Darcy.")

Anita had mocked him during the second call by saying that one's spawn did not prove one's virility. Maybe Dante wasn't even his, she'd suggested. She'd never said *that* before. On this call, he'd heard what sounded like merry-go-round music in the background ("Relentless. Too fast").

Ginny returned from her 8 p.m. Pilates class off the downtown mall (masked; skylights open; six feet between mats) only moments after he hung up from the third, most recent call. Anita had mentioned the garden again, then recited something (he searched for the right words) "poetically pretty"—she'd rhymed "rude" with "solitude." Ginny Googled "poem, garden, rude, solitude" and found it immediately ("Yes! That's it!")—but what of it? Though Anita *had* taught literature. Darcy's theory was that his father needed the calls, so he'd invented them. More likely (Darcy couldn't resist snideness, which was not a good trait), it had been a telemarketer coming down with laryngitis. He couldn't take it seriously. There was no afterlife (Darcy only attended church on Christmas Eve to keep the peace). But he didn't dismiss Pascal's wager, so if he *might* be wrong, why not assume his mother was in the afterlife, smoking her pastel Nat Sherman cigarettes through her cigarette holder inlaid with mother-of-pearl, their old dog, Sandy, curled at her feet instead of lolling her tongue while seated on bony haunches, like Blanche DuBois, the beagle. Darcy tried to change the subject: How was the dog? Leaving aside the old man's delusion, how was his father doing, confined so much to the house?

"Okay," she mumbled, sounding to herself like a reluctant teenager.

"Not a line of questioning you enjoy," Darcy said. "Understood. How's your job hunt—did the position at the library open up?"

"No one's hiring," she said. "Everything's on hold."

"That gives you time to work on your novel."

"That tone of voice sounds very condescending, Darcy."

Touchy, touchy! He tossed the ball back in her court: "If you won't let me read even the first page, how can it seem real to me?"

He was giving her good advice, in the voice of Jack Nicholson, when the call dropped. She'd called Verizon twice about this problem. They weren't scheduling any appointments; you couldn't go to a store. She'd done everything the tech person had instructed her to do during their previous call: at the top of her screen, two bars out of four were darkened, which could have been better but should have been *enough*; they didn't live in the boonies; the iPhone 11 had been her birthday present from Robbie. The doctor was quite right to have kept his reliable landline, even though he'd capitulated and now also had a cell phone.

Darcy didn't call back. She hated the phone, she was thinking, as Robbie cleared his throat before tapping on the den's doorframe. She'd left the door ajar. A streetlight had come on and illuminated two of the stained glass panels. One was of spring: stars glittered above willow trees as a woman in a wide-brimmed hat and apron carried her multicolored basket across a green lawn, the basket spilling branches of forsythia and what might have been peonies. The other was the least interesting panel, autumn: several women bent low in a field, gleaning. She'd never heard the word before, but she understood what the title meant, in a general sense, by its context. Robbie had explained to her that all the glasswork was based on famous paintings—the autumn panel, inspired by a painter named Millet.

Now, he cleared his voice histrionically.

"Yes, Robbie?"

"Did I get lost today?" he asked, peeking in, but remaining in the hallway.

"Not that I know of. Do you think you did?"

"Was that my wife?"

"Your son, but the call got dropped," she said sulkily.

"Did you secretly get married before he went to Japan?"

Blanche, sighing deeply under the weight of too many chains and charms and a too-thick collar, appeared and plopped down at Robbie's feet. She seemed to lose her balance, rather than intentionally settling herself there. It was her burden in life to accompany him everywhere.

"Why do you ask?"

"Because Will Carmody said he saw you back when everybody could still go out. You and Darcy were at Orzo, drinking champagne."

"That wasn't us," she said. "No, we're not married."

"Because if you were, I'd like a dance with the bride. That's a well-established ritual: to dance with your father-in-law."

She softened. She rose from her favorite chair. "I don't know why we have to wait. Let me put on some music." (He still kept his LPs and his turntable in the den; he was always happy if she played an actual record.) "We'll have a dance."

"How about something by 'Walk on By,' you know, Dionne Warwick. How about my remembering that, huh? Let's put on her other song, though: 'Don't Make Me Over.' That was playing at the dentist's the other day. Hygienist had never heard of it, let alone the upbeat, I guess you'd say 'upbeat,' Muzak version. 'Now that I'd do an-y-thing for you,' he sang in falsetto, planting his feet some distance apart, opening his arms as he hovered at her side. He often took her aback. In his own way, he was more uninhibited than his children—and, leaving aside Dante, that was saying something. "Oh, you don't really want to dance. It's, what is it"—he consulted his Swatch, on a neon-green band—"nearly eleven. My god, I used to turn in before now. Had to."

"I don't see Dionne Warwick," she said, flipping. The records were kept in an old wooden box stamped *Perry Brothers Seeds*.

"I think it's there," he said, "but I think a lot of deranged things."

"You aren't deranged."

"Oh, all you girls know how to flatter me."

She picked up her phone and tapped the microphone icon. "Dionne Warwick, 'Don't Make Me Over,'" Ginny said.

There it was. She selected the first YouTube video, pressed the play arrow, and thumbed up the volume. Blanche DuBois scrambled up as the doctor walked toward Ginny, arms again extended. "I'm beggin' you," Dionne Warwick sang to the ceiling from her position on the chair cushion, where Ginny had tossed the phone.

On "Accept me for the things that I do," Blanche tried to wedge herself between the doctor's legs and Ginny's. They'd been swaying, lost in the music. He smelled of Neutrogena. Ginny opened her eyes. "Do you want to get in on this, girl?" Robbie asked. "I'd scoop her up if I could," he said, grinning.

"She's jealous! Look at her!" Ginny said as the doctor bent to scratch Blanche's ruff, setting her doggie information tinkling, as the song concluded.

"We saw Dionne Warwick sing that at the Rainbow Room with some famous fellow," Robbie said. "Anita might not have gotten her diamond earrings soon enough, but never did I fail to celebrate an anniversary. Have you even heard of the Rainbow Room?"

"Of course I have. In Rockefeller Center. Look!" she said, picking up the phone. She turned it toward him so he could see the screen: dollhouse-sized Dionne Warwick and Burt Bacharach clasping hands, walking forward, smiling intensely, to the appreciative applause of the crowd.

"Will you look at that!" he said, the tip of his nose almost touching the screen. "Jeffrey Epstein!"

"What? Are you kidding? It's Burt Bacharach."

"It's not the one who hung himself?"

"It's pretty obvious he was murdered," she said. "The cameras were—"

"Horrible. Every aspect of it," Robbie said, slightly breathless. "Can't imagine what will happen, with the queen's favorite child—so they say—being sought by the authorities. Posing with that young girl. You have to wonder if the queen was spared that. Don't think they can extradite a prince, or whatever he is, but you never know." He was muttering either to her, or to Blanche; in either case, Blanche was much more receptive, wagging her tail. He leaned over to touch his beloved dog. When he stopped scrunching her fur, Blanche licked his hand.

"Well, thank you for this entire lockdown, I mean, *dance*," she said.

"My pleasure," he replied, bowing.

"Robbie, I know I shouldn't bring it up again, but look at the things you remember. I really don't think there's anything wrong with your memory that isn't"—she floundered—"expected, at your age."

"I accept the compliment, as is age-appropriate to do," he said. "Not only that, but I'm going to whisper in Darcy's ear about the sort of bauble you should have while you're still young, *and* I'm going to let the dog o-u-t."

She picked up the *Daily Progress* from the footstool, folded it, and dropped it in the trash basket. She dropped her phone in her sweater's deep pocket. At night, regardless of the weather, Robbie turned on the outdoor lights, opened the screen door, and surveyed the fenced yard before letting Blanche out. They'd recently called a trapper, who'd set a series of traps to catch what turned out to be a mother skunk and seven babies. They had apparently been living under the back porch. This had been done before they, or the dog, had any encounter with the skunk family—the doctor had only seen one skunk, several times, outside the living room window, near the still-dormant hydrangeas. One time he'd whispered for her to join him at the window, putting his finger to his lips, and she too had seen the skunk nosing around only a few feet away.

Now, from behind, Ginny noticed the doctor's sloped shoulders, his carefully calibrated movements, turning just so, to retain his balance while holding back Blanche with one leg as he perused the yard. It was dense with periwinkle (his alternative to having so much grass that needed mowing; to Ginny, it looked like a field of plastic). It might have been a bright star she saw over his shoulder when he turned toward her, after letting Blanche proceed. Or it might have been light beamed from a tower, maybe even the flash of a car's headlights. She didn't often feel isolated, except in moments when she glimpsed some other reality outside the house: the white flash of a skunk's tail; starlight; a beacon.

"Ginny," he said, stone-faced, "did we just have a dance?"

She must have looked stricken. Then his expression crumpled and he said, "Gotcha!" and turned toward the staircase, proud of himself. Since Blanche so loved her late-night explorations of what Robbie called "the kingdom," he left it to Ginny to lure her back in. She wasn't sure how that routine had evolved, but it had, even during winter's coldest nights. She wore no watch, but she checked her phone. Around eleven fifteen she'd begin whistling for Blanche, then do anything necessary to get the dog inside. It was the least she could do. He'd been more than gracious about her moving into his home, he'd been insistent: his house was spacious and safe; he was delighted at the prospect of her as the newest family member; she must "hibernate" with him. "A great pleasure," he told her, and all of his children. To Darcy, he'd added (Darcy himself had told her his father had asked this more than once), "Why would a man go so far away and work for so little money, just when he's found the love of his life? Don't you think Fate might be sending you a message, Darcy, to take shelter with your loved one at this perilous moment, that's sure to be far worse than the Spanish flu?"

*   *   *

GINNY'S RETURN TO Charlottesville had been just that, a return. Nine years earlier, she'd attended UVA's MFA writing program. Her favorite teacher (a former model; she had gobs of shiny, deep-brown hair) had since received tenure. Jeanette was a thoughtful person; she never capitalized on her still riveting appearance. Knowing Ginny would be back in town, looking for a part-time job that would give her time to write, Jeanette had contacted a friend at the Albert and Shirley Small Special Collections Library, who'd written Ginny a nice, welcoming note—an actual note!— regretting that the position she might be suited for was currently on hold. Jeanette also volunteered to read the manuscript she'd been working on, accepted unquestioningly that Ginny did not yet wish to show anyone anything at all, then suggested Ginny sit in on her twice weekly Zoom classes with the MFA students ("I'd be bolstered by your presence, Ginny. You're such a good reader. Please feel free to comment too"). It was wonderful to be able to interact with Jeanette again; that inevitable imbalance of power between teacher and student had somewhat inhibited them in the past, though now they could just be friends.

How did she look to the students? She felt like an interloper, regardless of what Jeanette said, and rarely spoke during the classes. As she remembered it from her year in the program, everything had been more intense, every detail of every story or novel over-analyzed; if you resisted, your classmates came back at you like green-headed flies. In retrospect, she'd been a little unstable back then, knowing she wanted to be nothing like her mother, but not sure whom she might model herself on. During her earlier time in Charlottesville, she'd left town before getting her degree, running off with a twenty-years-older cinematographer she'd met during Thanksgiving break in Aspen when she flew there to stay with the person who was then her best friend and the girl's family. Ah, those days pre-Covid. After a wild few days with the man now known as The Narcissist, she and her friend had returned to UVA. Ginny's friend had sulked a bit because she'd seen so little of her, once she met the cinematographer, but they'd patched things up by the time they returned to Virginia. At the end of the semester, Ginny and the cinematographer remained entirely sure they were soul mates and their relationship was meant to be; he'd landed a private plane on what was then the Kluge estate to pick her up and fly away with her.

But, believe it or not (some days she didn't), she'd been more smitten with Darcy, from the moment they met. He was funnier. He didn't seem full of himself. He certainly didn't tell her what to wear, let alone try to change her mind about becoming a writer. Everything had seemed propitious: her roommate in Brooklyn would be moving in with her boyfriend, as soon as he got rid of *his* roommate; she'd be escaping the other roommate, a poli sci major who did tequila shots with doughnuts. Charlottesville was Southern enough but not too Southern, liberal, much approved of by the travel sections of glitzy magazines—a "bubble," though of course the rally had put everyone on edge; and though she realized how lucky she was not to have to worry constantly about money, she still tried to put the subject entirely out of her mind, rather than admit how relieved she was to be getting an almost free ride.

And then Tinker Bell's wand turned out to be sprinkling not stardust, but teeny-tiny particles of coronavirus.

Who, really, were the people in Jeanette's class? Rich or poor? Admitting privilege or determined to write well enough to change their lives, if they had to? Several recent graduates had rather stunningly demonstrated the possibility of that working. The writing program was highly ranked, with good reason. A few New York agents still kept an eye on the program. Covid, though, made everything problematic. The graduate students could no longer count on augmenting their income by waiting tables. Part-time jobs had to be avoided, for fear of contracting the virus.

The faces of the new students on her screen were postage stamp–sized: the young woman from Sierra Leone; the tall boy— he really did look like an adolescent—whose exposition got tangled in the complex net of figurative language he'd cast; the twins, whose haughty manner made it obvious that they considered themselves the prose-writing equivalent of the starry Starn twin photographers, though to Ginny, each was horribly prosaic; the middle-aged woman writing about a fire she'd narrowly escaped by jumping three floors into a net, leaving her with only two broken ribs, a broken thumb, and a dislocated shoulder, who always joined the session late because of technical difficulties; the square-faced, muscular boy from Baton Rouge (Jeanette had told her he cut himself) with tattoos of the Joker and Batman on the backs of his hands, nails gnawed to the quick, who alternately wore a visor or an engineer's cap, one wrist accessorized with a Slinky-high tower of bracelets made of hemp, silver, copper, plastic—all androgynous. It was rumored he had a drug problem. Jeanette would not confirm or deny this, or the rumor that the same student had had his car towed when he'd parked by a fire hydrant, and that later he'd gone to pick it up and had made such a scene, the police had been called and given him a Breathalyzer test he'd failed, so that when he managed to wheedle his way out of that situation, he nevertheless had to have a device installed in his car that he was required to breathe into before the car would start. But the virus was a bitch, everyone was stressed-out; life went on even when it didn't much resemble what things had been before: people stole shopping carts from the Barracks Road Kroger; someone entered the closed university library and threw thirty books out of the second-story window, whose spines fractured and let go of their pages.

Back in her bedroom, after enduring the withering look Blanche gave her upon returning, Ginny climbed into bed to see that Darcy had forwarded a couple of Cassie's emails. Even from Tokyo, Darcy had been having disagreements with his sister. This exchange had been precipitated by his writing a group message to his siblings saying that their father would need live-in help when Ginny left, to which Cassie had replied—Darcy thought, with particular insensitivity—that whoever came from Meals on Wheels would be able to make sure Robbie hadn't fallen, and that he shouldn't infantilize their father. Ginny herself thought his email had raised a false alarm. Darcy also seemed to be only half joking when he wrote to say that now that Ginny had discovered who the most interesting man in the family was, what must he do to win her back?

During the winter, Robbie had twice prepared what had been his signature dish, beef Stroganoff. She'd never had it before—she wasn't vegetarian, though she tended to avoid red meat. She considered his stew the most delicious thing she'd ever tasted. He'd prepared dinner once a week; on weekends, they'd eaten takeout, or had pizza delivered. Far from being demanding, Robbie enjoyed a cheese omelet for dinner, or praised her for adding fresh snow peas and bean sprouts (with a slug of sake) to packaged ramen noodles. ("Thrifty!" he'd complimented her.) Their wine drinking went unmentioned, though from what she read, *everyone* was drinking more.

She leaned back against her pillows and clicked on the day's newest video of Darcy as Brutus. His delivery of some lines was too adamant, almost a satire of a lesser actor, underestimating the audience: "Our hearts you see not; they are pitiful; and pity to the general wrong of Rome. . . ." His gestures, too, were odd. Off. Until she watched a second time and realized he was joking. It wasn't a real performance, but something he'd done just for her, an imitation of—of course!—his father's expansive gestures, the way the doctor resembled a showman about to begin a transparently manipulative pitch (though, in the den, she'd walked so happily into his arms, and she really had liked their little dance).

LOL she texted Darcy.

Ping! (It was thirteen hours later in Tokyo. He was responding at two forty in the morning.)

                                        hey amazing you got it right away

No u got me thought you
were having off night

                                i'd ♥ to have any night with you

Who told you to take
job in Tokyo???!!!

                                you told me not to just like
                                dear dad, but its been amazing

He says you should buy
me jewels. Bring back jade.

                                        we're back to lol

x

                                                phone sex?

x bye

She waited for his reply, but no dots appeared. That left no excuse for not opening the most recent attachment from the older woman whose manuscript would be discussed the next day. The title was "Fifty Ways to Jump," though who could say if she'd keep decreasing the number downward; she'd been unable to revise two jumps to please her classmates, and had finally deleted them, as well as the one she disliked that had impressed everyone else. Of twenty jumps written so far, she was down to seventeen.

But first, Ginny hoped to get an energy hit from Gene Kelly in *Singin' in the Rain*. She'd watched that with Robbie and Darcy, the night he introduced them. That great moment, when Gene Kelly stands under the gushing downspout, then whips off his hat! The policeman's sudden appearance, arms folded across his chest, so that Kelly stops, closes his umbrella, then walks off, almost colliding with an extra who'd always be able to say, *I'm the person in the rain Gene Kelly almost ran into!*

She took a deep, calming breath, then exhaled. She opened the attachment and read:

[REVISION, PART 1] Most nights in my dreams I jump. People with sleep disorders jump out of bed in the middle of the night; we disapprove of people "jumping to conclusions." Let's take it out of the human realm. A horse jumps a hurdle and we think, "Good horse, good jump." If you say the word "jump" aloud, some of you will jerk your chin back as you say it, the same way many of you will raise an arm as you say "tall." But what does "jump" really mean? Does it mean you have a death wish? What if it means you're destined to become a writer. Should I "jump" to the end of this story, when ending it is the thing I most fear because what it will really mean is that it's over and I'm still alive? [HEY, NO WORRIES, DON'T CALL STUDENT HEALTH. 100% NO DANGER TO MYSELF, JUST TRYING NEW APPROACH TO BEGINNING.]

Ginny felt irritated. Her impression might have been different if the caps had been omitted, but the writer wanted it both ways: to startle, and to soothe. It was total self-absorption. Or: it put the reader in the position of the skeptical, drenched cop, standing with folded arms, the bad cop ruining someone else's big moment, exhibiting what her former boyfriend (Narcissus, Jeanette called him) had said about the self-inflating power of judging others under the guise of offering helpful criticism. He'd flunked out of two colleges before winning an award for his first movie, made before they met, a success never repeated, as far as she knew. When last she heard, he was living in a container house, flying people around Utah in his Cessna—rich people from the East who were suddenly desperate to buy land, even if they were surrounded by Mormons. His actress girlfriend threw him out for spending his days "playing Snoopy in the cockpit." A surprise to Ginny that, years after ghosting her, he'd forwarded the actress's kiss-off. Ever since—even though she'd made no response—those times he popped into her mind at all, she'd envision the black tip of his snout, his geeky helmet, and his dashingly flipped-back scarf, which made her stifle a laugh. Or not.

When she got up to go downstairs, she nearly scraped the bedroom door against Blanche; the dog yelped as she scrambled up. What was this? The dog kept guard outside the doctor's bedroom, not hers. Ginny cooed an apology and worked her fingers gently over a pad of matted fur under Blanche's ear. She did have soulful eyes. "Do you miss Anita?" she asked the dog, who did not perk up her ears. "Do you wish Darcy was here?" Even though she said "Darcy" with special emphasis, the dog made no response to that name either. Was she perhaps going deaf? "Robbie?" she crooned, and the dog became instantly alert, turning her head to see if it was true. "Daaaaarcy?" Ginny said again, under her breath. As she suspected, the name Robbie got the only reaction. Well, she herself was put out with Darcy. But so what? Wouldn't they be together soon and take up where they left off? If only some job would materialize. If only she had a backup plan, in case he called and said he was in love with someone else. That was the first time she'd wondered about that. Not all late-night thoughts were wrong; it was just that, in her experience, they tended to be very right or very wrong. If you tried to deny them in the morning and couldn't, they were probably very right. He'd said, some months ago, that one of the Japanese actresses squealed with joy when she saw his impersonations, even though she had to be told who Christopher Walken was. Why didn't Darcy at least adopt the persona of someone more recent, like . . . well, Louis C.K. was out, but maybe it would be amusing to see Anderson Cooper morph into Brutus; Anderson Cooper signing off with the person he was interviewing, saying, "Be patient till the last." Or couldn't Darcy do a version of Brutus by stonewalling, speaking his lines officiously, like Mark Zuckerberg testifying before Congress. Both of those people were a much better idea—it was certainly more interesting *not* to pick a stand-up comic, because part of what actual stand-up comics were up against was the audience's awareness that they were stand-up comics.

She closed her eyes and tried to imagine who would throw half a shelf of books out a library window. The same people who drowned litters of kittens? Or had the person had one motivation initially—*Take that, Schopenhauer!*—then another, and another after that, as number three thudded down, number eleven, the twenty-fifth, the final book. An early morning jogger had found them.

Ginny tiptoed downstairs to get a glass of water, followed by a secret nip of sake. To her surprise, Robbie sat at the kitchen table in the velvet dress shoes he now used as house slippers, wearing his pajamas and Barbour jacket. It was not the ides of March—they'd gotten past that without even knowing; it was April, though the nights were still very chilly.

"Ah! I am joined by another noctambulator," Robbie said, from where he sat at the kitchen table, eating peanut butter on a toasted Bodo's bagel.

"A what?"

"A noctambulator. A person who walks around at night."

She nodded. Robbie loved crossword puzzles. He reveled in finding the perfect word. He'd once sat in on a game of anagrams in Key West with James Merrill and Richard Wilbur, and other men—all men—whose names she didn't remember. But no game was going on now, Robbie seemed sleepy, it was late, and she was tired. "Smells delicious," she said.

"May I make you one?"

"No, thanks. Just came down for a drink of water."

"Like a quick waltz around the kitchen?"

He could be so sweetly amusing. "Too tired," she said. "We can be Fred and Ginger tomorrow."

She took a clean glass from the dish drainer. She flipped up the tiny lever on the faucet's side to filter the water. As she drank, she noticed, in her peripheral vision, the doctor lowering his hand to feed the dog a bit of bagel. Blanche had descended so quietly, she hadn't heard her above the sound of the running water.

"How many times did you and your wife run into each other down here late at night?"

"Well, back then I didn't live in this house. But in answer to your question, often enough. Of course, she slept beside me, so I was never too surprised because I sensed that she was gone."

She nodded. She opened the liquor cabinet, removed the sake, unscrewed the top, and poured some into a small juice glass delicately painted with tiny oranges the size of raisins. She sat across from him, curious to see if he'd react. He continued eating. Blanche walked away and returned carrying Monkey, her favorite toy. It no longer squeaked. Monkey's banana was missing the tip. Blanche carried it delicately between her teeth, disappearing under the table.

"How come you're not wearing your robe, Robbie?" Ginny asked.

"Because if the queen comes in to have a snort, I'll be dressed and ready to suggest a bit of midnight pheasant hunting," he replied. He pulled a paper napkin out of the plastic dispenser and gently patted his lips.

"You're even funny at midnight," she said. "I was reading . . . a vignette, I guess you'd call it, written by one of the people in the class, who jumped from a burning building at the last minute and lived."

"Then I guess it wasn't the World Trade Center," he said.

"Jesus, Robbie!"

His eyes were red-rimmed. He looked quite different without his glasses. His beard had already started to grow in. On the table in front of him was the headlamp he'd received for Christmas, its bright light aimed at the wall. He saw that she noticed it lying there. "It won't turn off. Switch is defective," he said.

"But why is it even there?"

"Heard something I thought might be an animal, another damn thing that might have taken up residence to procreate and cost me a fortune. Didn't have my glasses, so I thought I could see better with that stupid thing. Like a surgical laser! Extremely unpleasant." He opened a magazine and folded it over the top of it. A tiny glint of light escaped and shot back onto the wall. She wondered where the headlamp had been since Christmas. She thought of how much time had elapsed since their opening their presents, with the "Hallelujah Chorus" playing, the two of them drinking green tea from Sri Lanka, sent by a grateful patient.

"Would you pour that same amount in a glass for me?" he asked.

She got up immediately to get the bottle and a glass. She set the glass down and poured.

"Thank you. A good idea. Lighter than brandy." He took a small sip and set the glass on the table.

"Were you hungry? Are you feeling all right?"

"Fine," he said. "I had a hunch. You know how it is, when your subconscious tells you something? Of course you do. That's what it was, I knew I was going to turn out my light—my normal bedside lamp, not that damned thing—then Anita would call. Though I realize the greater consolation is that she didn't, so you can be reassured I'm not losing my mind."

"I've never thought you were losing your mind."

"All the girls . . ." he said, letting the sentence drift.

"Before I came down, I was thinking about my former boyfriend. Jeanette calls him Narcissus. Did I tell you he was a director?"

"Darcy did. Said he flew his own plane."

"Years ago, and it was a rented plane, but yes. I don't know whether he owns a plane or not now. He flies people around Utah, looking for land."

"Must be a fair amount of it to discover."

"People are moving there. I mean, the way they're moving everywhere."

"Kind of envy that. This is the kitchen where I'm taking my last stand."

"Oh, *please*," she said. "You're not even seventy."

"Memory problems set in," he said. "But were you going to tell me something else about this fellow?"

"Oh. That he sent me the snarky message his actress girlfriend wrote him, breaking things off, telling him he was a cartoon character. We'd been out of contact long before Covid. He just forwarded it without comment."

"Fishing," he said.

"Fishing?"

"I don't mean criminals on the internet. I mean fishing, as in— back in the day, we called something like that a fishing expedition. Putting out a feeler, to see if you caught anything."

"Oh. Sorry. I thought you might have meant p-h-i-s-h-i-n-g."

"You don't have to spell it. Don't have to spell anything but o-u-t, so as not to excite you-know-who."

Blanche was aware that she was also called you-know-who. Her tail beat the floor under the table: *slap, slap, slap.*

Ginny smiled. Drained her glass. After one sip, he'd ignored his sake. He blotted up the last few bagel seeds. He put them in his mouth, savored them, and swallowed. He said, "None of my business, but was there any one reason why you and this pilot broke up?"

"I was young, I romanticized him. The movie he got an award for was shown at Sundance. He knew Robert Redford."

"One time Anita and I took a car trip out west—last trip we took—but we never made it to Utah. Bryce Canyon—I always wanted to see those hoodoos. We went to Billings, Montana, where Anita's favorite cousin lived. A taxidermist. Anita did most of the driving. Beautiful out there. A lot of people asked about her Southern accent."

"Robbie—you don't have an accent, I just realized."

"Educated out of me. El-o-cu-tion, I should say. Before I got married, I had an affair with a speech therapist. Where I ended up practicing, it wouldn't have been any real disadvantage, ironically. My dream had been to start out in New York, at Sinai, or maybe New York–Presbyterian. In any case, very little works out the way you expect it to, I've learned by now. And as for rapport with the patients, I guess for some of them, you're not tall enough to seem authoritative, or you're too tall, so you're intimidating. Maybe you don't draw a picture of what will happen during their gallbladder surgery that makes any sense to them, or they just don't like you on first sight, like that writer said: Malcolm Gladwell. He said that people form an impression of you in the first six seconds after you walk into a room, or something. Could make you wary of entering a room for the rest of your life. If they don't like you, they don't. Nothing to be done."

"What was her name?"

"Whose name?"

"The speech therapist."

"Clara Huddleson. She got hit in a crosswalk in New York City. Couldn't have been forty."

"Awful." She shuddered.

"I'm glad I never kept a diary, because if I had, Cassie would have unscrewed the lock and taken it off to Kinko's and assumed that all the years of our marriage, my real love was Clara Huddleson. Though in my experience, I can't think of one man I ever knew who did keep any sort of diary. But I guess these days, if they've got a memoir in them, they write it. That *Running with Scissors* fellow was certainly talented. And I was impressed by that book about the firefighters, that was one amazing book, written by that lady married to my friend Francis Steegmuller."

"*You knew him?*" At Cornell, she'd read a book Steegmuller had written about Flaubert. It had been assigned by her favorite professor, Alison Lurie, who was lucky enough to spend winters in Key West. She'd probably known the anagrams players. Robbie actually *knew* the biographer? How amazing.

"Friend of Peter Taylor's. Our local Charlottesville writer— those times he wasn't off at Harvard. You know Peter Taylor's work?"

"My friend Jeanette's a big admirer, but—"

"Well, get on it! He won the Pulitzer. Wrote about how the folks in Memphis didn't understand the folks in Nashville, and vice versa. His wife was a brilliant poet, though she never got her due. They lived in Faulkner's house on Rugby Road. Very convivial people. His real name was Matthew, but when he was a baby, somebody gave him the nickname Pete, and Pete stuck. *Convivial*, there's a word you don't hear anymore."

He got up, unsteadily. His hand brushed the magazine on top of the light. He resettled it, this time taking care that no light escaped. "If you're hiding your light under a bushel, then do it right, by god," he said to her. She'd heard the expression before, but didn't know what it meant. If he'd been kidding, though, he'd have smiled. He left his jacket on, and left his chair pulled out, the empty plate on the table. She thought about washing it when she washed her glass, but the cleaning person would be coming the next day, and she was tired. Was Robbie leaving without saying good night?

"Sleep well," she called as she stood, pushing in his chair as well as hers.

"And to all a good night," Robbie called.

She waited for him to ascend the stairs, Blanche silently joining her, minus Monkey. They looked up to see him on the landing, turning toward his bedroom with its en suite bathroom. For some reason, it very much amused him that the bathroom had this designation. Blanche glanced at the front door more out of habit than need, Ginny felt sure. It occurred to her, suddenly, that she missed so many people: her roommate at Cornell; Alison Lurie; Alison's painter friend, Gillian; and Alison's writer husband, Edward. And, of course, now she missed Darcy. She hoped he wasn't involved with the Japanese actress. Was that even possible, or was she being paranoid? But if she and Darcy married, how could she leave Robbie and Blanche? It would have to be an outdoor wedding so Blanche could attend, beribboned. Did fathers-in-law ever give the bride away? She didn't think so, though perhaps, yet again, she was a deficient feminist. Who'd have thought that she'd feel she almost always understood anything Robbie was saying, whether or not he spoke the words? In spite of his age, in some ways she felt closer to him than she did to Darcy. She and Robbie had watched, hands clasped, as Trump preened outside the White House, after his release from Walter Reed. She felt as though she and Robbie had endured things together, that they'd weathered times she and Darcy hadn't, however privileged she and Robbie were, how disgusting, in some people's eyes: Robbie would be the man who'd stayed far away from Lee Park during the Unite the Right rally; he belonged to the country club; there was a cleaning person.

Robbie was not hopelessly forgetful; he'd remember, he'd be front-and-center at their wedding—if ever there could be such a gathering again: if only the virus would disappear. Like Robbie, she felt sure it wouldn't.

It had to mean something that Blanche curled beside her bed and beat her tail, as Ginny was plugging in her phone to charge it, loosening her hair from the scrunchie, lowering the blind, then climbing carefully over the dog to get into bed with its puffy duvet atop it, with no intention of giving any more thought to someone else's fifty possibilities about anything. It was really a relief to just tune out. Without wanting to admit it, she'd known for some time, even if only subconsciously, that she had two possibilities: either to marry Darcy, or not. If she dwelt within *Pride and Prejudice*, things would eventually become clear, but Jane Austen wasn't orchestrating her life. This was Charlottesville, Virginia, mid-April 2021, and while her Darcy really was something of a cad (talk about old-fashioned words!) for putting his acting career first, no one could have imagined the whole winter under lockdown, the chaos with the airlines, if they flew at all, the desperate wait to get the vaccine, everyone fearing Trump's reelection. Any intelligent person had been driven half mad. Robbie had gone to a dinner near where Ginny had first lived with Darcy, at Queen Anne Square, a gathering of Yellow Dog Democrats, double-masked, furious, others Zooming in. Back in January, the former owner of Robbie's house—someone who worked at the Pentagon, who'd used the house in Ivy as his weekend place—had called and offered Robbie half again as much as he'd paid for it, if he'd sell it back to him. He said he missed the backyard where their son had once jumped on a trampoline, the smell of the air;

his wife missed the stained glass panes she'd commissioned her friend at the McGuffey to make (though he still had his doubts about the downbeat autumn panel, which lacked the instant recognition you felt when viewing the original painting it copied, in its dreary colors). "I didn't press the point, but, you know, his reaction might have been for the same reason people didn't take to that painting that glass fellow—glass artist, I mean—meant to copy: Who wants to see laborers, even if they *are* women? That was pretty much the reaction when the painting was first shown. The painter, Millet, sold it for a pittance. Today it hangs in the Musée d'Orsay. Joke's on us. Not that I'm likely to get to Paris again, to see it up close with my evolved perspective." That had been the same conversation in which she'd found out that Robbie's favorite course in college had been art history. Robbie's grandfather and father had been doctors. His father had told Robbie he'd disinherit him if he didn't follow in their footsteps. ("Just what I needed to hear, to go off on my Wanderjahr. Always intended to return to Planet Earth, though.")

THE JUMPER NEVER LOGGED ON the next day, though one of the twins, wearing an ESPN jacket, had written a 309-word humor piece he wanted to send to "Shouts and Murmurs" at the *New Yorker* and volunteered to send it *and* to read it aloud on the Zoom call ("Yeah!" the student from Sierra Leone cheered; Jeanette had mentioned that they were an item). In the moment, though, flustered, Jeanette hadn't managed to say no fast enough.

From the den, Ginny watched as her face, and the other tiny faces, adopted expressions ranging from bored to chagrined, though the tattooed student from Baton Rouge twice exploded in laughter that greatly delighted the writer. The piece was about the difficulty of booking a mani-pedi during Covid.

"Very amusing," Jeanette said, at the conclusion. "But as you know, I find it difficult to take in what I'm hearing, rather than having the opportunity to read it. We all appreciate your filling in, though. If anyone hears from Justine, please let me know. We're clear about who's on for Thursday? Oh, and Douglas," she said to the other twin, "many congratulations on your story being accepted by *Sewanee Review*. I assume everyone's heard, but if not, there's the day's good news. Kudos."

"I've got another one!" his twin volunteered, though Jeanette wasn't having it. It wasn't her job to train them for Comedy Central. Some days, she viewed it as a liability that the brilliant Tina Fey had graduated from the university.

Jeanette called Ginny fifteen minutes after the class ended: "Well, if she jumped, UVA Hospital doesn't know about it, Martha Jeff doesn't, and neither do the cops." She sighed. "What's so hard? If you want to be a writer and write about your life, you have to accept feedback. Why wasn't Justine there today? Some of them really are snowflakes."

"She's a little old to be a snowflake," was all Ginny could manage.

"Where's it snowing?" Robbie asked, walking into the room the minute she hung up. He picked up an old *Daily Progress* from the trash and scanned the front page below the fold. Ginny knew that in his opinion, this was where the really interesting stuff appeared; they were obliged to go with the flashiest headline.

"Aspen." She didn't feel like getting into it. Really, if Darcy loved her as much as he said, why was he staying in Japan, hoping the theater would reopen? The actor from Berlin had jumped ship. Calpurnia had flown back to her parents' house in Buffalo. How could Darcy pretend his performances mattered, and that they had to be delivered from Tokyo—really done on-site, in Japan, in that particular auditorium—when the whole world was out of focus? Night after night, there he was, waiting to reimagine the role of the betrayer, Marcus Brutus, from halfway around the world, Caesar's role recorded nightly from a bedroom in Burbank (technically, on the previous day). Maybe her mother had been right, and happiness wasn't likely to result from meeting someone in a hotel lobby and going off to have a drink with them. So what if they both loved to kayak, if they'd had sex at least twice a night before he left, preferred dogs to cats, agreed on the pizza topping (extra cheese only; the doctor liked onions and olives), and secretly, shamefully, drank Diet Cokes?

First Darcy had learned that he couldn't fly back from Japan until August. Then that plan was revised: the date became May 11. He might return in only about three weeks, but now that too seemed unlikely. He was excited that someone from the BBC who was making a documentary about Americans in Tokyo during Covid was going to film one of his performances and interview him. She reminded herself: *We're not competitive; we both like to swim laps and to take long walks; we have compatible astrological signs.* The truth was, he'd begun to fade away. Sometimes, as she watched the videos, her only thought had been that she was watching an actor, acting. It made her remember her mother, Louise, and the time she'd said, "One time at the mall, your father was walking toward me, and I thought, *Who's that man in that cow flop hat?* And it was your father."

Ginny's last serious relationship before meeting Darcy had been with Carl, a carpenter from Red Hook, the polar opposite of Narcissus. They'd met at a friend's birthday party in Park Slope. Carl had been a real guy-guy, though he always included her when he went out with his buddies, and fuck 'em if they didn't like it. Now he lived with his wife and child in Proctor, Vermont, working at a marble factory and playing bass with a jazz quartet in Burlington—though she imagined that wasn't happening these days. They'd seen each other for about a year, while she lived with her roommates, working at Macy's and taking a writing class at The New School at night. He'd broken things off when he decided to go back to his high school girlfriend. He'd told her after picking marigolds and geraniums from someone's window box, half still dangling roots: a bouquet he must have thought of as consolation flowers. Jeanette had tried to one-up her by saying that her college boyfriend had stolen a carton of Tampax off the back of a truck and presented them, saying, "I thought you'd like these."

Robbie was the only parent any boyfriend had ever taken her home to meet. She'd made no attempt to introduce Darcy to her mother, because when she and Carl had been dating, they'd met Louise once at an Italian restaurant her mother suggested.

Obviously, Ginny's showing up with a boyfriend had put her mother out of sorts. Just before the entrées arrived, her mother had excused herself to go to the restroom and exited through the kitchen, sticking them with the bill. Apparently, she'd found Carl condescending, though she'd refused to give an example, and had hung up on Ginny when she called later that night to ask what had happened.

"You are *not gonna believe* how much my father isn't like your mother," Darcy had said, laughing, when she told him that story. "For example: my younger brother fathers two kids, one with a girl from high school when they were both at CHS, the other one a few years later. What does my father do? He talks to his lawyer, gives number two a *lot* of money, *and* his car. Off she goes, with child support thrown in. When my mother died, Cassie was given first choice about anything she wanted. Jewelry, sure, but he made it clear that he thought it best she had first pick of everything because she was the firstborn, and they ruined her childhood by having the twins. Which, if you ask me, also ruined their marriage. Cassie took his sofa! But go figure: it was a standing joke that my mother rolled her eyes when I cried in my crib and never got up to check on me. He was really the one who brought me up, busy as he was, and Dante—he was born nuts. What does Robbie do? 'Robbie,' because once we started high school, he told us to drop the 'Dad.' Anyway, he buys Dante a Jeep Cherokee! I was living in DC, in Foggy Bottom, working, well, I might as well have been the Kennedy Center's custodian. I was in a one-bedroom with two roommates, one of whom routinely climbed into the kitchen sink and used the spray hose to 'shower.' Kitchen turned into a little pond. I finally got up my courage to tell the old man I'd like a car. You know what he said? 'Nobody who lives in a city needs a car.' Then he announces I'm his favorite son, but that he only makes foolish gestures toward foolish people, and that I'm smart and have good *character*." "He sounds sort of mean," she'd said. "Oh, no. No, no, no. Sorry to give the wrong impression. He's his own man. You'll see."

So what was Darcy doing now, abandoning her to his father (okay, nobody could have predicted how awful things would become), and to her plan of *maybe* writing a novel that, true, she'd told him nothing about. She'd written more than a hundred pages, but found it hard to proceed, because it seemed so clear that everybody had their own crazy story. Darcy had been so (she hated the word) supportive. He'd insisted she continue, because he felt sure she had something unique to offer.

She was writing about her father's going to jail for embezzlement, which left his girlfriend, called Laurel in the novel, to raise Ginny and her brother. Jeanette thought she should write the book as a memoir, but what about the legal problems it might cause, with her mother *not* just slinking away, but bringing on a team of lawyers like the Furies? As a teenager, Ginny's brother had become a Scientologist and disappeared into the Tom Cruise ether. Of course she thought her parents were married. There was a photograph on display, until her father went to jail, of what Ginny assumed was their wedding day, though her mother later told her they'd put on borrowed costumes at a photographer's studio and exchanged "commitment vows" against a background of Mount Vesuvius erupting that he'd used for the previous photograph of a men's travel group. Ginny began pulling out her hair strand by strand in fourth grade, her father gone and her mother working two jobs and crying when she wasn't.

Darcy didn't know about any of this (only that she and her brother lived in near poverty after someone stole money from her mother). Ginny thought that the past was so intertwined with her writing that if she told him, she'd be talking her book away. She hadn't explained that her missing brother was involved in Scientology. She might have shown Darcy the zippered cosmetics bag filled with her hair—how really weird that she'd kept it all those years—except that when she moved from Brooklyn, she'd emptied it out the window, onto the front stoop.

Her father was suddenly a criminal, her mother went more-or-less crazy, and Ginny had the good sense, with the help of her high school guidance counselor, to get a scholarship to Cornell, the same school her best friend, who was from a wealthy family in New Canaan, had chosen. That summer, she and her friend had gone to Wesleyan's summer writing program (her friend's father had paid for both girls), where she'd had an affair with the workshop leader, who subsequently called a friend at UVA, recommending her to the graduate program. That friend was Peter Taylor, retired from his job because of heart trouble, though he remained influential.

Jeanette knew the circumstances of how Ginny came to town, but nothing else except for a passing mention of how traumatic life had been at home, when Ginny's brother disappeared into what she could only think of as a cult and there was so little money. In those days, a few English department women got together once in fall semester, once in spring, to eat pizza or Thai takeout at ugly sweater parties. Ginny had never gone, but she could still remember running into recently hired Jeanette, in jeans and a sweater decorated with a family of black poodles in rhinestone collars, framed in a heart. Ginny had been walking into the pizza place, Jeanette had been leaving in a rush with a pile of boxes, and Ginny had just thought, *Well, I guess when she's off work, she's off work.* She'd kept in touch with Jeanette (neither was on Facebook, though Jeanette posted on Instagram), once or twice sending an actual Christmas card. When she was still in Brooklyn, Jeanette had flown to New York to introduce one of her own former teachers from Iowa at the 92nd Street Y, staying at a hotel, where she'd bought Ginny and herself late-night cheeseburgers and vodka tonics. They'd bonded, so when Jeanette got engaged to a stockbroker from Wells Fargo Advisors not long afterwards, Ginny had been invited to the party. She'd taken the train, the endless train, arriving hours late into Charlottesville, where the brother of the groom-to-be fetched her in a green Volvo and took her to her already-paid-for hotel (!).

In the lobby, Darcy had been saying good night to his father's friend, another doctor. He'd reached around her as she was checking in to hand the receptionist a pair of glasses someone had dropped in the lobby. He'd bumped her shoulder, turning away. "Sorry," he'd said. "Not yours, are they?"

They had a drink at the bar. He'd been at Live Arts, auditioning for a play, after which he'd picked up his father's friend at the airport to drive him to the Omni. Ah, she knew the town! He'd grown up there. So changed. She'd soon discover the proliferation of coffee shops everywhere. She asked if Heartwood was still open. "Yes. And Art's behind the counter! Knows the entire inventory, off the top of his head." A dish of red-skinned peanuts was placed on the bar between them. She said that she'd loved the Halloween she'd spent on the Lawn. She reached into the dish of nuts. They were salty and delicious. He said it was odd the bartender had brought them without asking if they were allergic. She had to agree. He reached into the dish. There was a mural in Cabell Hall now she'd have to see, he told her: one of the panels was of that annual gathering of students, faculty, and community. It absolutely captured the spirit of the celebration, the wicked little costumed children, the Fellini-esque chaos. "One more?" he'd asked. "There are plenty of coffee places on the mall to sober up tomorrow."

IN OTHERWISE MISERABLE, frightening 2021, Ginny had lived like a rich person in Charlottesville, with adequate heat; the use of Robbie's comfortable, reliable Saab; takeout food as good as such stuff could be, or groceries bought from Foods of All Nations, so the terrible lines at the other stores could be avoided. There was a cleaning person, Mrs. Fox, who came every week after picking up the doctor's dry cleaning (that hadn't been possible for months; the business was closed) and took away their recycling. Ginny paid only her own phone bill, and for whatever she needed from the drugstore. She had a dog (sort of); recently, she'd even enjoyed a couple of dinners at the Boar's Head Inn, outside under heat lamps, the tables arranged spaciously apart, with Robbie and one of his doctor or lawyer friends, inevitably a man with good manners, married to a woman almost sure to like her. Ginny was engaged to the doctor's son and, my goodness, writing a book! Then came talk of the connections. They'd usually know who Jeanette was even if they didn't know her personally, if not from the university then because of her work on behalf of literacy. They'd say they still missed the old C&O ("Oh, that coupe glacée," Robbie interjected), then agree that traffic had become horrible. Why did they bring in that woman as president of the university? someone would wonder aloud. Imagine letting white nationalists onto the grounds. Though maybe more people did finally get a much-needed wake-up call, after that ghastly parade at the university, to say nothing of what happened later downtown, the doctor sometimes pointed out.

One night, doctors who'd moved to Charlottesville from Brookline insisted, in an ever-so-polite way, that it was incomprehensible that with all the posts on social media and the warnings zinging through the air like arrows, the police were unprepared to deal with the actions of the crowd. "Someone wanted the town to blow up," a woman—a doctor named Bronwyn—said. "We all act like this was a tsunami, but y'all know there were constant warnings, the mayor had to know, the university president must have been aware of what was brewing, the police. Why do we always want to think things happen because of ignorance, rather than collusion? That, or city government's full of anarchists." Her husband had tried to shush her, but she was having none of it. "Hush up, darlin'!

It does no good to pretend. We didn't go to medical school to become actors. We might be deficient in more ways than we'd like to think, but if someone told me to expect a surly patient, and—"

"But what can we do after the fact, Bronwyn? What will make next time different, do you think?" one of the wives asked.

Bronwyn thought nothing would alert anyone. That they didn't want to be alerted. "Paul Revere has been replaced by misinformation shouted shrilly on Facebook," Bronwyn said. Ginny was as taken aback as everyone else, though she admired how forceful the woman was. Bronwyn insisted there were more Trump sympathizers than anyone realized, and that worse was sure to happen next time. "Charlottesville's always congratulating itself," she said, "and if it can't do that, its default position is to be noble and brave, like the whole incident was out of a Hemingway novel, the running of the bulls in Pamplona—except that no red flag was being waved, only the flag of the Confederacy, and it was a young woman who'd gotten killed, not a tortured animal. And after the chaos in Lee Park everyone went away, commended by the president of the United States. Read James Baldwin," Bronwyn had said. "*The Fire Next Time.*"

After one such evening, Ginny asked Robbie (he again in the Barbour jacket he preferred to his robe; she in his fleece jacket, pulled on because it was the nearest warm garment) if he thought that once summer came, more people would want to socialize the way they had in the past, or if they'd still be too anxious, even with the vaccine, to attend an outdoor concert or go see a movie. He smiled and asked if she was contemplating making her own "great escape," and asked how his son really seemed to her, how she was doing herself, because he was quite aware, living in such a literary town, of the writer's struggle.

"One midnight sake doth not a drunken Faulkner make," she'd replied.

Then the phone rang. This call would be the one that would prove to be the giveaway. Ginny was indeed there. She was still warming up after a walk with Blanche, who seemed to run out of energy after about ten minutes, then reinflate if she was patted and encouraged, and the walk continued. In the winter, the doctor, observing the first half of this routine for the first time, had misjudged, carrying her home tucked under his arm. Robbie had entered the house panting; Blanche had been smirking. Really, she had.

"Hello?" he said, holding the receiver to his ear.

Ginny waited for him to give an indication of who it was, but he never looked her way. "Anita?" she finally heard him say. He'd come downstairs in nubbly wool socks. She could see his shoulders slump. "Just take your time," he cajoled, before falling silent. Ginny's own phone sounded, startling her: a notification from CNN. A judicious statement from Dr. Anthony Fauci. A message from the *Washington Post* about how to safely pump gas.

"May I remind you of what a great romance we had?" he asked, his back still turned to Ginny.

She wasn't sure if she should go away or pretend not to be listening. She reached for the napkin container, fidgeting by pulling one out, and the container broke apart. He heard it collapse, frowned, then turned away. "Yes, I'm listening," he said. "May I remind you that you very much wanted another daughter? Do we both remember the same thing?" He shook his head ruefully. "Dante has some psychological problems, yes, but you can't seriously believe that a two-year-old was *beyond help*."

The carousel music that suddenly blasted into his ear made him hold the phone away. It was followed by a very loud voice. The doctor so hated noise—leaf blowers, power saws . . . no wonder he looked horrified. It was his son-in-law, the CPA, drunk. "Let 'em have . . . Sistine ceiling, my finger's pointed right atcha, Doc. You . . . you . . . Cass, all that grief. Right now your girlfriend's probably gesturing, *Hang up! Hang up!* Oh, you've . . . somebody's always protecting you, Doc. Cassie never drank until . . . therapy, now she's morphed into *Psycho* . . . channels her mother and thinks she's her. Shut up, Cass! Doc? You hear what I'm saying?"

Ginny had never seen such an expression on the doctor's face. She couldn't tell if he was shocked, angry, amused, or all those things. She was surprised when he finally spoke, because while his eyes flashed with fear, his gaping mouth made him look almost— what?—beatific. As if he might have been frozen in time, singing with the choir.

"What's that music?" Robbie asked.

"This is what you . . . to know? You care . . . sound track? This is *my* paintball, with *your* daughter, *your daughter*, participating in what . . . much better therapy, running off her anger. Visceral animated regression therapy, it's called, and yes, we drink! We turn up the music . . . Planet Paintball, and driiiiiiiiink, you abstemious, self-congratulatory, preening jerk."

Robbie's face was pale. His free arm hung limply, like a broken wing. Toward the end, the voice had spewed out such a torrent of words, she couldn't believe that there was silence—that the call had ended. Visceral *what*? What had he been screaming?

"Oh, Robbie," she said, as he replaced the receiver.

"It's both of them?" he asked. "Both drunk, and Cassie's dodging paintballs he's firing at her? He considers this some form of therapy?"

She couldn't think what to say.

"I had no idea. I'll have to call Jenkins Irwin, get his perspective. What was that fool braying about? He says Cassie channels Anita?"

"I don't—"

"No, no. Not another word. I'm grateful you're here to back me up. He was in an alcoholic rage. Was he suggesting he was God, up on the Sistine ceiling? I've never heard such nonsense."

"I didn't know . . . I'm sorry. I even— I have no idea why this broke, I was just—" She stared at a jagged piece of plastic that had previously formed one side of the napkin dispenser.

"When did they become alcoholics? I wonder if it stops there, or it's drugs as well? This'll have to be dealt with." He sat in the kitchen chair across from hers, leaning both elbows against the table's edge. "I want you to know, I was never convinced it was Anita. I just let it play out. I'm a doctor. I don't believe in the spirit world." He cleared his throat. "Though, obviously, there's a bottom line here," he said, smoothing his chin. "And here's Blanche. There's my good girl. Let's hope she has no particular grievances tonight."

She would have laughed, but Ginny felt like a tourniquet was binding her chest. She'd seen the deified dressing table. She should have known they were nuts. She'd been told how upset Cassie had been when the family expanded. But this? What would Peter Taylor do with this? Had he lived long enough to see reality TV? Certainly he'd have known about alcoholics. His best friend was Robert Lowell, manic-depressive *and* alcoholic.

"I'm so sorry," she said.

"Sorry," he echoed. "Yes, indeed. That says it all. Maybe you'd like Blanche to join you, in case you have a nightmare?"

"She guards your door."

"That she does. Well, let's hope the phone doesn't ring again, which I can't imagine, though I've been brought up short about the power of my imagination."

"I never thought the calls meant you believed in the spirit world," she said.

"Well, some do. Brilliant man used to be at the medical center. File cabinets full of his investigations into the paranormal. You know, sisters separated at birth. They meet for the first time when they're thirty. Both have cats named Dinah and married men six feet tall who work in construction and drink Heineken. Maybe the beer choice isn't that surprising. He and I never met, the director of the, what is it now—the Division of Perceptual Studies. He died awhile back. When I left, they were in the process of renaming it, no doubt desperate to keep their funding. I'll see you in the morning."

"Can I ask you something?"

"Certainly."

"Did you tell Darcy he was your favorite child?"

"I shouldn't have? No, I shouldn't have, I guess. Places a burden, rather than being a compliment."

"I think that meant a lot to him."

"You do? Well, you take my word, so I'll return the favor."

"Can I ask one more thing?"

"Shoot."

"Could you find out if someone was admitted to the hospital today? The line for patient information never picks up."

"Lack of staff," he said. "Pandemic. Who did you want to know about?"

She said the student's name: "Justine Kendall."

Surely he'd ask why she wanted to know. "Okay," he said, walking back into the room. He pulled out a cabinet drawer. He pushed aside a ball of twine and removed a piece of paper, running his finger down a list. He picked up the phone and dialed. "It's Dr. Anderson, Robert Anderson," he said. "Is this Brian?" Again, he listened. "I know it," he said. "Difficult times." He listened awhile longer, nodded, but didn't speak. "You hang in there, it'll be okay," he said, then asked if they'd admitted anyone with the last name Kendall. There was certainly no carousel music as he waited.

"I appreciate it. You too. Take care," he said, replacing the phone. "Michelangelo!" he muttered to Ginny as he walked past. "Isn't that what he was alluding to? Imagine: that jackass, putting himself in the position of God, creating Adam! What would he do but create him, then hunt him down, for a little recreational sport. *What a jackass.*"

He'd understood better than she had. She hadn't even tried to sort out what the hysterical voice had been shouting.

"Thanks for making the call," she said. Of course, the information wasn't definitive, but at least the most obvious place hadn't admitted Justine Kendall. She texted Jeanette before going upstairs. The message was delivered, but she received none in return. Nor was there any new message from Darcy.

The *New York Times* lay unread on the seat of a chair. Bad news about increasing hospitalizations of younger people in Michigan.

As she walked upstairs, she heard the shower running. Blanche had already thumped down in front of the doctor's bedroom door, waiting for him to get out of the bathroom. He usually left the door open a crack, but he'd closed it. "Did I shut you out?" he asked, feigning shock as he stepped out into the hallway, naked. "How could I do that, huh? Come right in, come in." The doctor, ever the gentleman, naked! He'd have been so embarrassed if he'd seen Ginny standing in the dark, where the stairs curved. The dog disappeared into the room.

Ginny went to bed, angry not at Cassie's husband (though the call had made her afraid of him), certainly not angry at the doctor, but rather put out with his son. Though the performance space was now closed because the Japanese government had begun to worry about Covid, Darcy often went to a place called the Washington, DC, Cherry Blossom Bar, on the floor above the space where he recorded his nightly video. But he hadn't sent a selfie from there, or called again, or texted.

She'd once gone with her mother to the Tidal Basin to see the actual cherry trees blooming in early spring. It was one of the few trips they'd ever taken. Some politician's girlfriend, running from the cops, had jumped into the Tidal Basin, her mother had told her; the woman was named Fanne Foxe. Her mother had laughed aloud at that. Fanne Foxe had jumped, fully clothed, into the water, after exclaiming that she was "just a country girl from Argentina." *Wilbur Mills*. That was whose girlfriend it had been, her mother exclaimed. Her mother seemed to find this, too, hilarious, but to Ginny, it had been just another anecdote she couldn't make sense of. Who was Wilbur Mills, why did the girlfriend break away from him, what did it all mean? But telling the story had put her mother in a much better mood.

It had been a cold day for springtime, windy. Sometimes, after the trees had already blossomed, snow fell, her mother had told her, choking up as if it were a tragedy. Her mother's mood often swung between being highly amused by something Ginny couldn't understand, and crumpling under the weight of her despair when the next topic was introduced. Her mother was always so emotional, so out of control. Now she lived with her sister in Havre de Grace, and was on oxygen because of her bad lungs. The sister's husband had left the family shortly after Louise's arrival and now lived with *his* brother, in northern Maine near the Canadian border. Every year, he sent his wife a pop-up Christmas card, Louise had told Ginny solemnly. Ginny waited for a description of what this card said or looked like, but her mother said nothing more. She'd only met her aunt once when she was a child, and her uncle not at all. He had stopped to play miniature golf while the women visited, the year Ginny started school. She should go see her mother. Ginny knew she should. Yet it was easy to pretend that she was the *doctor's* relative, that the safety and sanity he offered (even if not on this particular night) was her due—because, when you thought about it, look at who his sons and daughter were. This winter in Charlottesville had been grayer than usual, had been the general consensus, though it had rarely snowed. Her phone pinged and she picked it up, thinking it would be either Darcy or Jeanette. It was another notification from CNN, followed by one from the *Washington Post*. Both were about the virus.

She dreamed that there was another panel, a fifth season depicted in stained glass. Even in the dream, this seemed unlikely. In all the other panels a woman was featured, or women, but the additional panel was abstract: colors and forms that didn't fit together, the separate forms united by a scattering of what looked like ice cream sprinkles, though how could those adhere to glass. Finally, she woke up to see Blanche curled beside her, flicking a paw in her sleep—was *this* the dream? How, possibly, could the dog have gotten onto the bed without her knowing? Blanche never did that. She'd been trained not to jump on the sofa. Surely the dog's presence was, as the doctor had said, one of life's surprises you'd have no way of anticipating.

In the morning, Blanche nowhere in sight, Ginny peed and brushed her teeth, then went downstairs to find a note from Robbie, with the extinguished headlamp used as a paperweight: he was off having coffee with his old friend, Dr. Jenkins W. Irwin (the rest of the note was handwritten, but he'd printed the man's name in block letters); if she needed to reach him, he had his cell phone.

Robbie's daughter and her husband drank. Her mother drank. Her father hadn't smoked or drunk alcohol, but what would a seven-year-old child know? Quite possibly, she simply remembered incorrectly. After he went to jail, she never saw him again. She thought about the two glasses of chardonnay, so golden it had verged on green, that she'd drunk with Darcy at the Omni the night they met. Then she started the coffee machine. Robbie had filled it, she saw, but had left without turning it on.

Blanche crawled out from under the table and stood, shaking, tinkling. "Some night last night, huh?" Ginny asked the dog. The coffee machine exhaled its first sigh, then gurgled. This would repeat two more times. She'd begun to think that now she'd internalized the daily household rituals in her bones. "Out?" For some reason, she had to say it again before Blanche began to pad arthritically toward the door, as the coffee machine sighed.

Outside, it was a beautiful April morning. Here and there, tulips were blooming. Redbuds bloomed in the yard next door ("flowering Judas," to the doctor). It was killing Jeanette that her house wouldn't be on the garden tour this year, because there was no garden tour. She checked her phone: Jeanette had left a message, late, expressing her appreciation for what Ginny had found out about the AWOL student. It had now been revealed that the woman was in Baltimore pinch-hitting for a friend who worked at a recently reopened daycare center. She'd decided to take a break from the program. *Yeah, well, just don't fly off with anybody you think is your soul mate,* Ginny thought. Who was that girl she used to be? Younger (in a word). Blanche descended the steps and pounced on Monkey, though she would have sworn the dog had carried it in the night before. Or perhaps Robbie had let her out before leaving.

A plane passed overhead. During Covid, the sky had been almost empty. This one sounded small, though not like a helicopter. Its shadow passed over the hallway's oak floor. She paused as it lengthened and faded, then headed back to the door. Could it possibly be? Might his popping up again to send the email mean that he was thinking of her, intending to . . . impossible . . . but what would she do if he *did* set down in the doctor's backyard? It couldn't make the same impression as it had years before, at Morven, the old Kluge estate—that had been sold, and Donald Trump had bought the vineyard—but The Narcissist (hers, not Trump) had always been impulsive. What if he'd found out where she was from one of Jeanette's Instagram posts? What if, instead of just casting a shadow, the plane landed on Robbie's deep backyard, an acre flat enough that you could play boccie (Robbie had taught her how, one unseasonably warm night, a few weeks before). What if she morphed into Cinderella, minus the carriage, minus awful stepsisters, definitely minus her Scientologist brother. What if she and The Narcissist reunited and lifted off, while Charlottesville receded until the plane flew into dense clouds: No more in-ground pools, their blue-painted bottoms lit like stained cells forced to give up their secrets when examined under the microscope. No Blue Ridge Mountains, no tall, leafing trees, the springtime flowers—the ones

Jeanette kept on her desk, in a pink Roseville vase—shrinking until they were as tiny as invisible dust mites. No doctor, no Blanche, no virus—wouldn't Darcy be surprised to realize that while he was halfway across the world playing Brutus, his would-be Portia had zoomed right out of his life.

Mrs. Fox tapped on the front door. She was early. "Mr. Fox dropped me, I hope you don't mind," she said. "How are you this morning, Ginny? Isn't this a beautiful day, uh-huh."

"It is. Nice to see you. I'm sorry, we made sort of a mess in the kitchen with our"—she couldn't think what to say; had she put the bottle of sake away?—"our midnight snacks," she said. "As you can see, I just got up."

"That's all right. I sleep in on Saturdays, so I know what a pleasure that is. I didn't see Dr. Anderson's car."

"He went to meet a friend for coffee."

"I'm glad he's getting out. He'd have been so blue if he'd been here all alone during this difficult time, that's what I told Mr. Fox."

Mr. Fox, a retired policeman who, before the pandemic, worked several part-time jobs, had formerly been the night guard at the most expensive gated retirement community in Charlottesville—one that, in its naming, gave a nod to England, so that it would sound classier.

"It worked out for me too. It's hard to imagine leaving."

"Well, those who leave Charlottesville, if they come back once, they come back forever, they do. I'm cleaning over on Hessian Road for a man who was here as a student, I don't know how long ago, but I don't think he had white hair then, uh huh. He was here as a teacher too, then off he went. Now he's back again, commutes all the way to Richmond, because he had to get out of New York City, and he was a lucky one, he managed to get a job the same day he called his old company back in Richmond, so don't you believe there are no jobs. I have never been busier, but I ask did they get their shots. I promised Mr. Fox I wouldn't work for anyone who didn't. I'm so thankful for my second Pfizer vaccine, which Dr. Anderson got me March fifth, 2021, and I will always be indebted for his looking out for my welfare."

"You're glad he has my company, and I'm glad he has you to rely on, Mrs. Fox." All the time Ginny had been listening to Mrs. Fox, the woman had been kneeling to open the vacuum and replace the bag, repeatedly tucking her hair under a red terry-cloth sweatband she pulled on before cleaning. She wore black Mary Janes. She often wore a wide-skirted flowered dress, even in winter.

"Thank you, that's a kind way of putting it. You enjoy your coffee, I'll start upstairs," Mrs. Fox said, dropping the old vacuum bag into the trash, tentatively pushing it in deeper. "I'll be down soon enough."

"Mrs. Fox," she called after her, "I didn't hear Blanche bark when you opened the gate. Was she there?"

"She came with her tail wagging, yes she did, uh-huh."

Soon, water ran upstairs. She was eager to know what Robbie's doctor friend advised. She'd have loved to go along, but that would have seemed intrusive. She could have driven him, though. He was much more alert in the afternoon. She could imagine Peter Taylor writing a story about one doctor talking to another about how to address his relatives' alcoholism. Though Robbie might have been right. Maybe drugs were the real problem. Apparently when

Japanese businessmen finally left work, they sat in makeshift bars on certain streets and drank until they fell off their stools. Darcy had sent her photographs of men unconscious on the sidewalk.

Blanche scratched to be let in. With great purpose, the dog dashed upstairs, though her back legs weakened halfway up, which she protested by yelping. As Ginny walked toward the stairs, Blanche gathered her courage and continued her ascent, too proud to accept any help. At the top, she stood still for a moment, before gingerly padding down the corridor.

Ginny glanced at an old *Daily Progress* on the hall table. In an even older *New York Times,* there was a photograph of men in hazmat suits, digging holes for caskets, that took up almost half a page. Hart Island? There was such a place, right there, off Manhattan. Why had she never heard of it?

One of the doctor's conundrums was what to do about the home delivery of the *New York Times.* He disliked reading online, and he didn't want to risk going into a store just to buy a newspaper. However many times he complained, he found the paper thrown in the weeds far from the house, sometimes bound with a rubber band rather than a plastic sleeve, often missing the Sunday magazine. The *Daily Progress,* thinner each day, was always placed in the mailbox.

The vacuum roared on, which caused Blanche to dart out of the doctor's bedroom. Her legs buckled again, before she scrambled up and dashed past Ginny, embarrassed.

She didn't want to start writing. She was happy that as soon as she admitted that, Robbie's car pulled into the driveway. She looked over the railing to see him entering the house, flinching because of the noise, but looking much better than he had the previous night. In the quick moment before he closed the door, the world flooded in. The flowering trees and bushes had grown greener overnight. It really was springtime. The birds were singing joyfully, she heard, in the brief moment when the vacuum was shut off, before it roared back on again. Were the birds really joyful? Certainly, people often projected that emotion onto them. For all she knew, the birds were desperate about something.

"I got quite a bit of information," he said, as she descended the stairs to greet him. "Let me get some coffee—it does smell wonderful—then I'll tell you about it. By the way, I ran into your friend, the teacher. She was carrying one of those cardboard containers that held six coffees, and she greeted me with a kiss on the cheek. She did! What's the word from Darcy?"

"He hasn't written."

"I assume you're going to tell him about the phone call?"

"Would you prefer that I didn't? Until there might be better news, I mean."

"Do whatever you think best. He always said I spoiled Cassie. I guess it turns out he was right."

Ginny walked toward Robbie to help him out of his plaid jacket. He was fond of the jacket, which surprised her, because most of his clothing was so understated. He wouldn't wear a shirt he thought too widely striped. Until she moved in, he hadn't even owned a pair of running shoes. She'd bought him those—Nikes, as conservative as possible—for his Christmas present. He'd walked around, exaggerating how strange they felt, for laughs. His own son couldn't have done a better routine, though at the same time that he was amusing, she'd also thought he seemed like a child, trying to establish his balance before trying out a trampoline. Maybe she thought that because there really was a trampoline in the basement, a circular one, whose existence had recently been explained to her. Another little boy had jumped on it, back when it had been set up in what became the doctor's backyard.

She hung up his jacket. His jackets never wrinkled. Some, made of linen, he usually handed over to someone else at a restaurant, though he still never loosened his tie.

The aroma of coffee grew stronger as she followed him into the kitchen. She thought something else needed to be said about the phone call. Whatever his friend's advice, she wanted him to know that she too had been thinking it over.

"Anita wanted another girl," Ginny said matter-of-factly. "I wonder how Cassie would have reacted to a sister?"

"Oh, some days she wanted that. Then, like all the rest of us, she wanted all of them out of her sight. Just wanted to lie in a hammock in Bali. Darcy got shuffled aside a bit. I see that now. Anita was moody. She loved him, but she more or less turned him over to me, because the twins were so high-maintenance. Anita did everything to encourage them, though. She'd make them French toast at midnight, if they were still up doing their studies."

Ginny had never met them, but given what she'd heard, she had little curiosity. It was possible that he was not so much commending his twins as saying that it was unfortunate his wife had coddled them.

"Dante was an accident," he said, carefully carrying his mug to the table. He seemed relaxed. It was good he'd seen his friend. "That's Mrs. Fox upstairs, already?" he asked.

She nodded. He cleared his throat. He took a sip of coffee, then set the mug down. Napkins from the broken container lay splayed in front of it. He picked one up gently, blotting his lips before placing the unopened napkin on his lap.

"What I told you last night skipped over something. It's true I had an affair with Clara before I met Anita. But we also reconnected, I guess you'd say, after she was struck by the car. A year or so after that, her husband died of a heart attack. Heavyset fellow. I was in New York with Jimmy Bishop—Jimmy, who tried to line us up for a visit to Nantucket this summer. The guy you helped me set up the Zoom call with. So much for our vacation. Safer to stay right where we are, of course. Anyway, Jimmy and I took her to dinner after the viewing. Jimmy only had time for a drink and most of the bread basket. Flight to catch. OB/gyn. He's at Yale New Haven now. I walked her back to her place. One thing led to another."

"Wasn't she—didn't you say she'd been badly hurt?"

"Thirty-eight years old, her husband dead. She had a prosthetic leg." He gestured. "Below the knee."

"Jesus. Did you continue to see her?"

"Aroused your curiosity, huh? When Anita went to visit her sister, I met Clara in New York and we flew to Bermuda for the weekend. Then time passed, and I went to New York again."

"I'm glad she could travel. At first, from the way you told it—"

"I married the wrong woman. Simple as that. I *loved* Anita, but I married the wrong woman."

It crossed her mind that he might be able to read her mind, the same way she assumed she knew what he was thinking—though what he'd just said was proof that she wasn't highly intuitive at all.

"Too many good women. That's one of the many things men are resented for: so much ability to choose. Don't jump down my throat; I know it's all different now. But the point of my story is that it wasn't *such* good luck, as it turned out. Clara got pregnant. I had to tell Anita. One of the hardest things I ever had to do. Do you know what happened next?"

She was unable to do anything except stare at him.

"Clara had a miscarriage in New York, right after we'd had a big fight over Anita, me exiled to a hotel. That night she started to cramp and bleed. She called me and I rushed her off to Sinai, and that was that. If you've got all day, I could explain how things were never the same afterwards. Anita and I had different bedrooms. The twins were acting up something awful. Wouldn't stop competing with each other. Drove everybody crazy. One time Anita just ran out of the house. They got into physical scraps too. Got suspended from school. Darcy was afraid of them. He was just a little fellow. Clara? She insisted on being a martyr, sent me back to my family, where she said I belonged. Can't say that I didn't. Jenkins's former partner—Jenkins, the guy I met for coffee—was the one who covered for me while I was off in New York. But my family lived here"—he spread his arms expansively;

there it was, that familiar gesture—"my wife, my children, my practice. I never saw her again. Then, to my surprise, eventually Anita stopped hating me. We had Darcy, then Dante. She picked the names. The thing is, she did forgive me. Confided in Cassie about the whole mess, I always thought, but Anita denied it. 'Why would I lie to you? If I had told her, what would be so wrong with that, compared to what you did?' But, do you know—and this is interesting: for a long time she didn't write anything in her diary, turns out. You've seen it. The whole middle of the book, nothing but blank pages, dated, that she skipped over, then one day she started in again. What does Cassie make of the empty pages but that it was where her mother was changing—so, maybe Cassie didn't know anything about my affair. Cassie points at a blank page and says, 'This is it! This is where she's becoming a lesbian,' like her mother was a werewolf."

Ginny's hand flew up to her mouth.

"Go ahead, laugh. In some ways, the whole thing's a soap opera."

"I'm sorry. Your analogy was funny, not—"

"Anyway, things did get better. I took her to dinner at the Boar's Head, with the man who used to run the *VQR*. Good tennis player. It started raining, so we were nursing cups of tea. The three of us were laughing, and she pointed at a drawing of a boar on her cocktail napkin. 'Look at those tusks. Doesn't it resemble Robert?' The way she asked seemed particularly nasty, especially when I was seeing a shrink—I was!—and she and I'd been talking to the priest. Our friend just assumed she'd had too much to drink. Finally they started closing the restaurant, so he left before us, shaking my hand when I walked him out to the lobby, apologizing, as if *he'd* insulted me. I got her rain jacket from the coat check. They had a real person back then. I hadn't worn anything but my corduroy jacket. He took down Anita's all-weather parka, then he piled a London Fog on top of it, size forty-two long, and as I slipped into it, I felt like my whole body was different. Two days later, I took it back, 'Big mistake, ever so sorry,' then I left. I'd done the right thing. I wasn't in a good mood, though. I'd gotten a speeding ticket they weren't about to look the other way on because I was a doctor, and I was coming down with a cold. I could have afforded my own London Fog, but instead of going out and buying one, I ended up in that place in Barracks Road, across from where CVS used to be, and bought a Barbour jacket and a spray bottle to keep it water-repellent. I never felt right in it, though. Too stiff. But the other night I pulled it on and liked the smell. Fit perfectly. The spray bottle sat right there on the shelf, all this time. I assume the other guy eventually got his raincoat back."

"Your story isn't so much about the raincoat, is it?"

"Somewhat. I was displacing my anger onto somebody I never met, taking his coat. Not like me, I might add. Aberrant behavior."

"You returned to Anita, and you returned the raincoat."

"Never said you weren't smart. Anything else, Dr. Freud?"

"As a matter of fact, there is one more observation I could make, but you wouldn't like it."

"Shoot."

"When she said you were like a boar, she might have been making a pun."

"That's right! I think you got it!"

"But think about the story you just told. I can't believe you think you have a memory problem."

"That night at the restaurant? That's long-term. My problem's short."

"Who am I?" she asked, leaning across the table.

He grunted. He said, "Will you keep your name, or will you become Mrs. Anderson?"

"I have a feeling I'm not going to marry Darcy."

"Is that right? You're not kidding?"

"I'm serious. Maybe I should wait until we talk next and see if I feel entirely differently."

"I've been worrying this might be coming."

"Robbie, don't you think he hasn't made any attempt to fly back because he also has misgivings?"

"I don't know that. He might just be a coward, dodging Covid."

"That's crossed my mind."

"He's always been impulsive. His *going* was the surprise. He didn't get that from Anita or me. We certainly didn't raise the children to live for the moment. Though whatever you do as a parent, it turns out to be wrong."

Music drifted down from upstairs. Mrs. Fox was listening to her little transistor radio that she carried in her handbag. (*"Écoute, mon ami!"* Ginny would have said to Robbie, if she'd been Poirot.) Mrs. Fox didn't sing along, but sometimes she hummed or sighed "uh-huh"—her favorite way to conclude a sentence—when the music stopped.

"As you say, can't hurt to wait until he contacts you," Robbie said. "See how you feel. These times put everybody on edge. More coffee?"

"No, thanks. I'm supposed to go in to the library this afternoon, to meet a person Jeanette put in a good word with, who's going to tell me about a newly created job, if the university ever opens again."

"I think Darcy likes cities. He liked DC, though I wouldn't call that much of a city. I never cared about the place one way or the other, though I enjoy New York and have to assume that'll all bounce back. Tokyo! Everything about it interests him. He sent me some photos a few days ago of men in suits, sprawled on the street. Drunken businessmen, and he said some nights it looked like somebody'd opened fire on them. Not that that happened."

"I have to say, it was my good luck to meet you, and to be here where you've made me feel so welcome."

"'The horror, the horror!'" he said, waving his hands in the air. She got the allusion, but what, exactly, did he mean? Was he thinking of the passed-out Japanese businessmen, the horror of Covid, or something more existential?

After which another plane flew over, on a different course, so that the shadow it cast seemed more smudge than shadow.

"Robbie, I've got to tell you something," she said. "It could be him. The pilot from Utah. It's only fair I mention it."

"Oh yeah? Where'll he land, in my backyard?"

"That's what I'm assuming."

"You're kidding," he said, after a pause.

The noise diminished, then, unexpectedly, intensified. The plane was circling. Now even Blanche rushed into the kitchen as if she'd realized that, all this time, she might have been missing out on some wonderful game. She skidded to a stop and cocked her head.

Never would Ginny tell Robbie about what had happened earlier, when Blanche's back legs collapsed, mid-stairs. If there was any possible way to also communicate her discretion to Blanche, she'd like to try, but except for stroking the dog and whispering words of nonsense in her ear, she'd have to believe a dog was capable of reading minds in order to understand.

Robbie had gone to the window. He was leaning on the wide, stainless steel sink divider to peek under the valance, his arm sliding forward to brace him.

"Pegasus," he said. "Just as I thought. Let's hope they picked up whoever it was, far enough away that we didn't hear them landing."

The medical helicopter, Pegasus. That was what had passed over. She hadn't seen it for so long, she'd forgotten its existence. Had they suspended its use because of Covid? Or maybe it hadn't been much needed because there were so few cars on the road. Stores were closed, some with plywood nailed over the doors. Only a skeletal group of faculty and students were on campus. Of course car accidents had sharply declined, though it didn't fly only in response to accidents.

Blanche walked over to where Robbie was standing. She circled twice, then settled herself at his feet.

"I admire them," Robbie said. "Every time they're called out, it's a matter of life or death."

IN THE GREAT
SOUTHERN
TRADITION

The property on which they worked, this early October Saturday—Jonah, his aunt Monica, and her brother, Uncle Case—was still partially owned by Monica's English ex-husband, Ashton. Case had nicknames for most people and things he disdained, among them Delusional Folly for the house (named Devonshire by Ashton), and Lord Mishap for Ashton himself. In the divorce, Ashton had kept the New York loft, Monica had gotten the Key West condo (which she'd sold immediately), and in the spring both would mutually profit from the sale of the Virginia house and its fifty-two acres.

So, today Jonah and his aunt and uncle had assembled to plant tulip bulbs. At least, that was the ostensible reason: in spring, the flowers would be eye-catching to prospective buyers, and Monica would receive half of whatever Ashton received from the sale. The real reason he was there, Jonah felt sure, was simply that Monica liked to involve him in "family matters." Which said a lot about what had become of the family.

Monica had married Ashton in her forties, following their years-long engagement. Ten years older than she, he'd been her one and only husband. They'd had a wonderful time for a few years: ballooning, visiting nearby vineyards for wine tastings, taking tango lessons. ("Drifting around in the sky, dancing, and being drunk," as Case had described their union.) A few years into the marriage, Ashton had taken up with a polo player: younger, prettier, an oenophile. He and his new love had decamped to London, along with Sir James Hewitt (Ashton's ferret; even Ashton had been amused by Case's name for the little thing), and the woman's young daughter from her first marriage. Ashton left behind the photograph album of his and Monica's wedding, as well as forgetting the ferret's food and the child's favorite toy. Ashton had made the mistake, back then, of calling Case in Richmond when they'd landed, asking him to "do the right thing" and go into the house, find Hoppie, the green turtle, and mail it to London. Case had simply hung up on him.

"You know, I was thinking this morning that Mama died just about the time everybody stopped writing letters. Though we did get that thoughtful note from Dr. Anderson. And, of course, Carrie's condolences. I guess there were others. It just *wasn't* what I expected," Monica said. This long after the fact, Joshua's aunt still ruminated on her mother's death. Earlier, looking at the sky, she'd said, "Mama never did have any desire to get on a plane, bless her heart."

"Stop talking about her," Case said. "She died years ago."

Monica glowered. She said, "That response to Mama's passing is extremely disrespectful."

"This is a central issue for Monica," Case said, turning to Jonah as if his nephew were a camera eye, through which he could appeal to a wider audience. He gestured with fingers splayed, ever the lawyer. "She views the demise of her mother primarily as an opportunity to examine the shortcomings of others. If I'd known how much superficial consolation meant to my dear sister, I'd have invited everyone over to toast Monica with champagne and thank her for her long period of compassionate service. Heaven knows, *I* never tried preside over that circus. Champagne flutes are best for toasts, not those shallow glasses that encourage quiver and slosh."

"'Quiver and slosh.' Brilliant!" Jonah said. "Aunt Monica, how many years did you take care of Grans?" He asked because in the preceding years his own contact with the family had been intermittent.

Two squirrels ran up a tree trunk, pantomiming *barbershop pole*. Something small and hard fell from the tree and shattered.

"Two years, five months. Before that I had a job, as you recall."

"Will you rejoin the workforce?" Jonah asked.

He was digging with his trowel as Monica had told him to do, making sure the hole was seven or eight inches deep. Each tulip bulb's descent into the soil was preceded by the throwing in of bonemeal. "Ashes to ashes, dust to dust," Case intoned sententiously, as his sister and nephew worked. Uncle Case had yet to pick up a bulb. He checked his phone constantly. He'd said he couldn't miss taking an important call, which apparently (from the few cryptic remarks Monica had made when Case wasn't there) had to do with the possible removal of statues on Losers Row in Richmond. Really, leaving aside the great Arthur Ashe, with his aviator sunglasses and his tennis racket, children clustered adoringly at his side, who'd miss those overwhelming but paradoxically invisible statues of Confederates everybody already knew lost the war, riding their horses like something out of a teenage girl's wet dream? Case always seemed to be on call, Ashton had complained. He'd thought he was being so clever by whispering in Jonah's ear that, actually, C.R. (as he always called his uncle) was an obstetrician. Today's crisis had to do with *Monument Avenue*. It was *Important*. So okay, everybody was over there gawking at the statues like they were looking at a lineup: that one might be the mugger, or the carjacker, the rapist, the asshole who threatened them with a tire iron. *Oh, that's Lee, that's him, the one right there on the horse that probably only wants some hay and water, and to get the fucking saddle taken off.* Yeah, sure—Uncle Case was a great success, though in this family the bar was so low that only meant he'd gotten out of Charlottesville. One thing Jonah'd give him credit for, though: his new home in the Fan District was huge. Its bowed windows made it seem as if the house itself struggled to burst out from within, wishing to make an even bigger impression.

"Two years of unemployment does not help anyone 'rejoin the workforce,' as you put it," Monica replied. "I know I should be grateful that work isn't a necessity. I only did it because it was so much fun to spend time with Sterling."

Monica had been an employee at a lamp store that sold and repaired new and antique fixtures. The owner, Sterling Schuler, had closed up shop shortly after she left. How that job could have been fun, Jonah couldn't imagine. Sterling had made the bad decision—the images of blazing fires in California proved it—to leave Charlottesville for LA, where he hoped to restart his earlier (much earlier) career as a character actor. Jonah could understand that impulse, though at twenty-two he was too young to have anything that he might restart. To stay chuffed, Jonah tried to imagine himself an already famous playwright, one who wryly considered the strange actions of others, while wearing an assortment of fabulous scarves.

Jonah was currently on the waitstaff at Simpatico, around the corner from Lee Park, formerly Emancipation Park, now Market Street Park, near Charlottesville's downtown mall. Upon entering Simpatico, employees were required to drop their phones into an Easter basket filled with celluloid grass (Easter was the boss's favorite holiday) and take a new mask. The work benefits included a six-pack of Poland Spring every Monday and two monthly passes for Bikram yoga classes, taught by the owner's ex-wife. Jonah did these things, though chose to think he was just gathering dialogue as he charmed potential benefactors, while performing Downward Dog among them. That's what he was aiming for in his present reality: to see himself as brilliant, in a self-deprecating, Jeremy Irons sort of way. Jonah tried to demonstrate a gently mocking sense of humor that grazed the vulnerabilities of everyone he chatted up. He found it interesting that Monica was the last female family member standing (though, at present, she was sidewinding like a crab, if a crab might also be holding a tulip bulb). There'd been three sisters: Monica; Laurene (who'd moved to Colorado and drowned); and Cora, Jonah's mother, whom Uncle Case called The Mistake.

Aunt Monica had always had favorite-aunt status, which was a good thing, because the other aunt was dead. Monica remained his best hope for money that might allow him to spend a winter month at an artists' community called Civitella Ranieri, where he could write plays in solitude and stroll across something called the Russian Terrace if they admitted him as a paying guest, off-season. He'd dropped out of college before and was prepared to do it again, if fortune smiled. *Se la fortuna sorridesse*, as Alia, the waitress he had a crush on, would say—and had, so often, that after Googling it, he'd memorized the phrase. The sentiment sounded gentler in Italian. Alia had a live-in boyfriend who spoke only English. Ungrammatical English.

"Look out," Jonah said, swatting a bee that had landed on a bag of bulbs. It lifted off on the diagonal, grazing his ear as it buzzed.

"It's best not to anger them," Monica replied, reaching into a different brown bag to bring out a parrot tulip bulb. She'd interspersed their planting with bright-red pencil tulips. A photograph of them in bloom was stapled to the top of the bag.

Case was not helping at all. In fact, he'd walked some distance away, turned his back, and was peeing against a tree. It gave him something in common with one of the bronze horses he might be representing, protecting its rights if it was hauled away—though he supposed the horse would just let fly, forget the tree. Monica tipped her hat brim lower, avoiding glancing in that direction.

Springtime would be such a—what was the cliché?—a riot of color. Or was that fall? The redbuds would be blooming along the highway—the South's weedy equivalent of dandelions. After today, Jonah doubted he'd ever see Delusional Folly again.

But that wasn't what bothered him. What really worried him was that he'd never be as good a writer as Sam Shepard, who'd lived not very far from where Jonah was right this minute, back when Sam Shepard was with Jessica Lange. They'd lived there, and Jonah never even knew it.

THE PLANTING WAS DULLY REPETITIVE, so Jonah tried to entertain himself with *faux* murderous images of doing in his uncle. (He and his college roommate, Mark, had delighted in inventing bleak, cartoonish scenarios about people they found inherently ridiculous.) Right now, Jonah decided to adopt the perspective of the Road Runner. He'd collide with Case—easy, since the Road Runner was always running amok. His toppled uncle would see stars, while he, the Road Runner, plucked two stars from the air and affixed them to his own eyes, Elton-John-sunglass-style, then vaulted a fence, only to be chased by a dog with gleaming fangs. Oh, but that backward glance lingered too long: amid a burst of spittle, over the cliff he went! But wait (he set the trowel aside): this was a revenge fantasy about his uncle; what could he do to lure *him* over the cliff? He could pick up the trowel, which—if he squinted—took the shape not of a sword, but of a blowtorch. He'd set Uncle's thin, hairless ankles on fire (cargo pants! who would wear those, at Case's age?): as Case became engulfed in flames, Jonah would levitate to safety, emitting a cosmic laugh some might mistake for thunder.

"It's best not to swat bees," Monica was saying, again—one of those softly spoken mantras she was so fond of—her hat brim pulled even lower. Jonah's mother, Cora, The Mistake, had once fantasized about going back in time to become a painter on the Left Bank. She'd worked most of her life as a secretary at Money-Wise Payroll—she'd bought some painting supplies, when she was middle-aged, as well as a black beret, though she'd taken so much kidding, she'd only worn it once. Eventually, the brushes had been used for dusting narrow spaces.

"A penny for your thoughts, Jonah," Case said, returning.

"My *thoughts*," Jonah echoed, stalling for time. "Well! My thoughts runneth over, like a river swelling its banks: a river cluttered with Styrofoam containers filled with taco corpses, and acres of plastic discarded by insensitive day-trippers who respect neither the depth, nor the ancient beauty, of this canyon."

A squirrel streaked by.

This reply got not Case's, but Monica's attention. She'd been observing a tripartite bulb, which she tapped lightly on her palm, to see if the parts separated. She hadn't been able to find gardening gloves, so she wore gray angora texting gloves she'd taken from her glove compartment. Though she didn't text, her hands were often cold, summer or winter. She extracted from the bag a bulb larger than any others, its root whiskers like Spanish moss. "This one's an interloper," she muttered to Case, who crouched at his sister's side, finally, grudgingly, digging. He was a law partner at Mills, Crace, Hart, Fullerton, Donado & Miller who contributed to the Fresh Air Fund, but otherwise avoided the outdoors. Look at him: he had on cargo pants and a white button-down shirt. Black loafers, worn sockless.

"Madam," Case said to his sister, who adjusted the brim of her hat to see him. Ah, that routine again: his uncle was channeling a Southern gentleman. "Madam, what you hold in your hand I declare the winner of this year's Vidalia onion competition, a recent addition to our P'ettiest Bird comp'tition, as ever' bird thus far selected has regrettably become extinct. No more doves, no starlings, which of course were imported to our faaahn country, and a disastrous mistake that proved to be, no sparrows, our beautiful blue jays gone, every last bird but a mem'ry."

His uncle didn't go on quite that long. He'd shut up after exclaiming that theirs was a "faaahn country." Jonah had silently filled in everything else—he'd learned this in an acting exercise: how to channel the unspoken words of the other character so that they also informed your own performance—because it was so easy to follow his uncle's drift. His uncle was a ham. He'd never seen him in court, but of course he'd overplay everything, that was a no-brainer, and wish he could be wearing a wig when he did it, like barristers in England. Case would love to be over there—as so much of Charlottesville wished to be in London 24/7—where he'd hobnob with No. 10, the man with the enormous amount of visceral belly fat who retained his explosion of straw-man freak hair, uttering ignorant, Trump-like pronouncements that were nothing but mouth farts.

Now Case was rambling on, talking about a state fair he'd gone to as a young man, some Biggest Potato in Nelson County contest he and his wife, Janet, had stumbled into. Backstory: What everyone who met Casey Robert Fullerton (C.R. to his colleagues) for even five minutes knew was that his wife had died in his arms of a ghastly disease just after their fifth anniversary. Jonah's mother had resigned her job to help nurse her; everyone agreed that the young woman had been quite something. That must have been true, Jonah thought, if Cora had expressed such compassion for her. His mother had sent him to school with a fever of 103 and accused him of pretending to be ill when the call came to pick him up and he'd staggered to the car, leaning heavily on the school nurse. In high school, she'd told him to "buck up" and had refused to get his broken ankle x-rayed for a week. This many years later, at the end of a shift in the restaurant, the ankle still felt wonky.

Monica was now upright, embracing her brother, as sad memories of his day at the fair (or whatever it had been), overwhelmed him. Jonah simply stared, as Case tried to flip his grimace into a reassuring smile, which further contorted his mouth. They were both weeping. They did it all the time! There was medicine for people as depressed as Monica and Case, but they never took it. You could be saying something completely neutral, such as how nice the breeze felt, and all the while they'd be exchanging invisible signals, like singers at a Pentecostal church. Jesus, they were often very, very hard to be around, though for the sake of family togetherness, in a world where almost every family he could think of was fucked up and he didn't happen to know the ones that weren't (Alia had been sexually aggressed upon by her stepfather, the boy next door, *and* her priest, even *after* she left the Catholic church, she'd told him one evening, strolling past Lee's statue in the park). He felt obliged to see his aunt and uncle, who tried so hard to be surrogate parents, not because they were compassionate and successful at their undertaking, but because they had no clue about how badly they were failing. His uncle had given him cuff links for Christmas! Monica had given him a tie bar, which was ridiculous, even if it had belonged to her father. Also, there was the arts colony in Umbria he was desperate to attend, and at least his aunt might be sympathetic about that.

Monica's head rested on her brother's shoulder. They acted like nobody could see them. It seemed like a version of that old movie, where Demi Moore sits at the potter's wheel and sees her dead lover, which was either before or after her famous *Vanity Fair* cover when she was pregnant and showed her naked belly. Wasn't that pretty much what that movie had been about—the one he and his roommate had watched on TV, sharing a bottle of wine Mark bought because the label depicted two trucks colliding? For a ten-buck bottle, that had gone down smoothly after a few tokes, making the maudlin movie seem more like the comedy it was.

What was wrong with his aunt *now*? She'd torn a hole in her pants, kneeling, and Case had dropped down to cradle it—really, this was so hyper; it was like a marriage proposal or something—apologizing, all the while, for bringing up the past. She'd banged her knee on a rock. Well, ouch to that. She was maybe slightly too old to be doing what she was doing, though? "Miss Gloom" had been his mother's disdainful nickname for her sister. His mother hadn't exactly been the best example of equilibrium herself (after her husband's death, before her heart attack, Cora had lived with a Hawaiian alcoholic she met while betting on the dogs).

Back when Jonah was still very young, his father, The Old Man, had gone apeshit one Thanksgiving, when Monica asked everyone to join hands before dinner to observe a moment of silence, remembering (she'd glanced significantly at Case) "those no longer among us." This had happened at Jonah's parents' house, not at the so-called retirement community his parents later staggered off to. "Then what?" The Old Man had roared. "What? Janet rises out of her grave? Our fond memories resuscitate her?" "Please stop!" Case had said, pushing back his chair. Cora fled the table. But Janet hadn't even been buried: as Jonah understood it, her ashes had been scattered in his mother's rose garden. Later, the rest of them had been set floating on the Chesapeake, and finally sprinkled atop Crabtree Falls. (They'd been on a car trip, and Monica had taken The Old Man by surprise; she had Janet's cremains *with her*? His father had lost it: "No, no, don't tell me, Monica, don't even tell me. You want to let some ashes fly? Please do that while I take a piss. Your sister and our boy Jonah can weep and wail with you—he's been raised to think everybody collapses at the drop of a hat. Who cares about scenery? No, let's not waste time in the real world, let's have the day be centered on *you, Monica*.")

Yeah, Jonah thought, it was too bad Eugene O'Neill hadn't gotten out more. He might have met this family.

THAT MORNING, Jonah had pumped himself up by doing a few turns as the Mick Jagger rooster, elbows synced with jutting chin thrusts. He'd been helped by a shot of Smirnoff, tipped into the morning Tropicana (he'd learned the vodka-in-freezer trick from his on-again, off-again girlfriend from CHS, Frieda). That, and just the tiniest, most minuscule toke, in preparation for his day of working the land, in the great Southern tradition.

Of course, years before, he'd rebelled. He'd wanted to put as much distance as possible between himself and his bellicose (such a great word) father and his disdainful mother, to say nothing of weird Uncle Case and Aunt Monica. So it had been surprising to Jonah that after he'd dropped out of Penn, Monica had expressed real concern. She'd arranged for him to spend time in California, crashing at the famous Sterling's on an inflatable mattress she had shipped there, working the lunch shift at Bounty Burger and writing plays at night. That had been interesting, but after a few months he'd decided that what he was accomplishing wasn't enough: the family affliction, maybe, where everyone's internal refrain was Never Enough, Never Enough. Back home, Monica still hero-worshipped Sterling, who'd been her walker (what a word that was!) before she met Ashton. Sterling told rather hilarious, long-winded jokes, made crème brûlée, got stoned and decorated his Christmas tree the day after Thanksgiving. Once in LA, Sterling had gotten himself a new wardrobe that featured triangle-patterned shirts and argyle socks in shades of purple.

But really, whatever. It wasn't like he felt superior to Sterling. The man had always been very nice to him.

When Jonah moved back to Charlottesville after more than enough time in Philadelphia, he hadn't moved back to his parents' house. In fact, he'd only visited them once, with Monica, who begged him to do it. What a miserable time that had been, when Frieda wanted to go with Monica and him to meet the folks, and he'd refused. Oh, so he could just move into the basement apartment in Belmont she shared with her sassy, blue-haired barista roommate, but he wouldn't even tell his parents he lived with her? she'd asked. A few months later, The Old Man was dead, after falling off a roof at the retirement community: *They* were now countersuing the estate (this his uncle considered "ill-advised"; he'd put Ray Miller, the Oxford-educated, youngest, brightest member of the firm, on the case) because *Damn right, the guy wasn't allowed up there, but he didn't supply his own ladder!*

He didn't much like to think about Frieda, though she *had* smoked with him and dragged him along on train rides, once to the National Gallery of Art, where they'd viewed paintings and had sex (which they never did in the apartment) in a stall in the women's bathroom. (One chorus of Taylor Swift: "Ooh, look what you made me do.") His friend Mark, who'd later taken the train from Philadelphia to Charlottesville, had thought Frieda was bad news, but really: Jonah would never have considered applying to UVA to finish college if she hadn't insisted ("Your uncle will lend

you the money, I know he will, I know his type: type A, always
You-Can-Do-It; in fact, You-Fuckin'-Have-to-Do-It"). She'd been
right. If he hadn't done that, he'd never have found himself in
the totally inspirational Introduction to Playwriting class, taught
by Dr. Jorgé Bellavista. When Frieda moved to Amsterdam, he'd
found her absence hard to deal with. U HAVE ACCESS FREE
MENT HLTH CARE UVA, she'd texted from the flat where
she'd decided to live with the barista and that woman's Dutch
businessman husband, with whom she'd reconciled. They had a
threesome (as well as views of some canal)—no doubt, much
more interesting than his current situation, helping his aunt and
uncle dig up a lawn. At least Monica and Case kept in contact,
which was more than his mother had done. Oh, sure: she'd called
once to say he'd killed his father. It was amazing, the number of
guys whose mothers unfairly accused them of doing things they
hadn't done, such as burglarizing their, *ahem*, summer cottages.
Example: a five-bedroom, four-bath with solar panels in Bath,
Maine, with a wraparound porch bigger than any place Jonah had
ever lived; he and Mark had gone there from Penn on spring break.
Mark certainly hadn't broken into it; the guy was into Bikram
and Buddhism, and walked no-kill shelter dogs on his lunch hour
and worked in the community garden in springtime, so that was
insane. Or his friend Joe Fanelli's mother, who'd had a meltdown
and accused him of "terrorizing" his younger sister by telling her
she wouldn't get accepted into any college (all Joey had done was
suggest a few places that weren't Ivy League, so she wouldn't get
her heart broken).

Back when Jonah and Frieda had driven to Richmond for the Big Ask, his uncle had seemed pleased to see them, though they hadn't been invited to stay for dinner. Someone had been cooking in Case's kitchen ("Southern boys and their slaves," Frieda had huffed, in the car); they'd seen her briefly when she brought out—yup—a cold bottle of San Benedetto, which for some reason was *the* preferred boutique water in the family. To Jonah's surprise, Case had nodded encouragingly as Jonah made his pitch ("Yes, yes, resuming your studies"). Case had offered no resistance to writing Jonah a check that more than covered his tuition. He'd made a few brief remarks about how he himself had found it hard to decide what to focus on when he was younger, or whether to focus at all. He seemed as perplexed to be saying that as Jonah had been to hear it. His uncle had even written out and handed over the check before asking him, the minute Frieda went to the bathroom, "Unrelated, and none of my business, but your time in California. When you were staying with Monica's friend, Sterling? I wondered. I mean, it makes me wonder: Are you gay?"

"You're not yourself!" Monica was suddenly exclaiming. "I'm talking to you, Jonah! You aren't even listening. Did you hear anything I said?"

Whoa! The Monica avatar was right in his face.

"You don't want to be here, I know you don't, I know that," she said, grabbing his hand. "It must be so *difficult*, after your mother, well, my sister must have had a breakdown to take up with that man who was never drunk and never sober. When someone dies and things remain unresolved, it can be so *difficult*. I hope you don't think any of it was your fault. I can't believe I got us into this, this ridiculous day—that I thought it was an opportunity for bonding! It's not what a young person should be doing with his weekend. What's wrong with me?"

"Jonah," his uncle said, startling him by addressing him instead of Monica; already, Jonah imagined Case and Monica getting hysterical. "I want you to know that your aunt and I are proud of you, and even though you stand to inherit a bit of money once your mother's affairs are finally sorted out, you shouldn't think that you ever need to repay me for your tuition. I'm also very happy you didn't marry that woman who was with you in Richmond that day, because she radiated malice."

"We care so much what happens to you!" Monica said. Her right texting glove was filthy.

"'What happens'?" Jonah echoed.

"Well, we certainly botched things, didn't we? It's not like we've been able to set a good example for you."

"Monica, you need to clean that knee," Case said. "It's oozing blood, for god's sake. Go in the house and . . . Should I help?" His uncle looked at the tulip bulb he was holding, scrutinizing it in an "Alas, poor Yorick!" moment. Then he threw it. It rose in a high arc and plunked down an impressive distance away.

"It's just a scratch," Monica said quietly. She turned to Jonah. "But we'll have a lovely dinner!" she said. (Were those *tears*?) "What about the Ivy Inn? All those new buildings crowding it out, but it's still the same old-fashioned place. Jonah, you work so hard in school, and nights at that restaurant, and on weekends attending all those rehearsals. I understand. I think I understand that you're here today because you're the next generation, and as our family's sole representative, you feel a need to please us."

"What?" he said. It was as if his aunt was reciting lines from one play, while he'd been memorizing another. Or maybe she expected him to act some part he had no script for——one that was being written in the moment.

"But what do I really understand?" she said bitterly. She'd walked to an empty birdbath, felt underneath it, and was holding the house key. "Listen to me: 'I understand.'" Monica's bloody knee was visible through the cut in her jeans. Jonah instantly decided that behind the denim, it was really Curious George's lewd little red tongue protruding.

They'd been at this ridiculous task too long, Case was saying. And why did people not call when they said they would? This rarely happened when there were landlines, but a cell phone apparently provided the opportunity to blame technology. Was there, or was there not, a problem about the potential resettling of Richmond's statue of Robert E. Lee? He did the windup to the pitch and threw another bulb. He agreed entirely: Jonah *shouldn't be* wasting his time trying to plant flowers that might or might not bloom, considering climate change. *That asshole*, Case was saying, who ran off with that polo player——they *deserved* to be ruled by Boris Fucking Johnson, who was nothing but another tarted-up Trump on Halloween. Case strode off, frowning furiously.

Well, that was cool, at least: his uncle totally got the relationship between Boris Johnson and Trump.

Zzzyipppp!

The bee stung. Jonah heard it, *zzzyipppp*, the second the fucker bit his wrist. Where had it come from?

"Case, Case!" Monica was calling, running after her brother.

Ah, god: they were at it again—the ongoing melodrama. Just as well she didn't know anything had happened. He could just die of shock, maybe, if he was as allergic to bees as he was to cats—though in that case, he'd merely sneeze himself to death. But wait, wait—was this the moment when the day was going to turn into a horror movie? *Flip that channel,* he thought. *Reach for the remote.* But all he did was increase the pressure of his hand over his wrist. Was he supposed to see if it left its stinger in him? His entire lower arm felt scalded, but he dared not ease up on his grip to look.

THE SKY WAS TINGED PINK; the insects were angered that people still occupied their turf. Until the bee bit, he'd been sitting on the lawn so long with his legs outstretched that his butt had gone dead. It was still tingling back to life. He'd been reminded, when he tried to stand up, of the way he'd sat late at night, with a pillow behind him, on the fake cowhide rug at Sterling's, after his own stint at the hamburger place ended. Jonah had often made himself available with the script, in case Sterling needed a prompt. Sterling, whose best chance was being cast as a sentry who'd get his big moment when he clanked onstage in his armor to exclaim, "M'lord!" or something equally banal. Every now and then, just for the hell of it, Sterling had also practiced lines from *Hamlet,*

Macbeth: "My way of life is fall'n into the sere, the yellow leaf." Sterling, well past midnight, barefoot, wearing his lime-green pajamas in the rented house in Silver Lake, declaiming as if the track lighting was a spotlight.

Jesus! Look at that! he thought, startled out of his LA time-warp memory. For a second, even his wrist stopped burning. A dog stood amid the swarming insects, the bushy-tailed squirrels, and the chirping birds that still endured, regardless of his uncle's declaration of their extinction. It must be the neighbor's dog. Its coat was white, mottled with brown. One ear sat cocked, the darker one dangled. It took him another few seconds to realize the dog could come no closer because an invisible fence separated the properties. Well, *who knew*? Didn't they mark those things with little flags on stakes? Even out in the county, everybody had to draw their line of demarcation.

The dog eyed him, debating its next move. Memory had no doubt kicked in: what you'd get, versus the pain you'd endure to get it. "The art of life is the art of avoiding pain," said Thomas Jefferson. His mother loved to quote that: a man so certain, while simultaneously so cynical. Sure, Mom: and how had that worked out for Sally Hemings, giving birth to Jefferson's children?

Alia had had a baby when she was fifteen and gave it up for adoption, she'd told him one night, drinking a glass of wine they'd been comped after an extra-long shift, as Tom, the owner, turned away and called his wife from the far end of the bar, begging her to take him back.

To deflect attention from its cowardice, the dog feigned interest in pawing the ground. It dug, dug, dug, its snout disappearing. It couldn't resist seeing if Jonah was buying the act, though; the dog glanced up quickly, snorting at the same time it ducked its head, but it was really sneaking a look at its audience before immersing itself with increased vigor in its important task: *Oh, there might be a bone down here. Okay, forget the bone, there might be a roast beef, or do you care about money? There might be gold! Yeah, probably there's gold. Or a hidden stream. With judicious dredging there could be a pond, a wonderful pond for skaters, or to play ice hockey, to slide on with anything handy, a tray, a magic carpet you can lift off on if you don't give a shit about ponds, and what you'd really like is to get out of town.*

Monica reappeared at his side. Was she going to minister to him, exclaim about how terrible it was that he'd been bitten by a bee? No, she wasn't.

"G'boy, g'boy, come over, come over here," Monica cooed, patting her thigh above the bloodied rip in her pants.

He made Don't-Do-It eye contact with the dog, who stood with narrowed eyes, pretending to sniff the air. The dog hesitated. Then, less energetically, it resumed digging.

She didn't get it. She would, if the dog decided to run toward them, but then it would be too late and what happened next would become just another family story about bad judgment.

JONAH SENT A TELEPATHIC MESSAGE to Sterling describing the situation, in which he, his aunt, and his uncle had utterly run out of energy, but were without any way to retreat from one another: *Monica cut her knee; I got stung by a bee; Case is exhibiting his usual superiority.*

The response came instantaneously: *Snow dome.*

Okay, *snow dome.* He could work with that. He cupped the possibility in the palm of his hand. Gripped it. Shook it hard with his dominant hand, but *wow, did that hurt.* His forearm was becoming as bloated as the Pillsbury Doughboy's. It was warm to the touch. His lips tingled. But he wasn't going to whine to Monica and Case; the point of coming had been to show support, to help—though how? How had he thought he might do that? As he looked again at the dome, he saw that one of the two tiny figures had turned upside down. It made sense that it was Monica—and that her hat offered some cushioning.

It's a small world, he realized. He jiggled it again: Uncle Case floated crookedly to his sister's side. The snow swirling slowly around them made it obvious the snowflakes fell not through air, but through viscous water. He concentrated hard, sending one last message to Sterling: *Am I supposed to be in there?* Whoa! This could have been an outtake from *Being John Malkovich.*

Take a pass. You don't belong, came the reply.

He looked up to see the dog bounding off across the field, one ear flapping. Though he could no longer see its face, he imagined the creature with a furrowed brow, baring its teeth, saliva dripping, happy to leave the humans behind as it raced toward home, imploring the heavens to know why it had been born into such a world.

NEARBY

Midway through the semester, Rochelle stepped in to pinch-hit at the university for a teacher she'd never met, though she hadn't taught before. CFS, the famous visiting writer claimed: chronic fatigue syndrome. How excruciating it had been, he'd reported, sitting on the edge of his bed, frustrated to tears at the exhausting prospect of pulling on his socks. ("Maybe he should have forgotten the socks," Jeanette, who ran Creative Writing, said witheringly to Rochelle.) It was assumed by much of the faculty—at least, those who knew he'd been there—that since his new love had been his only topic of conversation, he'd flown back to Ireland to reunite with his girlfriend.

Rochelle Warner-Banks (her husband was the well-known lawyer Reggie Banks, who'd argued several times before the Supreme Court) had gotten Jeanette's desperate call only the day before the abandoned class would next meet ("Please, please; just come once, see if you like it"). What a surprise! She'd hung up and immediately texted six women in her book group (Jeanette had belonged to it, until she got too busy) to say that she was sorry, but she wouldn't be able to make her presentation on *The Waves* the following afternoon because she'd been called into service at UVA. She called Sage Versa, and asked—since she knew Sage had loved the book—whether she could step in. The world suddenly seemed like a merry-go-round of substitutions. Fortunately, Sage was very smart and didn't fear public speaking. Forty-five years before, when Reggie was attending law school in Ann Arbor, Rochelle had worked at an ad agency and made monthly presentations to one of the firm's biggest clients, because her boss considered her so "amazing"—and the client had been a New Yorker, by definition hard to please.

You can do it, you can alter the syllabus, you can find a way, she silently reassured herself, though the pep talk made her feel like she was talking to a horse.

For the first meeting, she'd worn a long-sleeved tunic over the regimental black winter tights. Everyone in town wore Arche shoes, and so did she. She'd entered the classroom accompanied by Jeanette, who'd introduced her and explained the situation. Apparently, most of the students never picked up email messages, and Jeanette wasn't reassured by a smiley face in response to a text message. Jeanette's husband was a stockbroker. She and Jeanette had played mixed doubles at the Boar's Head a few times. They crossed paths at ACAC. Jeanette had brought a bunch of flowers to welcome Rochelle, which she plunked down on the seminar table in a vase improvised from a wide-mouthed iced tea bottle.

Her predecessor turned out to have been more than a bit odd. He'd asked, "If this character could be a twee, what kind of a twee would he be?" which, he'd informed them, was not an entirely joking question: it had been inspired by a lisping American interviewer who'd routinely asked such things of famous people on television. (Thank god television had improved; his imitating the lisp, though, had certainly not been PC.)

Surveying the students' faces as they attempted to suspend judgment, she realized the other teacher's eccentricities might work in her favor. Indeed, she did not care if a story offered clues about a character's astrological sign.

She'd been forthcoming: She'd explained that while she'd had jobs that seemed to involve aspects of teaching, she wasn't going to pretend to be an experienced teacher. "I majored in English myself. I belong to an excellent book group in town, and I do freelance editing. I used to work in advertising," she told them. She added that in recent years, she'd more than once had to introduce her own husband at public events ("a well-known lawyer")—and if they didn't think that was intimidating . . . She'd let the sentence drift into its silent, implied meaning.

"Why couldn't he introduce himself?" a round-faced student asked. Several bracelets on his wrist clanked when he raised his hand before speaking, though the gesture seemed more like a reflex—what a person would do if a door was about to slam in their face.

"I think because having someone else introduce you is a formality."

"So, did you say what kind of a twee your husband would be?" (This was how she'd found out about her predecessor's tic.)

Her expression must have indicated that she didn't get the joke. Most of the young women glanced tiredly at the questioner, who nevertheless smiled at his own witticism.

"Fritz always goes off-point," a young woman sitting near her said.

She'd gotten through the first two meetings pretty well, and Fritz had gone silent. One of the girls who frowned most deeply turned out to ask thought-provoking questions. Reading the *Cavalier Daily*, she discovered that another of her students was organizing a protest in DC.

She began to fall into her new routine of teaching. She didn't like the long walk to the building (barricades everywhere, even if you were on foot; if you were driving, forget it), but the students' generally alert manner (eight were female, four were male) was encouraging. She told them she was happy to be there, because it had gotten her out of having to explain *The Waves*, a notably complex book by Virginia Woolf. After class, Lauren Li asked where she stood regarding Michael Cunningham's *The Hours*, vs. *Mrs. Dalloway*. (Later, though she had assigned nothing by Raymond Carver, Lauren had asked what she thought about Gordon Lish's "extreme" editing of Carver's stories.)

Soon the semester was half over. (Her initial condition for continuing had been that she could add some books she liked and forget about *The Executioner's Song*; no one could care what tree the murderer Gary Gilmore would be, and the book was interminable.) This day, when class ended, she'd started down the hall, when Fritz came up behind her. He wanted to know if he could ask her a personal question.

"If I don't have to answer, or if I can lie," she replied, straight-faced, pushing the elevator button. It seemed better than impulsively saying yes or no. Her husband, Mr. Always Give a Question Three Beats Before Answering, would be proud of her.

"The thing is, I teach karate in Staunton tonight, and I've got my brother's car, but the tire's sort of bald, and I got a warning. Like a ticket thing when the cop walked around kicking the tires? But, so, I've got to get there. Is there any way you could possibly loan me forty dollars?"

"Yes," she said, simply. (He considered this a personal question?)

"Great! I can have the money back to you by the end of the month. I just got a job at Crazed, and the tips are good. At least, when certain bands don't play."

"What's the relationship between tips and bands? Customers leave more if the band's good?"

"No. I think, like, okay, for example, Nate, who used to be with Girlyman? So, everybody watching is whatever, transfixed, and everything else goes out of their mind: hooking up later, tips. They tend not to leave a decent tip because it's not like Nate himself's going to get it."

"Ah," she said—though what he'd said only further confused her. Her husband would have warned her not to enter the labyrinth of speculation. To wait and see what was revealed. "I'm afraid I'll have to go to the cash machine, though. Can you walk over to Bank of America with me? And maybe you can give me a ride to my parking lot afterwards? I'm in K-2."

"Oh, sure thing. It's the least I can do. This is really nice of you. Thank you," he said. "My roommate offered me fifteen bucks, but I already owe him twenty, and he's down to eating oatmeal for dinner, so I just couldn't."

"That was kind," she said, ignoring the oatmeal information.

"I live over in Belmont," he said. "Near the Local. I have four roommates, but never see half of them. Nobody goes to the university. One guy, over the summer he moved in his girlfriend and she had fleas. We had to get the place exterminated. K-2's the name of a notoriously scary mountain in Nepal. That's where you said you parked, right?"

"What? Oh, the parking lot. Yes. Are you a climber?"

"It's cool to think about, but I'm more into other stuff. I just want to say, we really lucked out. I mean, I could do without Alice Munro, but you see a lot there with how those women characters think one thing and do another, I get that."

"You're not persuaded, though."

"Pizza and snails."

"Excuse me?"

The office door closed. She pulled the handle to be sure it had locked.

"People prefer pizza, most do, but other people prefer escargot, which are snails."

Again she noticed the bracelet collection when he crawled his fingers through the air.

"I've eaten snails," she said. "Once, in Paris. Those were the best, but maybe it was the restaurant, and it was my first time there."

He didn't offer to help her on with her coat when she paused to put it on. She managed fine. She reached into her pocket for her cashmere hat with the two tiny moth holes and pulled it on.

"You were in France to introduce your husband, or something?"

"No. Actually, we were on our honeymoon."

"Oh. Wow."

"It's my husband's favorite place. He wanted to show it to me."

He didn't walk ahead of her to open the door as they exited the building.

"My mom's had three husbands, or sort of husbands. The first one died. The second one was the brother of the guy she'd been living with. When she got pregnant with me, my father joined the army, but it turned out she got a thing going with his brother, and when my dad didn't come back, Pete married my mom. Hey, that's Lauren! You know her mother's a famous pianist?"

"I didn't know that."

Lauren, walking toward them, faltered. She adjusted her backpack, shrugging it higher onto one shoulder. There was no way she could pass by without speaking, though, in spite of her contortions. In all the wide-open space, she looked cornered. She said, "Hi, Ms. Banks, I mean"—she blushed—"Ms. Warner-Banks. Hi, Straight Punch. That was an awesome class, Ms. Warner-Banks. I never thought about the beams of the house being like the scaffolding of the story."

"I love it when something like that occurs to me after I've read a story many times. Munro does that: she finds something that seems ordinary, that you can point to, that actually carries clues about her story."

"Like a mystery."

"Exactly. They are mysteries, in a way, aren't they?"

"Oh! I am so late, excuse me, goodbye Ms. Warner-Banks, bye, Straight Punch."

"Later," Fritz said.

Lauren had dropped a mitten. He picked it up. She thanked him profusely when he caught up with her, before she began running.

"'Straight Punch'?" she asked, when he returned.

It was his nickname, he told her. It was a karate move.

"Her mother's fighting to get custody of Lauren's sister, this baby she had when Lauren was in high school? It's in, what's that place, Dabai?"

"Dubai?"

"Right. The husband works there. He kidnapped the baby."

This seemed too complicated to pursue—more like a case her husband would tell her about. She prompted him:

"You were telling me about your mother?" The path sloped steeply; she avoided an ice patch.

"Yeah. She married one guy when they were eighteen who died when he was twenty-one in a race-car accident. He was infertile due to German measles. When he died, though, she found out he'd only been seventeen when they got married. I guess they didn't go to Paris on their honeymoon. She saw a snail then or now, she'd stomp it! The husband she's got now was my dad's, my biological dad's, brother. Turns out I was one of two kids she had with my dad, but she'd sent the other one to Baltimore to her mother's. Then she married Pete, and my brother came back. They were also business partners."

"I'm sorry. Who were the business partners?"

They'd entered the crosswalk. Every car had immediately stopped.

"My father and his brother. Pete's at Wintergreen now, running the lifts. He's not afraid of heights. That's why he climbed up the Stonewall sign. Before Wintergreen, he was assistant manager at a sporting goods place by the railroad tracks in Staunton, then he fell and had to get a hip replacement that got infected or something, and they let him go. He can still get stuff thirty percent off, if you want any North Face."

She said that she'd never been to Staunton, but that she appreciated his offer. Reggie had a fleece North Face jacket, so she knew what they cost. She waited three beats, then said, "You mentioned Stonewall? Did you mean the bar in New York?"

"Bar? No. Oh, I get it. You've never been to Staunton. There's a hotel called the Stonewall Jackson. Everybody's saying it's going to have to change its name because he was in favor of slaves, so the sign's got to go. Somebody called Pete to inspect it. They sent him up in a cherry picker, over to a ladder that went to another ladder. Sucker's really up there. Nobody knows what they'll call the hotel."

She nodded. Even in Charlottesville, there seemed endless complexities related to long-unfinished buildings, air space, height restrictions. Her husband's pet peeve was that when a park was renamed, it then had a *second* renaming: "All right, it's not Lee Park, that's entirely understandable, but what was wrong with Emancipation Park? Now it's Market Street Park. You know, one of my colleagues said that when his wife put their house on the garden tour, she was told that there were new nicknames—nicknames!—for the roses. Not to use their old-fashioned names."

"Pete's got two sons from a previous relationship living with them now, so I don't much stop by. They're always fighting. They know I do karate, so they leave me alone."

Finally, the person withdrawing money from the cash machine stepped away, still staring hard at the receipt. She unsnapped her wallet, reaching into the pocket where she kept her credit cards. She slid out the red BoA card.

He stood far back from the cash machine as she withdrew two hundred dollars. A receipt curled out; she glanced at it and pushed it into her pocket, thinking: five roommates; two jobs, in addition to his class work; his father vanished, the man who would have been his uncle now his stepfather. A brother. Two stepbrothers. Could he always remember this without effort, like someone who'd long ago memorized "The Twelve Days of Christmas"? She turned and walked back to where he was standing. She held out two twenty-dollar bills, saying, "Here you go. Good luck with the tire."

"My car's right there," he said, pointing toward an area where three cars could nose in next to a bicycle repair shop. "Let me give you a ride to your car."

"Thanks. Do you know where K-2 is?"

"Yup," he said.

The car was so old, he opened the door by turning a key in the lock. Once seated, he quickly lifted the lock and pushed open the passenger door. "Your chariot awaits," he said. "Did I already tell you this is a loaner? From my brother? Like I said, my mother gave him to her mother in Baltimore before she had me. Apparently, when Pete married her, he thought that kid was out of the picture. Bro didn't come to Staunton until I was walking. A year or so ago, he was an extra in a Netflix movie shot in Richmond. Now he goes on a lot of dates."

"Amazing," she said. Such an avalanche of information. Reggie, of course, would only have nodded slightly. He disliked stand-up comics because he never registered the conclusion of their joke as the punch line. When she pointed that out to him, he'd done a double take before admitting it was true, and cracking up.

"There, the silver car," she said, pointing.

He said, "I heard there's supposed to be more snow coming day after tomorrow. Nice car you got. Okay, thanks again. You're totally saving me. I'm going to give Alice Munro another try."

"Drive safely," she said, getting out.

As he drove away, she beeped open the Lexus, got in, clicked on the seat warmer, and retied her scarf. No need to check her phone; she'd be home in fifteen minutes. Now that he wasn't talking—now that there was lovely silence in the car (she decided not to turn on NPR)—she wondered if, in his agitated way, he'd been telling her what he took for granted, or if he'd meant to test her reaction. It was as if he'd wanted there to be some, what . . . some dissonance between them. Some acknowledgment that they were nothing alike. Every reality of his life clashed with hers: She was an only child and had had an almost idyllic childhood, except for kidney surgery. She had a stable marriage; no children. (Reggie's son from his first marriage, Edmund, was an architect in Sydney, Australia. They spoke every couple of weeks.) What would Alice Munro write, if she wrote the story of Rochelle and Fritz? Too easy, to have the mismatched pair fall in love. Munro would never do the obvious. But maybe things could flip, and she'd be (as she was) financially secure, yet needy, and he, with no money, would turn out to be stable. *Centered.* That would be the word. But Fritz certainly wasn't that. His gushing talk made him seem immature—friendly, but with an edge that scraped like a dull knife.

She'd pulled out of the parking lot and began driving down Main Street—fortunately, no rush hour traffic yet—past the old Sears, whose building was now university-owned, used for shipping and receiving. Just beyond that was her former hairstylist, though the salon had moved off 29 North. The tire place was just past that building, and there stood Fritz, *Straight Punch*, in the lot, talking to a man: *Saved by a mere forty dollars,* she thought—*ah, youth.* She pulled in without thinking, as if they'd always intended to meet up. "Oh, *hi,*" he said. "Hey, this is my"—he paused—"friend, who really saved my ass," he said to the man. The man wore a hoodie and an orange cap, pulled low. His glasses frames were rectangular, so smudged she didn't know how he could see.

"This boy needs two tires, with them back ones rotated forward," the man said matter-of-factly, without greeting her.

"He does?"

"You don't want your son driving on tires with no treads," he said. "We sell the best used tires in town. Them front ones gotta be replaced and rotated. That's still just going to buy you another five hundred miles."

"You said it'll drive with one new tire, " Fritz said, sounding frustrated, embarrassed. Newspaper pages blew across the lot. A wind was whipping up.

She did not correct the man and say he wasn't her son, though it seemed to her that he'd made quite an odd assumption. She said, "How much would that cost?"

"Forty plus forty's eighty. Plus tax. No charge for tire rotation. If I said the seventy-two-dollar brand-new Goodyears were superior, you'd think it was a hustle, so best keep it simple."

"Fine," she said. "Two forty-dollar tires."

"Oh, jeez, you can't," Fritz said. "No way."

"Mama don't want you skiddin' off Afton Mountain."

"That's right," she said.

The man said, "Why are we standing here? Step inside."

Walking beside Fritz, she said, "Let me have the money back, and I'll put it on my card. It'll be easier that way."

"I am *so* sorry," he said, reaching into his pant pocket and pulling out the folded money, along with ChapStick that fell to the ground, and two pennies that rolled some distance apart, which he quickly plucked off the asphalt.

Would Reggie have picked them up? Only if he'd felt like he was littering, she thought. Would she have? No. Simply, no. "I'll be glad to have the cash if the prediction about snow turns out to be right," she said.

Inside, there was a space heater. Near it lay an old dog, sleeping atop a pile of newspapers. The dog never opened its eyes. She felt in her purse, found her wallet, removed her credit card, and said, "I'm running late. Would you mind processing this now?"

"Glad to. The faster I get paid, the better." A landline—a red desk phone—was ringing. He ignored it. He ran the card and handed it back, the bill already curled into a tube. When he lifted his thumb, the piece of paper looked like a lavish shaving of white chocolate to decorate a cake. She took out her own pen to sign her name. The man gestured to a coffee can with a hand-lettered sign above it, stretched between two chopsticks: TIPS THANKS. The can's rim was covered with duct tape. She reached into her wallet again and took out two one-dollar bills. She folded them and dropped them into the jar.

"Thank you kindly, now to work," he said.

"I really appreciate this," Fritz said. "How did you know where I was?"

"I didn't. I drive home this way. I live at the far end." She gestured, and as she did, she realized that she could have been standing in a different town, the five or six blocks seemed so far away, where Main Street ended and you had to decide which way to go.

"You mean down by the Omni Hotel"—he pronounced it *Om-i-ni*—"where everybody's suddenly got an objection to that Indian statue?" the man asked, snorting, as he rolled a tire into the garage.

"Nearby," she replied.

"I guess General Robert E. Lee up on his horse Trigger"—was he kidding?—"ain't enough to object to, you also got to get rid of two great American explorers because there's an Indian girl's bent over near them."

"Sacagawea," she said.

"Sack a whatever, sack a potatoes, sack a Scrooge McDuck's gold coins, maybe. Personally? I'm hoping they object to all them one-way streets and make 'em run the way they used to. Let 'em fix that too, during their break from swinging tire irons and topplin' statues."

She bit her lip, raised a hand to signal goodbye to Fritz (Straight Punch; what move, exactly, was that?), and hurried outside. Why hadn't she initially suggested he go to the tire store on Preston Avenue that Reggie always used? No matter. Now she really did have to hurry. Dinner would take awhile to prepare, and Dr. Winston— David Winston and his wife, Dr. Bronwyn Winston—would be coming, to check in on how Reggie was doing after his knee replacement. No doubt, David would take in the beautiful view from their window (the part not obstructed by the tall building under construction, whose panes of glass turned lavender at sunset), which offered (not for long) one of the higher vantage points from which to see the rooftops of the houses and buildings that now seemed so small, so antiquated. As well as the wine, there'd be

Reggie's insistence on tap water ("Of course, others should enjoy Perrier, as they please!"). And she'd wear something a bit more dressy—did anyone call putting on a dress being "dressy" anymore?

"Best view in town," David Winston always said, sipping his old-fashioned (minus the cherry), silently toasting the sky, the trees, the mountain, followed by his wife's inevitable "Let's not allow the green-eyed monster to take hold, David, darlin'!" Bronwyn, Reggie's primary care doctor, was from Mobile, Alabama. Her husband had been born in New England. Years earlier, they'd relocated to Charlottesville from Brookline, Massachusetts.

Hunched against the breeze (*how* had the pansies in the big pots escaped getting frostbitten all winter?) she punched in 3-3-3. Mary Ralston Cooper was waiting for the elevator. She had no coat, so she must have come down to check for mail. Mary Ralston lived on the fourth floor; Rochelle and Reggie lived in the penthouse. Again she took out a card, the one to slip into the slot to access their unit. Mary Ralston asked immediately how Reggie was doing.

"A little more pain than he'd admit, but he was up for company tonight, so I guess that's an improvement," she said. She liked Mary Ralston. Her indolent middle-aged son, who spent his days listening to conversational Norwegian with Bose headphones clamped to his ears, she could do without. Mary Ralston's husband, twelve years older than she, had died the year before. He was always the elephant in the room or, in this case, the missing presence in the elevator.

"You have a wonderful night. Tell Reggie he can always call downstairs, you know. If he might need anything and you're not here, I mean."

"Very kind . . ." she was saying, as the elevator door closed.

Two dollars had been too little to leave in the tip jar, but she'd had to choose between that or a ten-dollar bill.

There were east and west penthouses. Theirs faced west, with a view of the mountains out the long row of sliding glass doors across the back, another bank of doors facing Main Street, and what had been the Greyhound terminal. During the past year, two attractive middle-aged women had bought the east penthouse, one a retired dental hygienist who was writing a mystery about a missing dentist (she'd learned this from Bronwyn), the other a mystery woman who left early in the morning, before 5 a.m. Bronwyn knew only that she was doing research at NIH she wouldn't talk about. She and Reggie had twice invited their now not-so-new neighbors to dinner (the women had bought the other penthouse as a cash sale, in a bidding war), but they'd declined with regret, giving no specific reason, which Reggie maintained was perfectly fine. She and he disagreed about whether they were being brushed off.

"I'm back, honey," she called. "I'm running a bit late. How are you?"

"Well, the damnedest thing," he called back, elbowing himself up to a higher position in bed, still wincing as she came in, unbuttoning her coat. She draped it on the bedpost. He looked sheepish, registering her surprise at not finding him in the living room. He hurried to say that he'd taken a quick nap (she could see that; his hair stood straight up on one side). "I got a call this afternoon from Bronwyn. She said they'd had a terrible fight, and not only could they not come tonight but, she said, 'Thanksgiving's canceled.' I said, 'Bronwyn, we just celebrated that. *Thanksgiving?*' and she said, 'Reggie, you can be such a pedant. I meant Easter.'"

"Oh dear. I'm sure that was a difficult call for her to make."

An orchid on a table caught her eye. Could the physical therapist have brought an orchid? she asked him.

"Yes, she did. Becky's an angel. Infinite patience, and kindhearted. But get this: it seems David's been keeping company with a woman he met at the Miller Center, all of it right out in the open. Bronwyn went into Feast, and there they stood, holding hands, surveying the cheese counter."

"*Really?* What did you say?"

"I don't remember. Can I help you put the groceries away?"

"I shopped yesterday. To be honest," she said, stepping out of her shoes, "I'm relieved not to have to cook." She slid into her sheepskin-lined black booties. She walked over to the plant. A tiny transparent butterfly clipped the stem to a green stake. The sinking light illuminated the flowers just so. "Lovely," she murmured. "We can have the Thai place deliver. But I think we should still open that new French wine."

"Sit down," he said, patting the bed. "I'm not finished. I've inhibited your impulse to question. Wait till you hear the rest."

"Oh no. What?" she said, sitting beside him. It was warm in the room. In a way, so much heat felt consoling. This seemed to be a day on which everyone could talk endlessly. The encounter with Mary Ralston, at least, had been mercifully brief.

"She said—and keep in mind that this came from a woman who didn't know what month it was—she said David resented being asked to dinner here. That he'd said we were insincere—that was his word. Insincere about what? And apparently—this really surprised me—she found out he'd been negotiating with the women across the way to buy their condo, and they were entertaining the notion. One of them does commute all the way to Bethesda. But David and his girlfriend came to look at the place a second time last Saturday, and while they were there, he realized that he didn't want to live near us. *Us!*"

"It sounds like he's had a breakdown."

"Yes. You're right! But I could hardly concentrate when Becky was here, even though I know it can't really have anything to do with us."

The baseboard heating came on with a tiny pop they'd never understood. She thought of the tire store's space heater, and the dog sleeping on the pile of newspapers.

"When I'm not at the office or in the courtroom, apparently I'm not at all prepared for daily life," he said, clasping her hand.

She lifted their hands and lightly kissed his fingers. "You always feel such things can't happen to you, right? But who knows? He and Bronwyn have been married, what, twenty-five years?"

"He's clearly in no shape to be working at the hospital. I wonder what will happen—whether Bronwyn feels she needs to deal with it, or whether she's gone off the deep end herself."

"Should we call her?"

He looked skeptical. "That's like asking if we should take in a cat in the rain."

She did a double take. "Reggie!" she said. "The Hemingway story?"

He looked confused.

"'Cat in the Rain.' Were you thinking of Hemingway's story?"

"I suppose I might have claimed credit for the allusion. I blew it."

"It's a mistake to pretend you know any story when you don't. You always get caught," she said, standing. She picked up her coat and draped it over her arm.

"Is his story as good as one by Alice Munro?" he asked. He was trying to gently, gently slide his leg off the bed. His hair made him look like he'd been electrocuted. His shirt was wrinkled. That morning, he'd let her talk him into wearing his gym pants, since they were baggier and easier to get on and off.

Was it as good? That was such an annoying question. Predictable, too, especially from people—such as her husband—who didn't read fiction. She'd read him several Alice Munro stories during his recuperation.

She ignored the question and said, "It's about a young couple in Italy, at the end of the war. It's raining, and they're in a hotel. But everything's left unsaid. It's all about displacement. And inference. The hotel looks out on a war monument. And the wife, who I don't think has a name, expresses her sadness and frustration about being there by saying what she wants. Things like candlesticks. She's meant to sound shallow, but also sort of desperate. There's a hotelkeeper, who finds out what she wants—the candlesticks I mentioned, and a kitty. Eventually there comes a knock on the door. The proprietor has sent one of his employees with a cat slung under her arm. She's there to give her what she wants, but of course it's all wrong. It's not a kitty. It's a big, wet, ugly cat."

"Those students are lucky to have you. Open some wine, why don't you"—he'd managed to stand; it was best not to interfere, to let him do it on his own—"and I'll toast your wonderful ability for description. If you can find that story, I'll read it tomorrow." He stood still for a moment to get his balance. She pretended she didn't notice his frown and preceded him out of the room, thinking that soon she'd order her favorite rice noodles with extra mushrooms; he'd get at least three things. Reggie's philosophy about food, slim as he was, was that more was always better (because of the medicine, though, he should really have only one glass of wine).

The sky was darkening. A streak of pink the same color as the orchid (did Becky have a crush on Reggie?) had slid across the sky. She listened to make sure Reggie was okay in the bathroom. In this case, silence seemed like a good thing. Her mind wandered back to the ugly tire store. There'd been something ominous about the way the man had mentioned, so casually, cars going over Afton Mountain—though, of course, that was a grim reality. On the other hand, she read too much, so that sometimes she found in banal daily life a foreshadowing of terrible things to come. Of course, there were many ways to think of everything—the sunset, for example—all involving projection. The sky might be sliced by pink. Tongued by pink. Flatlined with pink, as if the heavens were a vast ICU.

She uncorked the wine and poured two glasses, took down plates, pulled out the drawer to remove linen napkins. When next she looked, it had started to snow. It hadn't been predicted for another two days. Wasn't that what Fritz had told her? And hadn't he said his mother had had three husbands? Well, technically two. Though it hardly seemed the woman had gotten to know the first by the time he died, and it was probably her good luck that when the man in the military disappeared, his brother stepped forward.

At a certain age, replacing a man—friend, lover, or husband—became less and less imaginable. That was why, if your husband died, as they tended to do, predeceasing their wives, women expected to be alone, so that anyone, simply any man who disabused them of that notion, was not only acceptable but a gift from the gods, a miracle. That was the way Sage, in the book group, talked, bringing her husband into discussions of characters not even remotely related to his existence. Sage never stayed for coffee, but raced home to this Apollo, unemployed, in debt, a daytime drinker, one of those men who counted on everything being forgiven when he bought her a heart-shaped box of candy on Valentine's Day. Make that the day after, when it was half-price.

REGGIE HAD CHANGED into a fresh shirt underneath the cable-knit cardigan with leather buttons that his son had sent for Christmas. He'd combed his hair. His cheeks were razor-burned.

"You know, maybe you—"

He picked up the glass of white burgundy and raised it to peer through, so that to him, the lightly falling snow must be golden-tinged. She'd not yet taken a sip, she realized, and his lips had just touched the rim of his glass, so she said nothing about being cautious when mixing alcohol with pain medicine.

He said, "What were you about to say?"

"I thought better of it," she said. "I guess we can't get any reassurance about how you're healing, can we? Not tonight, I mean."

"You're exactly right that David must be in emotional distress. Surely his colleagues know. Someone must be doing something. Though I was thinking as I was shaving that we should call her. She was so belligerent, so really irritated with *me*. I think she could use a friend."

That was it. She needed a friend. Not Bronwyn; she herself needed a friend, because except for the occasional foray into the world, she did next to nothing—at least, compared to what she used to do when they still had their house. The Boar's Head was so stuffy, her ACAC workout repetitive, and this place—this spacious condo—wasn't Valhalla. You existed in limbo, regardless of all it overlooked: in one direction, West Main Street; in another, Carter Mountain. It was neither country nor city. (Why was she feeling sorry for herself? She'd never, ever admit that, just as no Alice Munro character would confess such a thing, though those women's sorrow was like gum they'd stepped in, a hard little gray ball, the accident that had been waiting to happen, cringeworthy in spite of how ordinary it was—really, because it was so ordinary: a nub of reality that must nevertheless be dealt with.) It was the Southern way to de-emphasize everything: your penthouse was your "apartment," your SUV your "car." Your Arche boots were "these old things." She could just imagine what the man at the tire store thought of her, driving in wearing her cashmere hat and her quilted down coat, a Charlottesville White Rabbit who was late, late, and had to leave.

"Why don't you make the call?" she asked. She supposed it went without saying that she lacked the courage.

He pulled out his phone without a word, swiped up, tapped the phone icon, began typing, stopped when he found Bronwyn's number, hit Home. She was near enough to him that she could tell he'd forgone splashing on the lemon verbena aftershave he liked so well. It was no longer available after the apothecary on Water Street closed.

If she could speak for Reggie? Among the things he wanted had been this iPhone 5000 or whatever number it was (it took great photographs); a glass of wine from the Rhône, by way of Market Street Wine. And she would like: a cashmere scarf to match her hat; Michelin radials (she'd immediately regift them); a first edition of *In Our Time*.

"Bronwyn, it's Reggie and Rochelle. We're concerned. We're just sitting down to a glass of wine, and we wondered—weather aside—if you might want to stop by."

"What part do you not understand?" Bronwyn screamed. "You're so sensitive, you're both so sensitive, but don't try to tell me you never knew what was going on. They were going to be your neighbors! And—"

His finger—either accidentally or intentionally—had activated the speakerphone.

"Bronwyn," she broke in, "David's had a breakdown. He's not himself."

"Himself!" Bronwyn gasped. "*You* know who he is? He's a man so hateful, he told me years ago to watch out for you, that you always sucked up—that you did, Reggie; he said it about you. *Of course* you wanted access to the great endocrinologist, and he might need *your* services someday too. Now I wonder, how paranoid was he? Who calls somebody back so soon after they've been hung up on? A glass of wine? Let him have that hussy, and all his important friends too!" She hung up.

"Good heavens! Well, she's really in a state. Who's going to intervene *there*? Though right now she's exhausted me enough for one day."

"It's so awful, it's funny," she said. "What if she's calling all over town? Remember Martha Mitchell, during Nixon's presidency—John Mitchell, the attorney general, incapable of muzzling his own wife?"

"Yes," he said. "Hard to believe there was a time when those antics seemed utterly shocking."

"My mother thought Nixon was the devil, to her dying day."

"She did? Well. In any case—we've done what we can." His pink cheeks had turned pinker. Bronwyn had really upset him. "Let's watch the snow fall and be glad they aren't here," he said. "She was so loud, my ears sealed up like I was on a plane."

"I had ringing in my ears today. I felt like I might get dizzy, but that passed. Maybe it was the fumes."

"Fumes? Where were you?"

"At the tire store. Near where I used to get my hair done."

"A tire store?"

"It's a long story." She poured more wine, unwisely refilled his glass, and sat in a chair next to his. "It's boring. It turned out—oh, the problems young people have; we've forgotten how hard life is for them. One of the students needed a tire, it was as simple as that, so I gave him, *loaned him*, forty dollars, and then for some reason, when I saw he'd pulled into the tire store, I turned in behind him. It was good I did, too, because he actually needed two tires. Reggie, he has no money. He's from a poor family in Staunton." Was that right? Did anything suggest they weren't poor? "He drives there in a broken-down car to teach karate."

"Well. That was a good deed, then. He got his tires, did he?"

"Two. The man explained that the other front tire was almost bald too."

"Without your even having to wear a Santa suit," he said, raising his glass to her, much the way David—had he come—would have toasted the sky.

"I had a premonition something bad might happen to him."

"A premonition? Based on what?"

"Based on, I think, poverty. The way things turn out when people have *no money*. And he was so guileless. It was as if he'd been betrayed when the man said he needed two tires. He all but said to the man that he simply wouldn't do it. I told you this was boring. Let's order dinner."

In the drawer where the takeout menus were kept, she saw a tangle of more green rubber bands than they could use in their lifetime. He cared nothing about string, but Reggie could never part with a rubber band. A little fruit parer she'd given up on finding lay right in front of her, its Bakelite handle protruding from rubber bands. She thought: *To my list of wishes, I could have added*

*the tiny, irreplaceable, sharp little implement I've been missing—the one
I'd convinced myself I'd accidentally thrown away.*

She glanced at the restaurant's flyer, but since she knew what
she wanted, she handed it to Reggie. "Seems like a vegetable soup
night," he said, "as well as a night when it might be nice to actually
nosh on something, so maybe the chicken satay, then crispy duck,
if you might share some?"

"You can always have leftovers for lunch," she said. The next
day would be Wednesday. She would not see Fritz again (Straight
Punch—it was good she'd omitted getting into that with Reggie)
until the following Tuesday.

"That's true," Reggie said, bracing himself to rise out of the
chair (that worked), picking up his phone, though it was almost
comical, the way he hesitated, as if touching it might make Bronwyn's voice explode again.

A cluster of lights below attracted her attention in the more
quickly falling snow. He gave his name and placed the order (they'd
know his address from the phone number; they ordered dinner
every week or so). "Thank you. Twenty-five minutes," he repeated,
disconnected, and joined her at the window.

There were five or six people. No, more; two men threw
open the back doors of a small car and jumped out. Someone else
stepped off the sidewalk and ran up the middle of the street. People
were once again congregating at the Lewis and Clark statue on the
triangle by Main Street, a statue that had been in place for a very
long time, now considered offensive because of Sacagawea's subser-
vient position. She was a tracker, that was why she knelt—though

some people viewed it differently, objecting simply because Lewis and Clark were white men, no longer held in high regard.

"Here we go again," Reggie said.

A light atop the truck arriving from the local TV station illuminated the statue. All these protests had begun after the white nationalists gathered at Lee Park in 2017, and would continue until every monument had been viewed in the most skeptical light. Someone carried a sign that jabbed the darkness, though it was raised and lowered too fast to read. Two figures linked arms and briefly danced in a circle, like a Cuisinart blade whose purpose was to turn everything to pulp. It was an open question as to whether the statue of Jefferson, the father of the University of Virginia, would remain standing on the Grounds. Her thoughts raced. It was certainly possible the sculpture would be taken down, even if Jefferson was not, at the moment, in complete exile. She couldn't fail to see the situation from another perspective that was at once valid and ludicrous; maybe a dirigible with Sally Hemings's face on the side could hover above the heart of the place as a reminder of the way things had really been, her visage looming above the grassy lawn that stretched between the Rotunda and Cabell Hall. She could look down on everything, like Dr. T. J. Eckleburg in *The Great Gatsby*.

Some of the talk below was audible: a shouted curse, a rhyming chant. Traffic slowed, as gawkers took in the scene. A tall man walked toward the statue with a baseball bat. That—a piece of wood—was going to effectively whack a bronze statue? Reggie squeezed her hand. When she looked again, she saw a man in an orange cap striding into the group.

"Reggie, that's him!" she said. "From the tire store! In the orange cap."

"Your student?" he asked.

"No, no—the owner. Or the employee. Whoever he is."

Then she saw the dog jump up, nearly knocking the man over with its big paws. She'd never have suspected it had such energy. The man pulled off his cap and swatted it. The dog turned and ran, darting in front of a car making a right turn, whose driver didn't see it. She and Reggie were too far above the commotion to hear the squeal of brakes (if there'd even been time for that). The cap lay on the ground. The man spread his arms and charged the car. She could look no longer. Reggie's hand squeezed hers so tightly, she had to say his name to make him release his grip.

But then she did look again. Now there were more women; they were chanting, *"Sacagawea shows the way! Sacagawea shows the way!"* as police cars converged. Through a bullhorn, a man hollered, "Bring the fuckers down!" Was Sacagawea included in his indictment, or was he only focusing on the two towering male figures?

The flashing lights cast polka dots on her chair and Reggie's. She felt sick. The dog had to be dead. It had run so fast. And yet, might that have been what she'd anticipated—not foreseen, she hadn't foreseen anything—but might *this* be the bad thing she'd anticipated back at the tire store?

When the buzzer rang, she'd entirely forgotten they'd ordered dinner. She went quickly to the control panel to unlock the doors for the delivery person, hazily viewed on-camera. She stood in the open doorway, waiting. Tonight it was a thin, black-jacketed Black man, various scarves coiled round his neck. He carried two bags, though one would have held everything.

"Shitstorm down there, excuse my language," he said, lowering his mask to speak.

"Yes, it certainly seems to be!" Reggie exclaimed, coming up beside her. He teetered slightly (she reached out instantly) as he removed his wallet from his sweater's deep pocket and paid in cash, no doubt giving his usual generous tip.

"Okay, folks, thank you kindly, you have a good night," the deliveryman said, offering Reggie a quick salute.

"He must have served in the military," Reggie said, after he closed the door.

Atop the contents of each bag lay the same scattered detritus that was always included, even if they explicitly asked that it not be: plastic forks and an excessively large pile of already half-damp napkins, plastic knives that wouldn't cut, packets of finger wipes that would reek of ammonia, spoons too shallow for soup. Under this foul plastic nest lay the recyclable boxes—small brown caskets filled with food, which she always emptied into serving dishes. Should they be having this feast, though, when everything that had created the opportunity for it had been discredited, when they were only ascendant because they hadn't yet died out? She hated to think that way, even if others did.

"Have a seat, I'll get bowls," she said.

Someone tapped lightly at the door. Reggie didn't react. He walked slowly toward the tiger maple dining table he'd been so pleased to buy at auction—how they'd laughed when he found a secret drawer in it, with a lavender thong stuffed inside. A thong and a penny and a dried-up pen. He pulled out a chair and sat down. He sat so erect, it looked like he was at church, or a schoolboy again. In winter they moved the table farther from the windows (cold *did* leak in), though the lights and the commotion below continued: the revolving lights atop the police vehicles, the (why had that come?) ambulance. Though since the ambulance was there, could they help the dog? Or was it possible—possible, if not probable—that the dog had escaped being struck by the car? All of it was happening in what now appeared to be a heavy snowstorm. And *who* was tapping at the door? It had to be someone from the building, because no one had rung them.

Rochelle put her eye to the peephole. She wanted it to be— though it could not be, it never would be—Straight Punch, alive and well, a present in himself, the mere sight of him compensation for anything otherwise lacking: candles unnecessary (she'd bought their candleholders, reproductions of the originals, from the gift shop at Monticello); no kitty wanted; of course he'd have no war wound.

She opened the door.

"I'm here to beg forgiveness. I was trying to work up my courage when Mary Ralston Cooper came into the lobby, poor thing, crying. Some protester said the nastiest thing to her when all she was trying to do was bring in groceries. These are terrible times, and I don't doubt that's a small part of why I've lost my mind, though nothing excuses what I said."

Rochelle awkwardly embraced Bronwyn while simultaneously guiding her inside. Again, Reggie appeared at her side. Bronwyn thrust out her hand. Inside the bag she held by its fake leather handles were two bottles: premier cru Chablis and Sancerre (said Bronwyn), separated by cardboard. Bronwyn reached around her to hand the bag to Reggie. "Rochelle. Reggie. Please accept my apology. I got so upset, I forgot to take my medicine, though that's no excuse for such rudeness." Reggie stepped back, allowing Rochelle to take the bag, his pleasant expression calculated not to match his pain, or how taken aback he'd been by what she'd said.

"Bronwyn, we certainly understand," Reggie said. "I must ask: Did Mary Ralston let you in?"

Rochelle and Bronwyn looked at him, each confused for a different reason.

"No, I came in, then I saw Mary Ralston crying, hurrying toward the front door."

"But how did you get into the building, dear?" he persisted.

"I pressed three-three-three."

"That's our unit," he said.

"Reggie, it's the code for the whole building," she said.

"It is? All this time, I thought it was our code."

"Well, I'm sorry to disabuse you of that notion. You know, I have two other friends living here. And an acquaintance," she added.

"Bronwyn, hang your coat over there," Rochelle said, gesturing as she put the bag on the kitchen island. "Reggie, dish up a plate of food for Bronwyn. And, my goodness, should we check on Mary Ralston? I'll just be a minute. I've got to make a very quick phone call, then I'll be right back."

"Please, Bronwyn, after you." Reggie gestured.

"It smells divine, Reggie," she heard Bronwyn say, as she walked down the corridor. Quickly she pushed open the bedroom door, then closed it. The orchid was lit by streetlights that also illuminated the falling snow.

She went to the bed, sat on one side, took out her phone, and silently rehearsed the question she wanted to ask. She tapped the screen. The phone was picked up on the first ring. Were there any reports of accidents tonight on Afton Mountain? she asked the policeman. There was a lot of background noise. "No, ma'am, not that we've heard," he replied. She thanked him and disconnected, though she continued to sit there, not so much gathering her thoughts as letting them float freely, imagining herself to be Hemingway's "American girl"—the unnamed young woman of his story. *Young!* So much for that!—a character who was in over her head, confused, angry, not knowing how to say what it was she really wanted. In time, you did find that out.

Fritz was safe. So, too, was she. And her husband. There was even a chance that Bronwyn would recover after a drink and some food.

She stood quickly. Instantly, something broke under her foot; she felt it through her thin-soled booties. Jewelry? No, her luck was not that bad. It was a one-winged, smashed butterfly—another of the orchid's tiny clamps that must have fallen off. The potted plant had been given with such generosity, such good intentions: a lovely gesture, an instant cheer-up for an aging man who was part of the old order—in which she had to include herself; she was his wife, who held many of the same beliefs, even those infrequent times she wandered slightly off the beaten path, then dared to look over her shoulder to see people noticing her for what she was, and for what she was not.

Had she been gone for only a few minutes, or had she been gone longer? Racing down the hallway, reentering the room, she saw Bronwyn's wineglass flash, filled with golden nectar. A more cheerful Bronwyn gestured as she spoke animatedly, and Reggie looked up and smiled, not so falsely.

"Ah! Here comes my love," he said, as Rochelle dropped the broken bit of plastic into the trash. So relieved was she that it was almost day's end, it mattered not at all that she'd pricked her finger.

ALICE OTT

I had an aunt named Alice Ott, who was something of an embarrassment to the family. As she aged, she was invited less often to family occasions. Sometimes, even then, she'd cancel on Easter morning or on Christmas, just because she did. Family members could put her out of their minds when a holiday wasn't involved (and, with the exception of my mother, did). When I was a child, I sometimes rode with my father to get her at her apartment on Jefferson Park Avenue, because she didn't like to drive in the rain, or after dark. My mother, who was fourteen years younger than her sister Alice, always took charge of the kitchen on family occasions, where Cousin Julie and my father's sister, Kay, made things from scratch, and assembled early in the day to do that.

I was a teenager when Alice moved to Belmont, a section of Charlottesville that had once been a modest working-class neighborhood of houses and small businesses, either freestanding or operating out of someone's converted garage, though by the time Alice left, bidding wars had begun for the old houses. Her house had come as a gift from Norman Ragle, a gentleman friend who went to her church. He told her that if she'd look in on him every day, he'd leave her his home when he died. This provoked much skepticism among everyone in the family, and while it was never talked about in Alice's presence, this "delusion" was much discussed by my father and his sister Kay, though less frequently by Julie and my mother. There was a general consensus that Alice was running herself ragged. The women, whipping and blending, slicing and chopping, had a lot to say about how Alice would never move into 133 Rein Street. She was foolish to believe what Norman Ragle said, and even dumber to take him homemade soup or her famous apple turnovers.

Yet she did inherit the house and its contents. When the will was read, she learned that his photography collection—some of which had been displayed inside the house—had been left to the Fralin Museum at the university (formerly the Bayly, which was what everyone in town still called it), and that she, Alice Ott, could move in. Norman's army buddy, who was left ten thousand dollars and Norman's army cap, seemed both touched and happy, but Alice was over the moon that day. The only other bequest had been an old Hoover upright, left to the woman next door, "who knows why."

Alice couldn't wait to gloat about this, and she was soon able to do that, because a week or so after Student Services moved what belongings she wanted to keep from her apartment on JPA, it was her birthday. It was decided that everyone must gather at 133 Rein Street (it was never called anything else), where there'd be a homemade birthday cake with Julie's boiled frosting that Alice loved. This would follow takeout pizza my father would pick up.

When we got there—my mother insisted I come, even though I complained that I had homework—the house seemed crowded with too much furniture. What I recognized of Alice's, though, looked much better, in part because it sat atop very lovely rugs, so that the furniture seemed to float. My mother was more than a little surprised because Alice never did anything quickly, yet she'd gotten rid of a lot of her furniture (some pieces were consigned, more were donated, and Alice's best friend, Esther, was given her entire dining set, including the drop leaf table, matched chairs, and carved walnut sideboard) without asking anyone in the family if they wanted it. Cousin Julie, who loved antiques, admired the Eastlake tables and torchieres that Alice had inherited, bought years before from Light the Way. I cared nothing about furniture; it was just stuff adults used to fill rooms. What got my attention was a black-and-white photograph hanging above the marble-topped Eastlake table. If the photograph was valued at less than some sum I no longer remember, it was to go to the museum, but if it was worth more, Norman had intended for Alice to keep it.

I was fifteen and knew nothing about photography; certainly, no one in the family hung photographs on their walls. There were only framed snapshots placed here and there. I had, therefore, never heard of Diane Arbus. Esther Straighter, Alice's birding companion, also came to the house for the first time that day. The next door neighbor stopped by with cookies and swore that she had no idea why she'd been left a vacuum cleaner.

"What's that supposed to be?" Kay asked, standing beside me, frowning up at the framed photograph.

What we were looking at was a woman in a wheelchair—I assumed it was a woman—who sat in front of a house onto which trees cast shadows. She was wearing a witch's hat, and held a mask to her face that made it look like she had many missing teeth, pointed eyebrows, and a big nose with widely flared nostrils.

"Don't let's look at that awful thing!" Julie exclaimed, and I let her steer me away.

The afternoon turned out to be a more informal family celebration than most, which pleased me because I hated sitting at tables with tablecloths, *and* we were getting to eat pizza. I went out to the front yard—there was almost no backyard—and walked around looking at the little figures in the scruffy grass: a mossy turtle; gargoyles atop ivy-covered cinder blocks; metal birds suspended from a metal stake that arched over an empty birdbath. One bird's wing lay on the ground.

My mother came out and said, "It's a lovely house, isn't it? What do you think? Was Alice his girlfriend, and she's just not saying?" My mother lit her one daily Camel and poked around with me for a while. "But the lawn looks like crap," she said. "Look at that over there."

She was pointing to a wooden animal, recognizable by the shape of its body, but missing its head: a decapitated giraffe.

"What was that picture of, inside?" I asked.

"That! Your father says it's worth a lot of money, and your aunt told me it has great sentimental value. Your father says the museum will get it, after the appraiser comes from Baltimore."

"But what was it?" I asked.

"I don't know," she said. "Somebody clowning around with a scary mask."

"She was in a wheelchair."

"You're going to see ghastly artwork in other people's homes all your life. Just tune it out, darling."

From what remained of the giraffe's neck, a tiny green plant sprouted.

"Why did he have all these animals?" I asked. "Did he have children?"

"Not that I ever heard of, but please don't question your aunt." She took a puff of her cigarette. "You know, I'll bet Julie's eating her heart out over some of that furniture. When she got divorced, Henry got the big house with all the really good antiques, and she got that condo she doesn't like a bit. And the house at the beach."

My father drove up then, so we went down the little pathway to the gate and pushed it open, though he insisted on carrying all four pizza boxes, saying, "I don't want you girls to get oil on your clothes."

My mother said, "Damned if he didn't leave her a very attractive house, Reynolds. You'd never expect it, with all the junk in the yard."

"Maybe that's how he kept people away," my father said as she held the door open. "*Aaaaalice*! Happy birthday! Your feast has arrived. *Venir à table!*" he called. The tomato sauce and cheese smelled awesome. As he strode toward the kitchen counter, I asked him about the picture in the living room.

"Diane Arbus," he said, opening a drawer.

"You *know* that person?"

"No, Leetle." His nickname for me was Leetle One. "That's who took the photograph. Diane Arbus was the sister of a wonderful poet named Howard Nemerov. She visited the grounds of a mental hospital, that's where it was taken. Let's hope it was on Halloween."

"The sooner that eyesore's gone, the better," Julie muttered. "It isn't at all fair to paparazzi people in wheelchairs. Come sit! Alice, you're the birthday girl."

"I see someone made a beautiful salad," my father said, nodding to his sister Kay. "Which will you have first, Alice? Was yours the mushroom and, what was it, artichoke, or the eye of newt and toe of frog with extra cheese? Leetle, you're up next." He turned toward Alice, beaming. "She happily gave up her volleyball practice to be with you today."

"That photograph was one of his prize possessions," Alice said, pointing to a chair to indicate that I should sit next to her. I did. "Don't you think it's enigmatic?" she asked.

"I'm not sure what that means," I said.

"*Énigmatique*, from the French, who very much approve of anything *énigmatique*. Mysterious. It means that something can't be easily understood."

I tried to be tactful. I asked my aunt if the photographer knew the person.

"No. There are many photographs in that series. Norman bought it from a distant cousin who lived in Malibu—and of course kept the paperwork."

My father broke in: "You know, there are photographs we take of our family and friends, but this woman was an artist. If you're making art, you don't have to know the person."

"Beauty is in the eye of the beholder!" Julie exclaimed, passing the heavy salad bowl.

"Did you rub a clove of garlic around the bowl and use the pink salt to make this beautiful concoction, Kay?" Alice asked. Kay nodded modestly. When Kay helped in the kitchen, she always brought a little nylon bag filled with her special ingredients to dress the salad.

"Tell me what you're liking at CHS. Is it a good school?" Alice asked, leaning in my direction.

"You have to go through security," I said. "We line up, but people push and fall all over each other." I said that on purpose, to see how she'd react. "It's okay."

My mother was giving me The Look.

"I see," Alice said, after a pause.

"It's a perfect day for your birthday, Indian summer," my mother said. "We were looking at all the tchotchkes in the yard. Surprises everywhere!"

Alice's friend Esther said she approved of any impediment to grass mowing.

"Did you like the little creatures out there, Leticia?" Alice was intent on talking to me.

"The headless giraffe," I said, hurrying to swallow a bite of pizza.

"One Halloween, boys came through with baseball bats and whacked its head off. Pointless vandalism. Norm could look right out the window and see them running, after he heard the thwack."

"Sickening, but fortunately not at all representative of the many truly wonderful young people there are today," Julie said.

"Ladies, excuse me while I make a brief phone call, but when I return, I expect everyone to be enjoying seconds," my father said.

I could still see the photograph from where I sat. Light coming through the window across from it made the glass reflective. I thought that all the women sitting at the table knew something because they were adults that I didn't—though this many years later, I realize that once too much has been said about something, more usually follows, as if whatever shouldn't have been said might be buried by words.

"You're a tolerant woman," Kay said to my mother. "My brother is *always* on the phone."

"Tolerant, indeed," my mother replied.

"Oh! I almost forgot!" Julie said, springing up. "Party hats! We have to put them on."

"All of you already think I'm silly, party hat or no," Alice said. "No one here ever thought they'd have a meal in this house, and that it would be mine."

"We're delighted for you, Alice. It's wonderful," my mother said.

"That's not what you think. You think a miracle happened. For years, you thought I was wasting my time. That's how everyone's always construed my good intentions. That's who I am in the family, the one who's not as wise or astute as the rest of you. Present company excepted," my aunt said, nodding in my direction.

Alice didn't really like me, I knew that. It was why she made so many attempts to cover that up, by asking questions when she didn't care about the answers. I was glad the conversation had taken a different turn, even if I was surprised Alice was being critical of my mother and her other relatives. Esther sat like an Easter Island statue (the subject of a recent paper I'd been forced to research and write), utterly silent.

My father rescued the awkward moment, bustling back into the house, dropping his phone into his pocket. "I see I've been left not the eye of newt, but the lizard leg," he said, peering at one of the few remaining slices. "Leetle, can you name that literary allusion?"

I frowned.

"Leave your daughter alone. We all deserve an evening off!" Julie said.

Kay cleared her throat. "Of course," she said, "eye of newt doesn't mean eye of newt, as in blinding a little lizard. The references are to plants, and an eye of newt is a mustard seed, isn't that right, Reynolds?"

"This is such a sunny, happy moment," Julie said. "If there's chaos in the world, for at least a little while we don't have to know about it."

My father had explained to me more than once that, far from being a knee-jerk optimist, Julie volunteered with a United Nations organization that supported human rights. Twice a year she flew to New York and stayed at a hotel near the United Nations. She'd been a friend of Hillary Clinton's in college.

The string of my father's party hat broke under his chin as he snapped it on. "All right, then," he said, and tossed it onto the table.

I was aware that my mother was watching him.

Alice said, "There are plenty of things you don't wish to know, isn't that right, Julie? Though I admire you for not sticking your head in the sand. No one would ever accuse you of that. Oh, and Reynolds, I want to tell you something: it's pronounced *Dee-ann*, not *Die-ann*."

"Is that so," my father said. "Then I stand corrected."

"That photograph's crazy," I said, sensing that under the new rules, I could say whatever I wanted.

"Happy birthday to me." Alice snorted. "What shall we talk about next? That I'm something of an outsider, after all? You looked down on Norman, Reynolds. You thought his African safaris were silly, harmful excursions taken by rich people. I remember you asked if they slept in a tree house with linen sheets. He was in the army, and we frown on that too. It's something *others* do. We regret people's inability to avoid military service. We go to Mensa meetings."

As I'd tell my therapist years later, I'd felt bad for my father because I knew he was embarrassed to have mispronounced a name. It was also disconcerting to realize that Alice was someone other than the aunt I thought I knew. She'd turned to me: "Your father pretends all meaning exists on the surface. I, on the other hand, believe in subtext. It's why I'm so mean."

It didn't occur to me that she was still discombobulated from having suffered a great loss. Norman, whom only my father had liked even slightly, had been dead for months when we gathered that day, and until my mother all but told me he'd been Alice's boy-friend, I'd never thought about it at all. I'd be lying if I claimed I was aware, in that moment, that inheriting a house had finally given her some power. What did I know? I adored my father, even if I loved my mother more. I was Daddy's Leetle, carefully creeping up to the edge of the cliff, trying to look down without becoming dizzy, hoping there'd be some way I could see what Adult Life really was down there. "If I understand correctly, you felt like you were looking through the wrong end of the telescope," my therapist would later say.

Just like that:

A telescope.

A looking glass.

Aunt Alice. There they'd been, the lawn ornaments, creatures from *Alice in Wonderland*, but because they'd been cobbled together and weren't part of some mass-produced series of figures, it hadn't been obvious. It was hardly a tribute like the Taj Mahal, but a recast, alternate world where Norman's Alice could preside, knowing the creatures were harmless, and that some might be inspirational in helping her find her way. No falling required. It was there in plain sight: text and subtext. A gift from Alice's lover.

YEARS LATER, when I returned to town, she no longer lived in the house. My father and mother had arranged for her to go to a nursing home, after the third or fourth time she went out walking and couldn't find her way home. He hired a company to make repairs, and a new roof was put on. Then, because prices were appreciating, he decided that he'd keep the place and rent it out. Alice insisted she'd soon return. But of course at some point things only move in one direction, and that was just a delusion. She lived in a room at a new facility said to be even nicer than Westminster Canterbury: Solace House. The name came as a cue—a sort of stage whisper to actresses who'd forgotten their lines.

Because my mother asked me to, I went to visit Aunt Alice. I'd returned because my mother was undergoing chemotherapy, and my father, who'd by then retired from the university, had flown to Belgium to be feted for his contribution to the development of a low-calorie, nutritional microbrew. ("To each, according to his abilities. We can't all be Paul Farmer.") Before my mother got the news that she had cancer, they'd moved to a tall, glassy building near the west side of the downtown mall, the same year I graduated with a degree in literature from the University of Michigan. Afterwards, I'd lived for a year with a man I'd met who was getting his PhD, though the relationship hadn't worked out.

Charlottesville was a changed town when I got back. The entire nation knew what had happened at Lee Park. It was hard to think of it by any other name. After what was in retrospect a too-long period of contemplation, it had been decided that the statues must be removed. There was even greater pressure to do the same thing in Richmond. It was going on all over. In Charlottesville, everybody had an opinion—living in the South was synonymous with having an opinion—though the bottom line had become that the provocative reminders of the South's shameful status quo of slavery must disappear.

On the day I went to visit Alice, I'd heard on the news about a plan: Lee's statue would be taken away and melted down. ("If climate change doesn't just do the job itself," as my mother said.) With my father in Belgium, she'd adopted his wry cynicism.

When I left the condo after talking with the visiting nurse and assuring my mother I'd get her a container of Bodo's Italian wedding soup for dinner (which I forgot), I'd walked down the mall to pick up the book she'd ordered from New Dominion, hoping, all the while, that my mother would be in less discomfort than she'd experienced the day before. She had friends in the building, a lawyer in one of the penthouses who was himself recovering from recent surgery, and his seemingly very nice wife. My father and mother had also both befriended a woman in the other penthouse, a doctor at NIH who'd urged her to let her oncologist know how miserable she was. ("I used to see patients. I would have taken seriously anyone who told me all their food tasted like sawdust.")

Hurrying along, I pulled up my mask and paused to look at trinkets displayed on a table set up near Violet Crown Cinema: small reddish Buddhas, strands of beads without clasps, and a number of animals—mice, onyx birds, jade-colored turtles, and a slightly larger pink hippopotamus, the odd man out among its fellow creatures. The vendor was carefully folding a scarf for a young man wearing a T-shirt that said *Tong Xue Men Zai Jian*. He wore round glasses and talked nonstop. The vendor slid the scarf he'd bought into a bag as if it were glass.

"In my country, I am a priest," the vendor said, nodding to himself after speaking.

What? A priest selling little carved animals on the downtown mall? How had this happened? I turned over the hippo, saw that it cost eighteen dollars, much less than I'd expected from its weight, and impulsively handed him one of three cash machine twenty-dollar bills. A present for Alice.

I picked up the Evan Osnos book my mother had charged to her account at the bookstore. She much preferred nonfiction, though she'd been moved to tears by *Hamnet*. She had to get better. She had to. It was inconceivable that she wouldn't. Her surgery and the follow-up treatment was the reason I wasn't sharing an apartment in Park Slope that very moment with my best friend, instead of buying a hippopotamus and going to visit a relative I'd never felt at all close to, who was a weight on my mother's frail shoulders. I'd have much preferred being in Brooklyn with Sophie, who had an entry-level job in publishing and was supported by her father, forever guilty for leaving her and her brother when they were only three and five.

When I got back to the parking lot, I put everything into my mother's car and started the ignition. Sickness, sickness. So much of it. It didn't have to be Halloween for the evil witch's wrath to get aimed in someone's direction. Covid *was* the witch's pointed finger.

*   *   *

THE GUARD AT SOLACE HOUSE fit my mother's description: large and awkward, with a piercing look. He told me his name rather officiously. Then George Matts asked to see my vaccination card. My mother had warned me about this. I produced it. He handed me a disposable mask that I could either put over my other mask, or use to replace it. He was double-masked. He asked me to sign my name on the clipboard and said he'd fill in the exact time himself. Visits were limited to fifteen minutes. I half expected him to salute. My mother must have called ahead, because when he saw my name, he acknowledged that I was expected. I carried my clutch bag in one hand and the hippo in the other, rolled in several layers of brown bags ("Please carry this way, you see, so it doesn't break").

"Our lovely girl," Alice said, looking up as I tapped on the open door.

She was sitting in a chair my mother had special-ordered, her aluminum walker, its legs settled in tennis balls, dangling two silver hummingbirds. "How is your mother?" she asked.

"She's had some nausea," I said. "But she's more than halfway through."

"I don't know why your father would be away at such a time," Alice said. "I can't understand his going. For what? Some celebration because he helped develop a new beer, in a country already known for having millions of different beers? Never in my life did I see Reynolds drink a beer. It makes no sense."

She'd pulled up her mask when I entered the room, but lowered it whenever she spoke in a near-whisper. *"It makes no sense"* had been one of those times.

Someone else must have visited recently. A pineapple sat on the over-the-bed table. It was hot in the room. The rooms of the elderly devolved into strange, semitropical enclosures, existing in a weird, Lysol-scented limbo, though the fruit and the heat didn't make it exotic enough to be convincing. We were in a nursing home in Virginia. I put the bag on her lap.

"You shouldn't have," she said.

I took the paper from her as she unwrapped it. There it was, the pink hippo, smaller than I remembered, lying on its side, as if already anesthetized.

"Look," I said, taking it from her and plunking it down by the pineapple. "If it's myopic, it thinks it's found a tree."

Alice smiled. She pushed it forward, and the hippo's head emerged on my side of the pineapple. Its butt was pinker than the rest of the stone. Quartz, it must have been. It reminded me of the lawn ornaments scattered around 133 Rein Street.

I asked if there was anything she'd like me to bring the next time I visited.

She looked me in the eye. "Is it true your father donated my favorite photograph to the Bayly as a tax write-off?"

I had no idea, but I wasn't happy to have the image conjured up. I took a deep breath and changed the subject. I said that a few days before, my mother had had enough energy to go to the park with Carrie, one of the aides—for once, setting aside her embarrassment about having to be pushed because of the distance—to see what Market Street Park looked like without Lee's statue. She'd told me later that it had looked emptier than empty. There'd been nothing but dirt where the statue once sat, only a single bouquet of wilting flowers in a coffee can. She was used to Civil War battle-fields redolent with ghosts, though she hadn't been prepared for the emptiness she felt, looking at nothing, where Lee had sat on his horse. She'd hurried to say it was good Lee was gone, even though she'd never again see the beautiful, regal creature he sat atop, its tail flying behind it.

"President Trump said the right thing," Alice said. "There were good people on both sides. Even when he said something sensible, they disparaged him."

This was startling. "Alice! Neo-Nazis, white supremacists . . ." I sputtered into my mask. "They came—"

"In my day, newspapers prided themselves on being objective. Those journalists bite you in the ass now, no matter that you're the president of the United States."

I couldn't believe she was serious. "The people at the Unite the Right rally wanted slavery to endure," I said.

"Please note that fifteen minutes have elapsed, and for your own safety, plus the safety of the residents and staff, I must request that you conclude your visit," George Matts said.

Alice lowered her mask. "Go away," she said to him. To me, she said, "I voted for Donald Trump because he's a man of the people. He's rich; he doesn't have to sacrifice his golden years"—could she have meant his hair?—"for our country. Look at his devotion to his daughter. You can judge a man by observing the way he treats his children." She looked at George Matts. "What are you staring at?" she asked.

Spittle began to dampen my mask. Did my mother know she held these views? If so, how could she speak to her, let alone send me to visit?

"Ladies—"

"Years before you were born, Henry Kissinger was President Nixon's White Rabbit, racing around the world, trying to achieve peace. He worked for the worst scoundrel of all the presidents in my lifetime, but Mr. Kissinger was his own man. He worked ceaselessly on behalf of his fellow Americans," Alice said shrilly, as George Matts backed out the door. Was he impersonating someone taking leave of the queen, was that what he was doing? Without thinking, I grabbed the hippopotamus and, no different from the Capitol rioters, felt the urge to hurl it through her window. I clutched it to my chest as I stalked out.

When I was finally outside, past the moving obstacle that was George Matts, my hand was trembling as I turned on the ignition. I sniffed back angry tears. My aunt was a horrible woman. Everything I'd sensed as a child from my parents' wariness about her had been entirely verified.

WHAT, EXACTLY, MADE ME DRIVE to Belmont then? What I really wanted was to have a drink at a bar with a friend, but Covid made that impossible. I didn't even know who was still in town. My friends were in Brooklyn. At first, I was driving with such purpose that I didn't think about why I was on South Street. I'd overshot my parents' condo. I should turn around. I brushed tears from my eyes.

But I soon had to admit to myself where I was going, all the while trying hard not to replay the discussion with Alice in my head. I drove over the bridge. Below, to the left, sat the little building that had housed Spudnuts. Which was the correct turn? I guessed, taking a left, and soon saw the Local, on the right—that was a good landmark—though I remembered some streets beyond Mas had become one-way. Which way was Rein Street? I looped around. *What are you doing?* I asked myself silently, angrily. What did I care about my aunt's old house? I had no fond feelings about the place, and no fond feelings about Alice either.

Parking wasn't easy. When I came to the foot of her street, I parked and walked. I'd stopped weeping, but I still felt ugly, confused, unclear about what I was doing. As evening came on, my mother got very tired. Shouldn't I be back there, talking to her and—I resolved—omitting mention of most of, if not all, the dismaying conversation Alice and I had had?

The house had been painted pale green, with dark-gray shutters. It was a nice little bungalow, though smaller than I remembered, with plaster half columns and an abundant fuchsia plant still blooming from a hanging basket below the front porch's overhang. I heard thrumming music from some restaurant, well in advance of dinnertime: heavy bass, at a volume that must have increased the neighborhood's pulse.

Alice in Wonderland hadn't been a beloved book of my childhood. I'd much preferred *Babar*—so much that my former boyfriend had given me *Yoga for Elephants* the Christmas before I ended things. He said I was remote. I knew he was narcissistic. Our relationship wouldn't have gone anywhere. Technically, he'd still been married, with a wife who'd hated Michigan so much, she'd returned to Albany to enter the family business. She'd made the right decision. I didn't have fond feelings for him, for his nightly scotch, neat, and his endless opinions, and his two tokes before bed. His refusal to even consider getting a kitten.

I moved closer and took my phone out of my pocket. I tapped the camera icon.

I saw the rabbit (I'd looked right past it until I saw it through the lens)—a topiary rabbit in need of trimming, its ears making it recognizable. It was later than ever for a very important date, though it wasn't going anywhere, strangled with ivy and pachysandra. I turned slightly. Was that the caterpillar? I wasn't sure. That shape, too, was obscured by weeds and ivy. If this was what Alice's beau had created as his way of expressing his love, who was I to say it wasn't an honor? Or that this gesture toward his Alice hadn't provided her with a respite from the angry, noisy world?

The birds were gone, though the Bandersnatch remained, guarding a child's discarded doll. (No; what I saw was only the doll's clothes.) I felt like knocking on the door and telling them I'd solved a riddle that they didn't know existed.

A couple passed by, holding hands. The one in orange high-tops was wearing over-the-ear headphones, eyes straight ahead. The second man wore some sort of leather harness and looked at me over his shoulder, calling, "No photos! No photos, please!"

It seemed entirely clear, when I looked back at the lawn, that I'd never get married, never have my own car, certainly never own a house. I reminded myself that I was part of a generation said not to want those things. What I wouldn't have given for a glass of wine with Sophie, though, in some cozy, pre-Covid Brooklyn bar.

I took one final photograph (the amorphous mound *might* have been the caterpillar) and started back toward the car. I climbed in, turned on the ignition, and began to retrace my route, remembering my mother saying that whatever it was people had been protesting, she hadn't wanted to see the crowd drift away, leaving her with nothing to look at but headlights. They'd begun to be turned on now. The light was going fast. I was in Charlottesville traffic.

As I got closer to downtown, I began to think again about the statues. In the time between leaving Virginia and now, Lewis and Clark and Sacagawea, near my parents' condo, had been scheduled for removal. *Poof!* Gone. Sacagawea? What Sacagawea? Lewis and Clark? Heartless, plundering, unreflective white bullies, off to impress the scoundrel Thomas Jefferson, even if Clark (*this was never mentioned*, as my father had pointed out) later made good on his promise, and paid to educate Sacagawea's infant son.

Would he have, if the baby had been a daughter?

I cracked open the window. It felt weirdly warm. Oh, the statues, the hateful, symbolic statues, monuments to men's aggression and heartlessness. Though now there was everything else in the world to worry about: melting icebergs; the ozone layer. I could only hope that Greta Thunberg was working on things. That she'd prevail where Colbert and the other prophets of late night hadn't succeeded.

*   *   *

AS I WALKED IN, Carrie touched a finger to her lips. My mother was sleeping. I felt like a five-year-old, rushing to report on my day at school. It was all I could do not to wake her. I left the room and went to the window, leaned my head against it, inhaled and exhaled slowly, fogging the glass. I repeated this, looking out on what was visible of Main Street. On a tiny triangle, the Lewis and Clark statue still stood. When I felt calmer, I drifted into the kitchen. It was as large as my entire apartment in Ann Arbor.

Carrie continued knitting. I asked if she'd like tea. "I am jus fine, thank you," she said, with her toothy smile. As she so often said to my mother, "You are gonna be jus fine. Those treatments they have now have come a long way from the old days."

I flipped back the electric kettle's cap and held it under the faucet, then replaced it, pushing down the lever on the base to heat the water. The half circle glowed orange. It reminded me of the Cheshire Cat's indelible smile against the night sky, which made me think again of 133 Rein Street. Cars; electric kettles; down-alternative duvets—my parents were privileged. Alice was my mother's older sister, technically her half sister from their father's first marriage. Though it went unmentioned, she was different; special language was used when talking about her: She was unwise; credulous; a romantic; easily taken in. We prided ourselves on being a liberal Virginia family, though, so we didn't emphasize the ways in which we weren't similar.

My mother, in her favorite green cashmere sweater, was propped up on her pillows, seemingly gazing at what had been the closed door, when I opened it to see if she was awake. I said, "Be right back," bringing her a cup of tea too when I returned.

"How are you?" I asked her then.

"Come sit, darling. Tell me all about your visit."

"Mom," I said, instantly breaking my resolve. "Why didn't you tell me that Alice was a Trump supporter?"

"Did she tell you the Chinese deliberately released the virus, or was it her admiration of Our Savior Henry Kissinger today?"

"Why didn't you warn me?"

"Darling, we're family. That obliges us to exhibit compassion, and to make allowances for other points of view. These views of hers came later, I'll grant you, when she started spending time with Norman. Your aunt has many good qualities. Also, if you try to distract her, you almost always succeed."

"She thinks Trump was right when he said there were good people on both sides, Mom. She said that. I can't visit her again."

My mother fingered her sweater. "She does seem different," she said. "I assume Norman was quite adamant in his views, and she bought into it. I don't know. She's happier in Solace House than she was at Our Lady, though."

"If she believes those statues aren't a continued endorsement of a mindset that enslaved and——"

"I'll visit her when I have more strength," she said. "Did you get my book?"

"Yeah, but I forgot it in the car. And the present I took Alice."

"You got her a gift and forgot to give it to her?"

"No. I was upset, I wasn't thinking; I grabbed it and left."

"Flowers?"

"No. A hippopotamus made out of quartz. I bought it from one of the vendors on the mall."

"That was thoughtful. But please don't be so hard on her. Forty percent of the country is in favor of him, you know. I do think her opinions express Norman's views, but we need to remember that he was true to his word and left her the house, including so many things of real quality. The rugs alone. The young lawyer who's renting it has a wife—an American girl, who grew up in Afghanistan because of her father's work. Oh, she must be so upset about the current situation. Reynolds said she could identify the villages every rug came from. That was what cinched his renting to them. He had some of that roll-out grass delivered, whatever you call it. He told them to just clear out the clutter on the lawn."

"It was a menagerie from *Alice in Wonderland.*"

"What? Those moldy things? Really?"

"Actually, I realized he'd assembled his little kingdom as an homage to Alice when I was seeing a therapist."

"A therapist? When was that?"

"In Ann Arbor."

"I didn't know that," she said. "I hope it was helpful."

"So Norman never hung out with us because he was a Republican? She could have explained we were a family who were obliged to be understanding and supportive, so we wouldn't have hit the trapdoor lever and sent him straight to hell."

She pretended to disapprove of her sarcastic daughter's remark. "About Alice. *Shh!* Let me finish. I'm not trying to, what's it called, *play the age card*, but as you get older, words don't always matter so much. I know, I know—language is the way we express ourselves. But there are other ways too. I hope people haven't stopped believing in omens and premonitions. That they listen to their inner voices. And that they still read body language."

I conjured up the photograph: the woman in the wheelchair, whose white hair could be seen beyond the mask's edges, communicating the essential truth: she was old. Old, incapacitated, her outsized wheelchair plunked down in a forlorn place. I asked what had happened to the photograph.

"Please don't tell me you're still obsessed with something you saw that long ago. It's been given to, oh, whatever they renamed the Bayly."

"Diane Arbus killed herself," I said.

"She did? I didn't know that." She reached for my hand. "That was an upsetting day," she said. "Imagine how much Alice thought was at stake. Your father was half at the birthday party, half somewhere else entirely. You'd raised quite an objection to coming, and I was worried you *and* your father wouldn't be there."

"Excuse me," Carrie said in a tiny voice, peeking in, "but it's time for your medicine. May I bring it?" What did she make of us, clasping hands in the near-dark? Did she see us as frightened, or as offering consolation?

"Thank you, Carrie. Of course."

Carrie nodded and hurried away, leaving the door ajar. My mother beckoned me closer. She whispered, "I'm on to her. She's knitting that scarf so she can make her escape out the window, down the side of the building, then disappear into the night."

Carrie returned, masked. She handed me my mother's pills in a little plastic cup and gave me a glass of water. Carrie fussed over the covers. Sometimes she spoke to them as if they were pets: *What are you doing down there? What am I supposed to do if you keep getting all tangled up?* I realized that my mother was worn out by our talk when I saw how feebly she reached for the glass.

No dinner, just sleep. Carrie and I both understood that.

My mother hadn't touched her tea.

The evening attendant arrived. He was clearly so trustworthy that my mother had told him the door code and given him my father's elevator card. Carrie's little joke with me was that he was so punctual that she could put on her coat and know that by the time it was buttoned, he'd be there: Charles Wu, who was getting a master's degree in psychology from the university, after leaving Stanford for reasons unknown.

I let him talk to Carrie for a minute before greeting him. He studied assiduously when my mother didn't need him, and she rarely did at night. Charles wasn't as warm or effusive as Carrie; he never said anything to suggest that things were sure to turn out well. I liked him because he was just there, doing his job. Sometimes, lovely as she was, Carrie seemed a little needy, but I understood that Charles was a professional. We weren't his priority.

Carrie left, pantomiming a hug to me. By the time I'd finished washing the teacups, Charles had moved the blue chair closer to my mother's bedroom. He'd tucked one foot underneath him. He was far enough away that he made no attempt to put on a mask. He was reading a thick book, a highlighter held between two fingers like a cigarette. It didn't suggest that he'd like to talk.

I felt like a petulant child, but I wanted his attention. Or, at least, someone's attention. I was in Charlottesville because my life had taken a wrong turn in Michigan, after which my mother's treatment scuttled my plans in Brooklyn. It had been a surprising day, but only now had I started to feel bad about fleeing from Alice. My mother had no doubt been right; I might have been able to distract her if I hadn't been on my high horse.

Charles wore half-glasses. What was it with men in Charlottesville, trying to look like bookkeepers in a Dickens novel? He wore black socks and black clogs—though at the moment his shoes were tucked under the chair. Five or six silver bracelets were piled up on one wrist, as if someone had successfully completed a game of horseshoes. My guess was that he was straight, but depending on the night, he looked more or less androgynous.

"Are you surprised the South has kept its statues up until 2021?" I asked. "Coming from California," I hastened to add. He'd told me that he'd come to the United States as a child.

"Korea has its problems," he said.

"Right," I said. "It's not like we're talking Tiananmen Square."

There was a pause. "No," he said. He tucked the flap in his book to mark his place. Clearly, he felt it was required to engage in conversation if that was what I wanted. He peered over his glasses.

"Do all the protests make you feel differently about living here? They must."

Another pause. "I did not previously feel any one way about Charlottesville," he said.

"I'm sorry, Charles. I don't mean to keep questioning you."

"Your mother says you are a little at loose ends. I know no one wants her to feel guilty for being ill, so I said that I really felt you were fine. That these are difficult times for all of us."

"I'm sorry I forgot my mask. I left it in the car, along with her book, but I don't think she'll be needing that tonight. I got both vaccines. Let me get a mask."

"Not necessary, thank you." He held up his hand. "If you were not vaccinated, that would be a different matter."

My phone pinged. Fern bar alert! Sophie texted. Earthling please proceed back to jungle. I turned the phone off.

"How's your coursework?" I asked. The chair I'd settled into smelled like my father: Ivory soap and his balsa-wood-scented shampoo.

"My work," he echoed. "To be honest, I'm somewhat distracted, but I did well on an important test. I engage in mindfulness meditation, to learn to better concentrate."

"She goes to sleep so early," I said.

"Sleep is restorative. She's proceeding through her treatment at a good hospital, with doctors interested in her care. In my experience, not everyone can finish this treatment."

"I have dreams about—whatever they're about. I'm following her, then I realize she's dead."

"I lost my mother when I was eight. It was an accident at the factory where she worked. I was then raised by my father. But, yes, I worried something terrible would happen to him, and I lost sleep."

"Do you think this is pretty much the way people talk?" I asked. "I think I might be a little out of practice."

He put the book on the floor. "I'm not sure. English is my second language. I have one male friend who's in my program, and I think we talk pretty much this way, yes."

"The stereotype is that men don't have real conversations with each other. Personal conversations in which they talk about their feelings."

"I think he and I are relaxed in the way we speak. Perhaps I'm wrong, and there might be more we could say."

"I did something silly tonight," I said, toeing off my shoes. "I drove over to see my aunt's old house. She lived there before she started going out and getting lost, so they had to put her somewhere safe. She inherited the house from her boyfriend."

He nodded.

"I didn't really talk to my mother about it," I said. "Going there."

"I neglected to say that Carrie wanted me to tell you that groceries were delivered."

"Oh! She must have put them away. I'll go check out the refrigerator. Maybe there's something for dinner."

I went back to the kitchen area and lifted out a box of frozen Stouffer's macaroni and cheese. There were also two turkey potpies whose packaging said that they should be kept frozen. In the refrigerator there was a large plastic box filled with baby greens, a jar of applesauce with no sugar added, and a bottle of extra-virgin olive oil that I removed and set on the counter, near a cluster of pill bottles. There was an enormous bag of carrots, as if my mother was intent upon befriending a horse. There was a bottle of albariño she must have ordered for me. Otherwise, there were only the individual cups of yogurt she complained smelled like dirty dishwater.

"Would you like a potpie?" I asked. "I'm not much of a cook."

"Thank you, but I shouldn't join in. We must be attuned to any needs of the client."

"We can crack the door open, Charles. You can hear her: She's snoring."

"I have to say, that's true," he said. "If you feel that it would be understandable that we eat together, I would accept."

"Good," I said. This was making more sense than anything I'd done all day. "Do you like wine? Maybe you could open the albariño," I said, pulling out a drawer and removing a rather cumbersome screw pull. "Are you familiar with these?"

"I'll try," he said.

"Would you usually drink tea with dinner, or is that harmful stereotyping?"

"I sometimes have green tea after dinner, yes," he said, examining the corkscrew.

He picked up a steak knife and carefully cut the foil around the bottle's neck. Though his hands were large, he had delicate fingers. I reminded myself that he was not a specimen I was observing. He was undoubtedly more conscious than I was of the power imbalance between us, though I couldn't do anything to alter that. At least, besides being human. I took down wineglasses and watched as he poured the same exact amount into both glasses.

We sipped. I put my glass on the counter and took out a baking sheet before I removed the pies from their boxes and threw the packaging away. I brushed off a few thin patches of ice on top of them into the sink, and placed them on the baking sheet. They looked quite naked and lonely. I turned the oven to 400, but put them in immediately, thinking they might bake quicker that way. If my mother woke up and wanted one, what would I do? Tell her the truth, and offer to microwave the macaroni? Why not? She only ate three bites of anything.

I asked him, if he could change anything about Charlottesville, what would it be?

As with everything else, he gave it serious thought. "Previously, I had a fellowship in Palo Alto," he said. "We slept four in a room, seven of us in a one-bedroom, where the living room had only lawn chairs and bunk beds, all of us coming and going through the night. But we understood we were very lucky to be there, because others commuted from Oakland and more faraway places." He extracted the cork. "In answer, I will leave aside the much-contested statues, and remark on something less fraught. That's correct, *fraught*? So, I would say people are pleasant, but everyone is in a hurry, with no time to meet. You also sense that people are very contented with that."

My expression must have revealed my surprise. Since the Unite the Right rally in 2017, the town had operated under a cloud of shame. It winced under the outside world's shocked attention—though at the same time it took pride in the many touristic ads, flaunting the bountiful apple orchards and the mist-shrouded mountains, Monticello under the full light of the sun—well, maybe not: Monticello had become problematic. Though there were the much-photographed serpentine walls at the university, the walled gardens where roses grew in December, as rosemary branches protruded from the snow. Now, instead of the cliché about Charlottesville's being a liberal bubble, people had begun to judge it with the same disgust they felt on any city street when they'd stepped in gum.

Charles's stool scraping the floor startled me as he jumped up, racing to my mother's side. "You should ring the bell, please! Always let me know that you wish to get up, because we might risk an accident," he said.

I'd overtaken him and was hugging her, self-conscious about the alcohol on my breath. I'd let her down in so many ways. She loved me, but so many things about me had turned into problems for her. When she'd bought me beautiful shoes, I'd developed blisters. When at long last I prevailed and she sent me to have my ears pierced like absolutely everyone else in my class, as well as throughout the universe, it turned out I was allergic to silver *and* gold. Would I ever bring up her book from the car? Could I even do that? To give her the illusion she was keeping up with things? Her shoulders felt bony. She smelled wonderful. It was Yardley shampoo. Carrie must have washed her hair.

"Sit, sit," she said. "I want to join you. I want to be part of the conversation."

"Great!" I said. "I can divide the dinner, there's plenty. It's going to be awhile before it's cooked, though."

"Pour me a little wine," she said. "You know, I like Carrie very much. She volunteers at the Blue Ridge Area Food Bank every Thanksgiving, did you know that? Her husband's fifty-two, and he's had two strokes. She has a lot to contend with. But she's *too* optimistic. I try to just let the optimism drift over me. If we lived in California, it would be smoke from the fire drifting over, wouldn't it? Didn't you tell me you were at Stanford, Charles? You must miss it."

"Stanford, yes. Please, come sit," Charles said, his hand lightly steering her forward.

"We'll have a drink and not assume I'm going to break, or die on the spot," she said. "I'll stop after one sip if I feel at all dizzy. Charles, is my shawl tucked into that bag? Carrie knits to deal with her anxiety, but she picks colors that would excite a bull."

"I see only this," he said, holding up the unfinished scarf.

"Well, that's all right." She looked at me. "I never taught you that fidgety activity," she said. "I didn't think I should constantly be instructing you. What about your own thoughts, your own abilities? Though I'd only give myself a seven for parenting. I was too rigid, because I was intimidated by having so much responsibility. If I had it to do over, I'd be more lighthearted."

We sat at the table with our wine. After her outpouring of self-criticism, she contemplated her glass. While negating everything she said about her deficiencies, I'd gotten up to get her a thicker sweater to put over the skimpy green one she wore over her nightgown. I'd seen it draped over the back of the sofa. It didn't look familiar, so Carrie might have left it behind. Charles had turned up the thermostat.

"What had you been talking about?" she asked.

"I'd just asked what he thought about Charlottesville, and he said that many people had good manners, but that he didn't find it easy to connect," I said, turning toward him.

"I have no criticism of this town," he said immediately. "The program I'm in is excellent. My professor has already invited me to join his family to celebrate his birthday. Professors at the university have been very welcoming."

"Well, why shouldn't he invite you?" my mother said. "He should be grateful it won't just be the same old people. In my day, the women were always in the kitchen, fretting over lumps in the mashed potatoes, even if we were all in Mensa. I don't know why I complied."

"What?" I said. "Who was in Mensa?"

"Excuse me. What is Mensa?" Charles asked.

"For people with high IQs," my mother said. "I was invited to join, as well as Kay. My sister-in-law Kay worked as a polymer chemist before her breakdown."

"Mom, what? Kay was a chemist? She had a breakdown?"

"Yes. Every woman in the family was always told what not to do, and in every case, complying served her badly. Kay would have married Izzy and they'd probably have been happy, but his family mounted such a campaign against it. He can't have been the right man, though, if he gave up the way he did. He moved to Montana, and he's single again, after three wives. He keeps up with Kay! Everybody keeps up with everybody now. He was so funny. He could throw his voice. What's that word? Snarky. He'd throw his voice when one of us was talking and offer an instant critique."

"Mom. She was in love with a man named Izzy?"

"It was his nickname."

"Why didn't anybody ever mention him?"

"What, and make your aunt even more morose? He'd had some illness, mumps, I think, and he couldn't have children. That wasn't the problem, though. His family sent the rabbi to explain to your grandparents why the marriage was a bad idea. Your father and Izzy had been chess partners. Afterwards, they still played chess by mail."

"I think that unusual, continuing that activity under those circumstances," Charles said.

The potpies began to give off a smell of butter, crust, and onions.

"Today, we assume people who care about each other will make accommodations. Kay was invited to Izzy's wedding. On the island of Maui! Of course, that insured she wouldn't be there. That marriage went kaput. He got married a second time on the rebound. That one was an heiress whose father disinherited her the minute the JP pronounced them man and wife, and she had to forfeit the Park Avenue apartment. That drama could have been an opera! Even your father lost touch with him, until he popped up on Instant-whatever-it-is, *Instagram*, back when Covid began, and he was lamenting his third divorce. Darling, I can see you're shocked.

But by the time the second wife left, Kay was giving thanks that they hadn't married. She burned all the letters he'd sent her."

"I am wondering if I should dish up dinner," Charles said.

"Oh!" I said. It was as if a spell had been lifted. "I'll do it."

I went into the kitchen and put on the pig oven mitts guaranteed to resist heat up to 475 degrees and lifted out the baking sheet. Juice had oozed out of one, leaving a charred puddle. I put it on top of the stove to rest for three minutes, following the directions. The big serving spoon was much too large. I settled on a smaller spoon with a pointy tip, then dug around ineffectually, making a mess.

"These smell delicious," I said, "but I sort of made a mess of the presentation."

"I was wondering why you selected a grapefruit spoon," my mother said.

"Oh. That's what this is? Well, now you know: I used to live on takeout."

Charles rose to help me carry the plates to the table.

"There were always odd situations in the family pertaining to relationships. Alice and her beau—Alice is my half sister from my father's previous marriage, Charles—set up a masquerade, in which she pretended just to be a helpful friend. All Norman's friends disappeared after he was diagnosed with Parkinson's. In this town! I never would have believed it. Dr. Anderson was still practicing back then, and he was stunned himself at the turn things took. Oh, how we miss Robbie Anderson! His wife was another brilliant woman who hung back. She'd read all of

Turgenev. I very much regret that I didn't join her book group. Anyway, Alice remained loyal, as why would she not? *'Why would she not?'* Listen to me! Then the poor man had a heart attack, and on top of that he was diagnosed with diabetes. It was all downhill from there."

"Mom, I don't understand. Why didn't she and Norman just get married?"

"Because he wouldn't break up his marriage, even after his wife took up with a builder. I'm not quite sure why his wife had to pay him alimony, but of course she made much more as an architect than he did. He got the house in the divorce too, on the condition that he live there alone. If he brought in another woman, his ex-wife wouldn't have to keep paying him alimony *and* the house would revert to her. In your father's opinion, he should have relinquished the house."

"What did his wife do?"

"She was an architect, didn't I say that? She and Norman had a child who was a drug addict; it took a lot of money, she was always in treatment. Anyway, she went off with the builder, and Norman filed for divorce when he fell in love with Alice."

"This is not a situation that would have occurred in South Korea," Charles said.

My mother laughed. Charles blushed, putting his hands over his face. My mother's laughter was contagious; I laughed so hard, I choked.

As we began eating, someone else knocked on the door. How had anyone gotten in without buzzing? I got up and looked through the peephole. There was Dawn Southwick, another aide. Well, the more the merrier. Maybe she too had a story to tell. The evening could turn into a latter-day *Canterbury Tales*. She was my age, but tried to act older in my mother's presence.

"Good evening!" she said. "How is everyone tonight?"

"I have a fifty percent chance of dying," my mother said. "Other than that, I'm trying to set the record straight, belatedly, about women's oppression and the ridiculous situations women of my generation got themselves into, and their sad inability to assert themselves. Dawn, would you like some wine?"

"No, thank you," she said. "I'm glad to see you up and about. You're looking well tonight. Hi, Charles," she added. "Things are good? Everyone's enjoying dinner?" She was looking at the aluminum containers. She'd moved to Charlottesville in 2017 from Louisville. She groomed horses in Keswick on weekends, though she was willing to forgo that for time-and-a-half. "I just got blocked by a jockey," she said. "We didn't even go out, we just talked about our astrological signs and drank coffee on our break. Then he left a weird message and left town. Now he's blocked my calls."

"People are feeling very antsy and jeopardized because of Covid," my mother said. "Though that's strange. I'm sorry, Dawn."

"I don't know," she said. "My whole life to this point was inventing my future. This is"——she began to shrug off her jacket; Charles reached over to help her with it——"it's sort of buzzy in here, you know? Like, strange energy's zooming around. Should I let you all talk and maybe come back later?"

"No, no," my mother said. She used the rim of the table to push herself up, then walked to the kitchen. I gestured to indicate to Charles to leave her alone. She lifted out another bottle of wine, red, and set it on the counter. Charles, unable to remain seated, walked quickly to her side to open it. "Dawn prefers red," my mother said quietly.

"There was . . . this has been a really odd night. Some girl out in the parking lot tried to get me to sit inside a car hooked up to another car with jumper cables. She didn't have a mask, and she kept hassling me to sit in the car to rev it, but I'm like, 'What?' She was asking if I was here for the protest tomorrow. Have you heard anything about that?"

"No, but no one rushes to give me disturbing news," my mother said.

"I saw something online I didn't read," I mumbled.

"I am not aware of a protest," Charles said, putting the wine-glass in front of Dawn. "Though that would not be surprising."

"She said she was staying with friends. In this building," Dawn said. "How likely is that? But you never know. I said no, I wasn't going to sit in her car or whatever, and kept walking, but I made sure she wasn't there when I put in the code. She had on a rainbow T-shirt and overalls. I mean, maybe I did her a disservice? Her car was sort of trashy. It was sitting there with the other car's hood propped open. I didn't really know what she was doing."

"Do you think I should investigate?" Charles asked.

"Yes," I said.

"No," my mother said.

"Thank you," Dawn said. She reached for her wine.

Charles said to my mother, "Maybe this is enough wine, though"—my mother was radiant—"because this would be counter-indicated with lorazepam." He nodded meaningfully at me.

I nodded gravely. But she was so much herself! It was exactly as I'd always remembered: when she wasn't where she was supposed to be, she was relaxed, direct, *droll*—charming, in her inimitable way. In the old days, she'd have been exhaling a smoke ring from her daily cigarette that would float for a second like the last remnant of the Cheshire Cat's smile.

When she faded, though, she faded fast. She'd begun to lean toward Charles, who deftly kept her propped up in the brief moment it took him to rise from the table. I was so much on sensory overload, I simply watched him help my mother to her bedroom.

Dawn was looking at me. Her glass held one more sip. "This was one weird frickin' day," she said. "But you know what? Your mother was more with it. Maybe she's a little overmedicated? I texted them about that, but I haven't heard back."

"I hope you meet someone, Dawn," I said.

"Thanks. It's not easy now, right?"

"No."

"Covid's made it next to impossible," she said. "I switched from the pill to Nexplanon." Her pleated mask sagged under her chin. She lifted her glass to toast no one and said, "Two shots of Moderna."

"Fully vaccinated. Pfizer," I said. I heard water running and considered going into my mother's room to help, but I thought she might want to be alone with Charles. Also, I was reluctant to hear what she might say next. Would I hear about her own subjugation?

"Do you know what the protestors are pissed off about this time?" Dawn asked.

"Offensive statues, I assume," I said.

"Haven't they all been removed? Over at the U., there's this strange statue that looks like an angel losing its balance. Will that come down because it disses angels?"

"I think that's an aviator. Some guy who died."

"Whatever," she said, taking a sip of wine.

"You know they're considering having Lee and his horse melted down? With the Lewis and Clark statue, they apparently offered it to Sacagawea's tribe, but they didn't want it," I said.

"Where do you think they'll store the thing?"

"I don't know. It seems like they don't want anybody to know where they'll be, like they hid the shark from *Jaws* in a huge barn on the Vineyard, before they shot the movie."

She bit her cuticle delicately. It was a way of avoiding making eye contact.

"Me and Charles hooked up a couple of nights ago. It wasn't exactly great. Did it show?"

That got my attention, but I didn't know what to say.

"You know, if you two have everything under control—"

"Stay, please," I said. "Unless it's whatever it is. Awkward."

She shrugged. "I feel like I walked in on something and I'm ruining the energy."

"Hardly. We were talking about my aunt, who's a Trump supporter."

"My ex voted for him. He thought he was a strong, fearless man. He also wanted to be able to buy any gun he wanted at Kmart, or wherever. Hey, is Charles making some sort of statement or something?"

"What do you mean?"

"Oh, shit," she said. "I have the midnight shift tonight, don't I?" I nodded.

"Shit," she said. "I screwed up. He probably thinks it was intentional."

If I'd been Dawn, I'd have opted for a thick fringe of bangs to cover my too-high forehead. Otherwise, she was pretty. I didn't know what to say. I found myself taking out my phone, saying, "Let me show you something."

"I knew I should have looked at the frickin' calendar," she said.

"My aunt's boyfriend, Norman, set up a tribute to her, or whatever you'd call it. Her name's Alice and the creatures were from *Alice in Wonderland*. I guess the two of them strolled around his shabby little yard and pretended they'd already been lucky enough to disappear down a hole into an alternate reality," I said.

"Wow," she said, taking the phone. She squinted at the screen, enlarged it with two fingers. "What's that?" she said.

"A Bandersnatch."

"Ex-*cuse* me?"

"I can't remember what it did."

"Yeah, well," she said, "whatever it's called, anybody with a shotgun would take that thing out if it was in their garden." She handed back the phone. "This is where?"

"Belmont. My aunt inherited the strangest photograph with the house, too. It had nothing to do with the stuff outside. It looked like it was taken on the moon—or at least, that's what I thought then. The photographer was"—I almost said it wrong, but corrected myself—"Dee-ann Arbus. She photographed patients at a mental hospital in Halloween masks."

"Transgressive," she said. "Was it hung up because it was a relative?"

I shook my head. *If it's art, you don't have to know the person* popped into my mind. I'd learned the word *enigmatic* that day. I'd felt so ashamed when I realized I'd failed a test that revealed to all the adults that I wasn't yet one of them. Though the person in the wheelchair hiding behind a fright mask looked nothing like me, I'd instantly understood that I was seeing myself, even if I'd have to wait most of my life to prove it. The photographer's arrival had obviously been the woman's magic moment: she *wanted* to be ugly, because that was what people thought of her. Halloween was an opportunity to disguise her anger as a joke.

That really was what I thought. That the *subjects* knew that for a brief yet significant moment, they could become someone else and give the finger to the society that judged them. It was a game that wasn't a game. There were so many of those, in a quick evolution from *Crazy Birds* to *Call of Duty* and *Time Crisis*. And for old-fashioned fun, Americans went to the funhouse to stand in front of warping, wavery mirrors that distorted them every which way. Then we got a president who was the embodiment of a funhouse mirror.

My boyfriend back in Michigan had found me *withholding*. That was because sometimes I didn't talk just about him.

"I'll come back," Dawn said. "You don't need me. It's cool. I'll see you later."

When I went into the bedroom, water was still running in the en suite bathroom, and my mother, who'd die of a stroke less than three months later, was propped up on pillows, still in the wig she'd inevitably dislodge during the night. Usually her aides would politely inquire if they should slip it off, as Charles still might. Her eyes were closed. She looked so peaceful.

"We shared a real connection tonight," Charles said quietly, coming out of the bathroom. "That's unusual, in my experience. I would say your mother was happy."

In just a few days it would be Halloween, with its mock-ghastly, Buy One Get One Free Target ghosts raised from the dead, pumped full of air to cavort on people's lawns. They'd soon be followed by Amazon's inflatable Thanksgiving turkeys, followed by crèches with Baby Jesus lying in mangers thick with real hay, flanked by Mary and Joseph, and sheep not at the moment busy providing milk for small-batch artisanal cheeses. There'd be the non-Democratic donkey and its friend the Elephant (maybe Babar on holiday), and of course the camels before they appeared on cigarette packs, along with warnings about cancer from the surgeon general. All those upcoming holidays, those significant, narcotizing occasions that allowed Americans to define themselves by whatever could be had cheaply, then climbed onto, inflated, or—if all else failed—passed off as a lame attempt at a joke.

"Were you hiding from Dawn in here?" I asked.

"Excuse me?" he said.

I didn't say anything. I just looked at him.

The next day, as we were finishing the wine, my mother told me my father had another wife and a son in Belgium. If she died, I'd lose him, she warned, though I wouldn't be missing much.

THOUGH SOPHIE AND HER BOYFRIEND had left New York for the Hudson Valley as the pandemic wore on, I did go to New York not long after scattering my mother's ashes, partly to see an old friend from high school who'd recently moved to the city.

For a few minutes before James and I headed downtown, we stood behind barricades on the west side of Fifth Avenue where tourists took selfies in front of Trump Tower, some of them asking people who weren't avoiding eye contact if they'd take a picture, then quickly removing their masks, the way my mother always finger-combed her hair before letting my father take her picture.

"At least it keeps them out of the water lily room at MoMA temporarily," James said.

We decided to stop for a drink on our walk, but then we didn't. We played our old game of trying to guess what people did—whether someone passing by was a plainclothes cop or a stockbroker. If the elderly man with the thin cane lived in Midtown, or was a day-tripper from Poughkeepsie. "Buffalo," he decided. He agreed with me that the tall woman approaching, who looked right through us, was a rich Park Avenue dermatologist. I remained unconvinced when he insisted she had a drinking problem and kept vodka in her freezer. "What flavor?" I asked. "Just Stoli," he said. "She thinks some things can't be improved upon." We held hands. After another few blocks, he hailed a cab to ride with me back to my boutique hotel (meaning: especially tiny rooms) near Union Square.

The bar was off the lobby—there was no one to seat us, nor were there two seats together at the little soapstone-countered bar, though someone leaving told James we could order and take our drinks to the lobby. James thanked him ("Worked at Fidelity, quit when his wife was diagnosed stage-three, works for an NGO"), then handed me two twenties and excused himself to go to the bathroom, asking me to order him a Heineken.

I studied the list of wines by the glass and decided on albariño, remembering the bottle my mother had ordered for me with groceries, when she was still in the glassy building in whose lobby she collapsed, with Carrie so stunned that it was another resident who miraculously appeared and called 911. Somehow, a doctor in one of the penthouses, a woman, also appeared. I couldn't figure out Carrie's account of how that happened, but there was no one else to ask. Carrie *still* called, still told me that before she fell, my mother had been wishing that Covid hadn't hit, that she could have lunch at the Pointe, in the Omni, though by then she simply went for tea.

A thought occurred to me, and I told the bartender there was no need for a glass with the beer. I suspected, based on nothing, that James wasn't in the bathroom, but calling his ex, whom he'd mentioned twice on our walk.

Two women who looked alike clinked the rims of their glasses. Then one lightly brushed the other's hair behind her ear.

In the strangely empty lobby, his drink and mine sat side by side on the table in front of a sky-blue sofa. The alternative seemed too intimate: two chairs facing each other over a table with a top as small as a pie pan, in an area too brightly lit by the chandelier. In the chair farthest away, a woman in white sat reading the newspaper.

Two issues of *Der Spiegel* and a copy of *Harper's*, as well as a large, light-gray book called *Untitled* lay on the table in front of me. The cover photograph got my attention. It wasn't one I'd seen before, yet it was instantly recognizable. I knew who'd taken it. I opened the book. There was no introduction, so I assumed it contained only photographs, which it did. They did, emphatically, speak for themselves; but after I looked at many of Diane Arbus's images—the photograph I'd seen at Alice's among them—I flipped to the back. Doon Arbus, Diane Arbus's daughter, had written something. Clearly, she never doubted that her mother had the right to intrude herself anywhere she felt compelled to look: "The photographs appear to be documents of a world we've never seen or imagined before—one with its own rituals and icons, its own games and fashions and codes of conduct—which, for all its strangeness, is at the same time hauntingly familiar and, in the end, no more or less unfathomable than our own."

Unfathomable.

You have to know and say something when your mother is dead.

MONICA,
HEADED HOME

From her townhouse on Second Street—lovely, everything she wanted; the rooms' discrete spaces separated by stairs, making the interior seem large, and a little mysterious—Monica considered her day. Jonah, her nephew, had said it best about her beautiful new home: you could view every area as a different stage, and become a different person as you ascended from living room to bedroom. The only problem with living on three levels was that a little planning was required before you went up or down. She left +2 drugstore readers on every floor.

The street was peaceful. Church bells rang on Sunday morning, the bats whorled into formations at dusk; young families in North Face outerwear (though their forays into nature usually consisted only of walking the downtown mall) crossed paths with older neighbors—stockbrokers, lawyers, university people—who could be relied on to exclaim over the contents of their strollers. Monica could tell that most of them found the blonde woman tedious—the woman who pushed her pug in a pram, up and down the rather steep sidewalk, the creature nestled in a Burberry plaid blanket until its owner lifted him out when they arrived at the dead oak tree to do his duty (as her late father called it). Neighborhood residents signaled to each other that they were in a hurry. Anyone who held a cell phone was in a hurry. Sometimes, of course, they did linger to comment on the changing season, or at least the recently revised, more optimistic forecast that predicted Charlottesville would dodge most of the fierce wind and rain from the hurricane about to whip the North Carolina coast.

Monica had decided that she would grow old alone. She commended herself for having such a mature thought. And for rethinking the inherent value of old vs. new—the townhouse was *new*—because change was good, it could be enlivening, illuminating. She'd assuaged her too-vigilant brother's anxiety by moving into town; it was obviously more sensible, because who'd want to rattle around Mama's house alone? Making this life decision had one big perk: no more dinners with Case's middle-aged male friends in Richmond who just happened by; no more pretending to herself that she might move to Los Angeles, that self-igniting fire pit, so she could hang out again with her soul mate, Sterling. Not that he'd suggested she do that. Anyway, how would she have mastered driving the freeways, whom would she meet? She was ancient by California standards; they'd assume she'd exhumed herself in order to relocate; they'd find her incomprehensible because she wouldn't do a Sun Salutation at dawn or drink imported teas steeped for exactly three minutes; there'd be no nibbling gummies before the evening's scant glass of white wine (never from California), no bamboo sheets, no orchid plants, no Swedish tights worn in a color formerly only seen in algae. She'd hang no wind chimes that tinkled one of the Brandenburg Concertos, as smoke rolled off the burning hills and the possums and coyotes fled as if they could hop aboard an ark. (No, no, that was just a prop for a movie that would never be made due to the director's old-fashioned problem with blow.) All she'd have going for her in La-La Land would be her glowing, keratin-treated hair and her thinness (it wasn't a struggle; she'd inherited her puny appetite from her mother).

Things seemed lonely, with her marriage to Ashton over, Mama gone, her brother in Richmond involved night and day in a case he'd been working on for two years that was finally about to go to trial, and Sterling in LA.

Not that she ever entertained the notion of anything romantic with Sterling, whose long-ago wife (they were twenty-one when they eloped; the marriage lasted little more than a year) had banged a colander—not even the proverbial frying pan—on his head when he confessed he had a crush on their car mechanic. It was why he had a little crescent scar above one eyebrow.

Even though she'd waited until she was middle-aged to marry, she'd had no better success than he. She'd kept the marriage inflated with hot-air balloon rides that made her feel like jumping beans the weight of stones vibrated in her stomach, at the same time that she became staggeringly light-headed. She'd pretended to love dancing, praying that her ankle straps would prevent injury. All those evenings ("Darling bunny rabbit, fire of my loins"—Ashton worshipped at the altar of Vladimir Nabokov, that depressing pervert—"it's *business*, I keep telling you. I really *do* have to talk on the phone in the evening. It's five hours later in England"), after which they'd have dinner much later than she liked, after which she'd usually substitute blow jobs for sex—she had to agree with Bill Clinton: that wasn't really sex—because she *would not* tolerate his other favorite thing.

What would Mama have thought? Could she have imagined her beloved daughter unfastening her bra during the first course— Mama had taught her the technique of unhooking the back, pulling one strap off over your arm, then pulling the bra out through the opposite armhole. Eventually she'd raise whatever top she was wearing over her head, then drop it on the floor. Oh, she'd flirted with her husband like the coquette she wasn't. She'd lied to him in so many little ways—the little ones were the worst—not so much with words as by her actions. She'd learned the trick of baking one Idaho potato at the beginning of the week, then scraping bits of it over the too-smooth-to-be-homemade microwaved mashed potatoes she'd bought from the refrigerated case at Foods of All Nations, to make them more convincing. He never knew, with that deep gulley of Irish butter he liked to dig in his potatoes, as well as his taste buds' inherent lack of sensitivity (though as waiters stood at attention tableside as he examined the cork they'd extracted before pouring an exquisitely small amount into his glass, Monica had sat attentively, feigning interest in her ex-husband's verdict).

Why had she married the wrong man? Well, because she wanted someone who was the opposite of her father, though she lacked the imagination to figure out what, exactly, that person's virtues should be. All she'd wanted was a man who didn't fart in the hallway the minute he left the room or drink two fingers of Johnnie Walker Black every night, before going down an increasingly sodden memory lane and deluding himself that his *girls* enjoyed hearing snippets of patriotic songs of the South . . . well, she should have looked farther afield, she knew that. Tall was better than short, cultured was better than men who spat—all she'd known was that she'd be alone when Mama died, and she didn't want to turn into one of those women out in the county who tried too hard to be charming by adding juvenile accessories to her wrists and hair, tying it back with an attention-getting Crayola-colored ribbon, before swirling her throat with Monet's water lilies. Also, the married man she might have returned to when she and Ashton divorced had written her a bitter note when she married—that, she could understand— *then,* after all his years of agonized indecision about breaking up his family, he'd left Miss Alabama and his ten-year-old son (who talked in riddles and picked his nose in public; she'd spied on the family from her seat at a Cavaliers game) and moved to Taos. He'd written her, snail mail, a scathing letter, and blocked her number. There had always been things about him that were less than ideal, but who was perfect? If she was being honest, she'd married a man whose eczema disgusted her—especially those elbows that looked like remnants of bitten-off pizza crust. He'd turned out to be vain—she might have understood that sooner, because it *had* seemed oddly charming that he had his back and chest waxed at Golightly Spa—but she'd thought he was one of those rare men who took care of himself. Not only himself: he'd *twice* stopped to transport wounded birds to a veterinarian. At their small wedding at Barboursville Vineyards, he'd promised never to be "all puffed up," which might have been prophetic. From the moment they married, things became inflated, from rainbow-striped hot-air balloons to the ridiculous soufflés she created to that not-at-all-funny moment at the gas station when she overinflated their crocodile pool raft and it exploded (Ashton's witticism: "Call Captain Hook! Tell him the assassination went as planned"), as she stood there, having peed her pants.

Sterling never liked Ashton. Back when they were courting, he'd derided her when she rhapsodized about Ashton's endearing traits and foibles by throwing back his head to look at the sky, saying, "Ay, very like a whale." She'd always disliked the way he invoked Shakespeare by choosing lines he could take out of context and deliver as implicit criticism. Men talked to themselves. They did. What *woman* muttered?

Now it was as if Ashton had been the passing cloud.

Today, in order to forget him—as she functioned every day, in order to forget him—she intended to do a social good deed, as opposed to a more modest one that no one would ever hear about but that gave her more in return than the recipient knew (she'd read interesting books she'd otherwise have missed, doing recordings for the blind). Truthfully, the bottle blonde, with her pop-eyed, Burberry plaid–swaddled dog that tongued its lips as if it had just turned away from a salt lick, wasn't worth her time, but those encounters were examples of *neighborliness*; that was what it meant when you stopped and feigned interest—such moments didn't qualify as good deeds. Once, years before, when a snowstorm delayed the grocery store's flower delivery, Sterling had impulsively bought three cyclamen plants and picked their pink blossoms so he could present her mother with flowers on her birthday. The plants themselves he'd tossed into Kroger's trash bin.

So, really, finding a man who could even be a reliable friend . . .

She and Sterling had had sex twice, once when they were young; then about ten years later—oh, all right, fifteen—with *Exile on Main St.* their sound track on Sterling's cassette player in a Virginia Beach rental, after a storm knocked out the power. Cassette players! By now, they'd probably even vanished from landfills.

In her twenties, she'd worn pointed-toe shoes with kitten heels. Now she wore round-toed ankle boots, neither attention-getting nor sedate: a shade of brown verging on bronze, bought at Scarpa for a million dollars.

All these random thoughts were not getting her to Solace House.

She'd get in the car and pick up a pastry at Albemarle Bakery for herself and her mother's dear friend Dorcas Johnson, making sure to buy a bag of their delicious oily croutons to eat later, like popcorn. One benefit of a solitary life was that she could indulge in compensations, even if it was a slippery slope from *Oh, I have*

to go to the dentist, so I'll reward myself with a chocolate milk shake to
The stock market's tanking, so how about a bottle of Sancerre?

It was going to be one of those days when she'd have to will
herself to function, she could tell. The doctor—the new man who'd
joined the practice, replacing Mama's longtime doctor, Robbie
Anderson—had taken her off Ritalin, which had always provided
a lift, because she'd had a couple of incidents of A-fib. Now she
had nothing besides caffeine to give her a little buzz, but at least
her nights were better, because he'd prescribed trazodone to help
her sleep. And of course she took her daily vitamin D and the B
complex, as well as biotin, which made a difference in her hair
between treatments, and even if she wasn't exactly Rapunzel, it
made her hair as lush as that of someone twenty years younger.

She put on her jacket, felt in the pocket to make sure she had
her mask, immediately rethought her decision and exchanged the
peacoat for a lighter one (Solace House tended to be overheated),
and picked up her car keys from the little navy-blue dish she
loved, which showed the night sky's constellation related to her
astrological sign.

Toward the end, her mother's pill bottles had crowded out her
jars of moisturizer and her precious tube of French eye cream,
the little amber bottle from England whose viscous contents
stimulated eyebrow growth, the tube of lavender-scented hand
lotion with a tufted purple button sunk into its top, as well as
the lighter hand lotion that smelled of vanilla. Sometimes Monica
envisioned all the clutter again as she was falling asleep, in what
seemed like a waking dream: Visine, Neutrogena for wrinkle repair

(the cosmetics industry seemed never to have come up with a good euphemism for wrinkles). All this presided over by Mama's guardian angel, an upright toy mouse wearing a pink tulle ballet skirt, its little paws outstretched. The spring before Mama died, it had sat inside her bedroom window, and a woodpecker had fallen in love with the mouse. Over and over, it hovered outside the window, or pecked the wood frame, darting glances at its love object. She'd tried so many times before finally managing to take a photo to send Sterling: the bird imitating putti, in midair; the mouse so comely, it satirized humans more than rodents. On impulse, she'd also sent a photograph of the rather heartbreaking mouse to her nephew—apparently, people Jonah's age were relieved because a photograph made no demands, and sure enough, he hadn't responded.

When Mama died (her fingers interlaced; no openhanded, openhearted mouse gestures for her), she'd left behind blood pressure pills, Tylenol with codeine, a different pain medicine compounded for her at a pharmacy in Richmond and brought to her by Case's long-suffering secretary. There'd been a package of sorrel seeds, the drawing of green leaves looking like dual Empire State Buildings, which she'd been given for contributing to a wildlife organization. There was also a bottle of San Benedetto (Mama liked the bird on the label) and two drinking glasses delicately etched with feathers, as well as omeprazole and atorvastatin calcium, a spray bottle of her secret scent, Coriandre (she wouldn't admit she used perfume and told visitors they must be smelling her shampoo), and a small photograph of her taken the day she entered first grade, in Washington, DC. Pink nail polish had marred it before the picture was protected by glass, which made it look like Mama, age five, had been shot in the forehead.

She'd photographed Mama's night table, not sure why she was doing it, except that of course it was kinder to photograph Mama's possessions than to aim a camera at the poor, fading woman. She'd sent it to Sterling, only to find out that he'd made a list of what was on *his* father's night table when he died (the "night table" being a yellow Cosco stool that was the perfect height for the bed; he'd placed his leather slippers on the lowest rung). There'd been an air plant settled into a miniature teacup; two pill bottles (Tylenol and an empty, capless bottle of Allegra); a small mahogany turtle with a spine inset with mother-of-pearl, carved in Taiwan; a paperback called *How to Sell Your House without a Real Estate Agent*. There was also a black plastic comb.

She and Sterling had so much in common. They really did. Anyone who'd grown up in the South in their generation might have seemed eccentric out of context, while among their peers, they were just being their vigilant selves.

As Mama neared the end, her sense of smell returned. She'd asked to sniff her perfume. Then she'd wanted to sniff the lavender lotion. Afterwards, instead of capping and replacing them, Monica had squirted, smeared, and sprayed their contents onto the back of her hand, presenting her hand over and over again to Mama, who'd been amused, as if they'd been playing a game. She'd pointed at the eye drops, and the two drops Monica had squeezed out helped make her hand into an abstract painting in white and yellow, with a bit of pink from the cheek gel. Mama was dying, and Monica had created for herself a Jackson Pollock hand. She'd folded back the covers and rubbed the backs of her hands over her mother's bony knees, making brushstrokes before massaging it all in.

All this, she was remembering while stopped at a red light. When it changed, she drove slowly down the ramp and merged into traffic, heading toward Albemarle Baking Company in the Main Street Market, thinking that it was a little strange that once you were an adult, no one really knew where you were in the world. Even friends who thought of you had no idea where you were on any given day, let alone what you were doing. At least, not if you were so unusual that you weren't on Facebook, or posting on Instagram, where everyone got away with talking about what they did, versus what they didn't do. Stories could always be sorted through in advance, so that embarrassing moments—oversleeping, letting a day pass without eating a meal—were all omitted.

At Light the Way, Sterling's lamp store, they'd always understood each other's references. Non sequiturs were another kind of shorthand for all that went unsaid, as well as pantomiming (he could do an excellent Case, one eyebrow slightly raised, to inform her that something she was saying wasn't exactly right).

She drove past the theater where her nephew had acted in Samuel Beckett's *Happy Days* when the actor who played Willie came down with meningitis. When she went to the performance, she realized, she'd been wearing the same coat she was wearing now, which she'd left folded on the seat reserved for Case, though he hadn't been able to make it, working late on his upcoming trial.

She remembered Ashton's saying that in England, *willie* was slang for penis. It had been distressing, seeing Jonah in that play. In a way, it only slightly exaggerated how unemotive he already was, put upon by the chattering, heartless Winnie, whose name—now that she thought of it—might have come from the sound horses make. What staging! Jonah and the actress had been plunged into matching mounds, painted to look like duplicate heads of Donald Trump, so that the audience instantly understood the political implications of everything they heard. Hadn't Beckett been one of those playwrights who insisted on having things staged exactly as he wished? Though, of course, he was dead.

She put on her turn signal and pulled into the parking lot, experiencing her usual confusion about where to park, amid the cars backing out in slow motion while incoming cars pulled around them, followed by all the tapping of brakes that further slowed the process. She opted for a parking place slightly away from the worst congestion and chaos, then looked in her handbag for her brush. Looking in the rearview mirror, she almost jumped out of her seat when a masked face loomed up at the car window. She had to remind herself—the damn cell phone was ringing, in the depths of her handbag—where she was, only to realize that she was *parked outside the wrong store.* Taking away the Ritalin had not been a good idea. It had *not.*

Under the baseball cap's brim, she recognized Jeanie, *Jeanette*, her stockbroker's wife, a woman who lived to do good deeds, but why had she left her house wearing an apron? Jeanette removed her cap, her dark-brown braided hair falling down.

"*The Wizard of Oz*," Jeanette said. "I'm Dorothy. We're reenacting scenes from classic movies today at Burnley-Moran. *Come say hello, Deirdre!*" Jeanette widened her eyes, saying a bit too emphatically: "This is my neighbor's *daugh*ter, who's made it clear she'd prefer to be Faye Dunaway in *Bonnie and Clyde*. But as you see, we have *Audrey Hep*burn from *Breakfast at Tiffany's*, minus the cigarette holder, of course, but with a hairstyle that is the essence of sophistication."

The girl backed up. "Tiffany's sucks," she said. "It's a monument to WASP money. *Breakfast at Tiffany's* is so old, it shows for free."

"Deirdre, where is your mask? This lady is a friend. Say hello."

"She looks sick. Why are we standing here?" Deirdre started hopping, her upswept hair threatening to collapse.

"We're picking up brownies," Jeanette whispered, this time rolling her eyes.

Monica wanted to tell her that children never liked her. Even her nephew remained distant. He'd been wary of her since he was three years old and proudly showed her his boiled-wool red monkey with its long, calligraphic tail, and asked if she knew who it was. Looking at its tiny pointed ears, she'd mistakenly said, "Satan." The correct answer had been "Toby the Monkey."

"What an interesting idea," Monica said. "Sounds like more fun than I had in school at that age. This isn't open to the public, is it? Not that——"

But Jeanette had turned away, clearly exasperated as the girl began twirling, almost colliding with an elderly man—— Oh! Was that Dr. Anderson, Robert Anderson, hurrying past, carrying a canvas bag to his car?

"Her teacher's husband was airlifted to Richmond and she went with him, so they desperately needed a substitute," Jeanette blurted out.

"Oh, I hope things turn out well. How nice of you to get involved," Monica said. She'd once had to consult Jeanette's husband about the amount of money that had disappeared from their joint account during Ashton's initial fling with the polo player. She assumed Jeanette's husband had told her. She always seemed to make Jeanette a little nervous. Jeanette raised a hand in farewell, as Deirdre ran into Foods.

Monica took out her phone and, standing by the car, called her doctor's office. She pressed many buttons, gave her name and birth date, and pressed the key that indicated she'd hold. Almost immediately (how unusual was that?) the nurse practitioner came on the line. He was from Bangalore, a man she'd met before. She was calling, she said, to see if the doctor thought her recent lack of focus might have to do with his having withdrawn . . . and then she couldn't think of the name of the drug.

He was exceedingly polite. He'd told her earlier that he'd dropped out of medical school in Indiana and entered the nursing program at UVA, which was where the doctor had befriended him. The only other thing she could conjure up was that he had two sisters ("I very much sympathize always with women"). She was sweating now—though that could be attributed to the sun. The storm had certainly passed by, if it was this sunny.

". . . because of climate change, as we know," he concluded whatever he'd been saying, as she pulled out what she hoped was a Kleenex to blot her forehead, but turned out to be a mask. She pushed it back in her handbag, irritated.

He said, "So, then, I will get back to you at approximately four p.m. Please have an enjoyable afternoon."

"Thank you," she replied—adding, so belatedly that it felt awkward, "Arjun."

Inside, she walked toward the aisle she guessed would have what she wanted. She saw the broken jar. Peaches had rolled under shelves. The quickly spreading rivulet splashed across the aisle. Of course, Deirdre had done it. She stood hiding behind Jeanette. Her hair was loose, and she'd lost a shoe. A man with a mop and bucket appeared, as a different employee who saw Monica standing there with her empty basket asked if she'd been splashed. No? Then would she mind coming back in just a few minutes, or could he get whatever she needed? He'd be happy to bring her whatever she'd been looking for. Jeanette, standing amid glass shards, was apologizing profusely, trying to take the mop from the employee. Deirdre stood behind her. Little monster.

Monica quickly retreated. Thank you, but no need, she told the employee.

Soon she stood at the checkout counter, holding a bunch of jonquils and a box of cheese straws (they'd be more nutritious than the cookies Dorcas liked), as well as a plastic bag of biscuits that looked like crisp little waffles dipped in chocolate that she'd picked up from the top of the bakery counter. Hadn't she been carrying a basket? The man ahead of her was paying in cash. No one stood behind her. Jeanette hadn't seen her. Everything was fine. Except—stupid, stupid—she'd been on autopilot, driving here instead of to Albemarle Bakery. Her handbag must be in the car—she hoped that was where she'd left it, but it must be. Just as he started ringing up her purchases, she asked if he could put the items aside for her, she'd be right back; and then, once outside in the fresh air, being careful to avoid an SUV backing up, she realized she could just leave.

So she did that; she drove away, relieved to be reunited with her purse (god, it could have been stolen; she'd left the car unlocked), and her phone beneath it, *good*. Seeing it there, she suddenly realized that it was Ashton's birthday. From the moment she woke up, she'd felt queasy. She'd tried to shake the thought that she was in the wrong place, that she should never have bought the too-small townhouse, that it was wrong to do what Case wanted and abandon Mama's house, which, agreed, could have used some tender loving care, though it had so many wonderful features that modern houses lacked. It was *five hours later in England*, but should she call him? Why pretend they'd parted on worse terms than they had? So he was a foolish man, and she didn't want any foolish men in her life, but all those moments they'd shared, those had been *real*. In the fall, when she'd gone back to their former house to "tart it up," as Mama would have said, planting tulips with Jonah and Case to make the property more attractive before it was listed . . . but the thought evaporated. He'd left behind their wedding album. They'd asked the guests (not that there were so many) to take pictures and send them afterwards. For a few minutes she'd thought, with a stab of horror, that she could burn the place down. What would she have done, asked Jonah to perform his Boy Scout trick of rubbing two stones together to get a spark?

Which reminded her of Bob Dylan's taunting "Strike another match, go start anew." Who ever thought matches would disappear? Restaurants didn't give them away anymore. What did it mean that toothpicks endured, but matches were gone? In any case, she'd never seriously considered burning down . . . oh, okay, *Delusional Folly*. As if a house could be the manifestation of a state of mind.

In that case, at least she could remember exactly how she'd gotten there to plant tulip bulbs. And her second visit too, when she'd agreed to show the dusty house with its many burned-out lights, with water in the basement because of a broken sump pump, to Hadden, a photographer from New York, who'd flown in to see if the house might serve as a good background for a fashion shoot. How funny would that be, to have photographs of gaunt women wearing mahogany-colored lipstick, their hair slicked back so tightly it was no wonder their eyebrows arched, standing near stubbly-bearded men with harshly framed glasses, posing in Missoni in the dining room where she'd regularly disrobed, or posturing in the now bed-less bedroom where she and Ashton had made love.

Ashton had brought the new girlfriend home, unannounced, for dinner. He'd thought they might have a threesome.

Hadden (the first name sufficed, apparently) was staying at the Oakhurst Inn, where, he told Monica, he'd later be joined by a friend, a famous female photographer (famous at least among other photographers) who lived outside of town. She intended to lead him to her house for dinner, because otherwise he'd be misdirected by GPS. ("Is that true? Are we in such uncharted territory?" he'd asked Monica with a wry smile.)

While touring the house, he'd told her the story of how he and his friend had met (Berlin) as Monica led the way through the empty pantry, where an ornate spider's web had been constructed between a cabinet and the refrigerator. Monica had wondered what he was observing, through *his* eyes. He'd told her his friend was bi; that he was also. She'd popped up again when he posted on Facebook that he was looking for large, empty houses that might provide good backgrounds for a fashion assignment.

"Did she know my ex-husband?" Monica asked. "How would she know about"—she almost said *Delusional Folly*—"my former house?"

"I think she has a real estate friend who told her it was about to be listed. I looked it up on Google. Along with a few other places. Her husband—I mean, before he was her husband—moved back here after he had a breakdown at a start-up in Mill Valley. His father flew him home. When he was better, he decided his new life plan was to study painting in Richmond."

"VCU?"

"That's it."

Monica nearly tripped over Donald Duck; it was the broken handle from a spoon.

"—and my friend, who was at that time living in Keswick, is it? Keswick. She went to Richmond to talk to a studio art class. When she left, she saw that she had a flat tire. He was walking through the parking lot. He went over, and called AAA. They chatted as they waited. And it was true love. *And* on top of that, the next year he got a MacArthur."

She felt like she'd been in a speeding car when someone hit the brakes, hard.

"That was quite the account, but why did you tell me that?"

"When I feel self-conscious, I deflect attention from myself. Particularly when I'm attracted to someone."

"Ah. So you're envious of this painter."

"No. Attracted to you."

It was the first time she'd realized that she was standing in a house in the middle of nowhere (*thank you, Case*), in fading light, with a stranger.

There was a long silence, during which she tried to pretend she hadn't really heard what he'd said. She was years older than he. Was this some bizarre joke?

She said, "The room with the William Morris wallpaper? That was the dining room. And the room across from it—what would people want it to be now? I suppose a screening room would be passé. Maybe a torture chamber."

He looked at her. He had ordinary brown eyes. It was amazing that he could be so handsome, when his eyes were ordinary.

"My ex-husband"—he'd never told her his friend the photographer's name, so why would she tell him Ashton's name, why would she?—"consigned the dining room table to an auction house. It was so beautiful. It sat right there, below the pendant light. It was tiger maple. It had a secret drawer. I heard some famous lawyer bought it at auction."

"I'm sorry if it's made you sad to return," he said.

He took a light reading, frowned, and dropped the light meter back in his pocket. "Do you know Deborah Turbeville's work? She sort of invented taking pictures inside huge places: palazzos, crumbling buildings in Havana. It wasn't like she cared about the lobby of the Ritz-Carlton."

He'd gotten in front of her. He was leading her down a hallway of her house!

He stopped abruptly, and turned back. He said, "She had a way of making you feel the breeze blowing through: diaphanous curtains. There were tall-backed, ancient chairs; potted ferns off in the shadows. Lots of unsilvered mirrors. The photographs were a kind of seduction, more like a seduction in a dream. Everything seemed tactile, but also improbable, like an opera. She photographed at Versailles. For *Vogue*. *Harper's Bazaar*. Places like that. Some critics came right out and said the obvious: what she was doing wasn't fashion photography, it was art."

"So you want to Turbeville this house."

What she hadn't said was, *Or first seduce me, so that will infuse every picture you take.* Like Mama's secret scent of Coriandre.

The problem was that she saw through men. Which made them less desirable.

WHEN SHE AWOKE FROM HER NAP, it was too late to visit Dorcas. She hadn't made it to Solace House. She was lying on the sofa—Mama's second-best, the one with the feather cushion—still in her jacket, whose seam cut into her armpit. She struggled upright, and as she did, her thoughts turned again to her mother, who'd always managed to spin straw into gold.

She knew what she'd do. She'd play the game (though Sterling always corrected her and said it was an *acting exercise*, not a game) in which you took an aerial view and thought of yourself in the third person, and tracked yourself.

(Monica walks into the bathroom, her bladder full. She pulls down her pants and sits on the toilet just so, to avoid having the edge of the seat cut into her thighs.)

That was a sad fairy tale to think of. The woman in "Rumpel-stiltskin" had been set up by her own father, who wanted to impress the king. She was locked up, asked to do the impossible not once, but always. She was aided by a little manikin who had the ability to transform things into gold, though naturally he exacted his price from the imprisoned woman, upping the ante, as men are known to do. All he wanted was her first child, and the only way around it would be for her to know his name. But she was saved because someone spying for her heard his self-congratulatory chant in which, dancing around *Twin Peaks* style, he said his name aloud. Victory! Problem solved!

(She stands, pulls up her pants, and walks to the sink. It's a nice sink, she thinks, shaped like a clamshell, with gold faucets that resemble fish tails.)

And the woman's great reward? That she can keep her child. But she's already married her torturer. She's wed to the king who'd imprisoned her and challenged her repeatedly: a mercenary, powerful man so arrogant, he blithely assumed that he'd be the great prize she'd win in the end.

(She dries her hands on one of Mama's monogrammed linen towels. She notices a tiny stain near the first initial of the surname.)

She found the game, the exercise, depressing—at least, without Sterling. It was better to wait to play it when something important happened. Few meaningful things were illuminated when a person went to pee.

Her phone rang as she walked down the hallway. She hurried to pick it up. Caller ID said MAYBE JONAH BUXTON.

"Jonah?" she said.

"Aunt Monica! I'm calling about something I maybe shouldn't involve you in, but it's really sort of, anyway, Uncle Case won't answer his phone, he's in New York and he's got it turned off and all, so I thought maybe you knew how to reach him because his secretary can't get him either. It's sort of bad because my friend's a really, really good person, and, uh, the guy she was living with is dead."

"What?"

"She found him last night when she went home after work. And she sort of went into shock or something. There was a note, and she was all fucked up—excuse my language—but it was super obvious he was dead. So, you know, I thought maybe Uncle Case could give her some advice."

"How did he die, Jonah?"

"She said he took really a lot of pills. He had medicine left over from his knee operation, and, uh, he took Alia's Ambien, all of it, actually, but there were blue capsules in his—this is really gross. Do you know what I mean? He'd written her this note."

"Where are you now?"

"Mudhouse. Outside Mudhouse."

"And for how long has Case not—"

"He just doesn't answer."

"I'm coming to meet you. Hold on."

"It was like, maybe he was involved in something, or something."

"I don't really know what you're talking about, honey. It sounds horrible. Where's your friend?"

"At the police station. When the ambulance came, so did the cops. I mean, what if they think she murdered him?"

"Jonah. From what you just told me, that isn't likely. And if they did think that, I'm sure it could be disproven. I'll be right there."

"This is really bad, because they were sort of maybe breaking up and now she feels guilty."

"Stay where you are," she said, and disconnected the call.

She was surprised but relieved that Jonah had contacted her, though concerned that Case wasn't answering his phone. He was in New York? Usually he left a message if he was leaving town. It would be good to talk to Case about whatever it was she was about to find out.

An awkward movement she made closing the front door caught her jacket. Damn! It tore the lining, but all she could do was lock up and hurry off, wondering what her mother would have done in this situation. That question was easily answered: Mama never intruded herself into anyone's life, even when asked. "Keep your distance, keep your friends," was her motto.

As she turned the corner and entered the mall, she saw Jonah holding a coffee cup, talking to a middle-aged woman in black tights topped with a long turtleneck sweater, her posture so perfect she looked like a broom. Little Jonah, whose wavy hair had made him look feminine as a toddler. Then, Jonah's mother was alive—Cora was still alive—as well as Mama. All was right with the world.

Jonah greeted her so naturally, it was hard to believe he'd just been so upset. He introduced the two women: "This is my aunt Monica. Monica, this is my yoga teacher, voted Best in Charlottesville, Jamie Feldenstein."

That was polite. An excellent impersonation of exquisite manners—though he *was* an actor.

Jamie was off to teach a class. Monica and Jamie said an equally cordial goodbye and the woman raced off, past a street person who was alternately singing and cursing.

"Jamie's my boss's ex. He tells her everything. 'People have more inner strength than they know.' Oh, sure. Like, if she was still married to Tom, she'd just call on her inner strength if he was dead on the floor?"

"Don't be so hard on people, Jonah. She was looking at you so kindly. I'm going to get a coffee. Do you want something else? Can you find us a table?"

Jonah nodded, but he was clearly too stunned to be functional.

She looked over her shoulder and saw that he was pulling out a chair from a table, though, as she hurried into the coffee shop. Her stomach already felt sour, but she needed coffee as a pick-me-up. For quite a while, she'd succeeded in putting Hadden out of her mind—no doubt just another man who regarded himself highly and assumed that if she hadn't succumbed to his charms the first time, she'd have second thoughts and contact him—but lately she found it difficult to get in touch with anyone, male or female. She attributed some of it to the move. There also might be an upside to that: she could avoid saddening, obligatory visits to nursing homes that way; there was something to be said for self-protection. Even afternoon naps, which were restorative.

She ordered a large cappuccino, wondering if a heart would be artfully swirled on top. "For here," she confirmed, then stepped aside to stand behind a Goth girl, already waiting, who extended one hand in a black mesh texting glove with part of a tattoo showing above it, to grab her big drink, apologizing so abjectly for nearly colliding with her that Monica felt the urge to reach out and hug her.

When "Monica" was handed her own cup (a bird quivered in the foam), she thought about adding sugar, or getting a little plastic stirrer, or a few napkins from the counter, though she wanted none of those things, they were just a delaying tactic. She, too, hurried out.

"Okay, tell me," she said, returning to the table.

"Alia, okay, so. She's on my shift. She was with this sort of loser, and he got in some kind of trouble, I guess, but whoa! To kill yourself? I mean, what if they suspect Alia? She's maybe going to need a lawyer? Not necessarily Uncle Case, I know he's a really big deal, but—"

"Honey, are you in any way involved in this?"

"*Involved*, in that she's a close friend."

"What does 'close friend' mean?"

"She's my friend."

"But are you involved with her?"

"Jeez! Are you standing in for Uncle Case or something? She and I are friends. Like you and Sterling."

She was startled by hearing his name. How different her days would be if Sterling were still in town.

"I'm sorry if I seemed to be prying."

"No, no problem, that's cool. I've never had a friend questioned by the cops. Alia's sort of fragile. I mean, not really fragile, but she's not up for a lot."

She took out her phone and speed-dialed Case. The call went immediately to voice mail. She hung up without leaving a message and sighed. There hadn't been anything between her and Ashton until there was. Her nephew looked so defeated. That little boy with rivulets of soft, wavy hair, who'd gotten hung up on words with an *n*: "Modica. Play a game, Modica."

Shouldn't she have stayed in Mama's quiet house, where her favorite horse, Ike, grazed in the field where the road dipped, and there was no real *next door*, let alone somebody pushing a pug dog around in a carriage, while noise from the Pavilion thrummed through the neighborhood on Friday night as drunks wove down East High Street? Lee Park—Market Street Park, by the library—was no longer a little area where non-neighborhood people gathered. The statue of Robert E. Lee remained, its base spray-painted with profanities or, more recently, with *Black Lives*

Matter. The statue would be taken down, that was clear; no one believed anymore that there was any other solution.

"Aunt Monica?"

"What?"

"Are you okay?"

"I'm fine, honey. Why don't we walk back to my place and continue our discussion?"

"I was thinking maybe I should go to the police station? As a show of support?"

"She might have left. Can you call her?"

That was brilliant. Of course he could. But when he tried, the phone rang once and sent him to voice mail, the new reality of his life. He looked at his aunt.

"What would be the best scenario?" she asked. It was a question Sterling sometimes posed when her anxiety kept building because everything seemed uncertain (really, *really*, a polo player with fake tits and chewed fingernails?)—his way of interjecting some positivity into a bad situation by making the other person realize that their worries might be a little excessive. He'd asked her that when Ashton first became smitten with his girlfriend. He'd probably have asked the same question if she'd told him about the photographer. *Oh, recently I had a chance to have sex with a stranger, back at the old house, but I shook my head—my head shook itself! I guess that was the best scenario, because I had no control over it—and then I left the room, which makes it a very boring story.*

Maybe the whole concept of a best scenario was ludicrous. Sterling must have been asking himself the same question, about now:

he'd moved to LA to become an actor. That hadn't exactly worked out. Now he'd taken part-time work giving lighting advice about how to best illuminate an entrepreneur's McMansion in Malibu.

"The best scenario would be that she'd never met him and I was married to her," he said. She'd asked. She'd *asked*.

"So you do have some involvement in this situation," she said.

His phone rang. It was Tom, who was back at his house with Alia. Did Jonah want to come over?

He most definitely, absolutely, totally did want to do that.

He thanked Monica for coming. God; she was so zonked, she'd once tried to lure a dog across an invisible fence, because she didn't realize dogs learned faster than she did. Maybe his aunt didn't even know there were invisible fences everywhere. You couldn't even join the country club in Charlottesville just by filling out a form. Did she realize there was an unspoken rule that street people had first rights to the benches in Market Street Park, as they waited before crossing the street to get their free lunch? All such lines of demarcation were invisible, because people understood unspoken rules. It was too perfect that outside city hall, near the Pavilion, a blackboard had been erected for the townspeople to express their grateful, privileged, PC, positive thoughts, but if you wanted to ask a question about something that was problematic? Or suggest a solution? Then somebody would erase it. That was what really happened inside the liberal bubble that was Charlottesville.

Monica gave her nephew a hug and watched him walk away. That expression everyone used now: *We've got your back.* Even American Express said they *had your back.* What was that supposed to mean? That somebody was sneaking up on you, but AmEx would save you? Jonah no doubt felt her eyes on him, but, like anyone else his age, he was intent upon casting no backward glance. Was that because he was male, or because his primary motive was always to escape? Or were those things synonymous?

She feared she hadn't helped him at all. Best to go home, try to gather her thoughts about whether there was anything else she could do. Best to avoid the park too, because you could never tell when contention would flare again. She stayed on the sidewalk alongside Lee Park, Hill & Wood funeral home to her left.

Trudging uphill, she saw the Altamont apartment building, now filled with hipsters who liked its high ceilings and spacious rooms, the abundant radiator heat. They liked the secret pull-down stairs that gave them forbidden access to the rooftop. Formerly, its occupants had been old people, some of them ancient, usually widows or widowers. One of the longtime residents had been a friend of her father's. On his one hundredth birthday, the corridors on his floor had been lined with printouts of calendars representing every month of his life, put up by someone else in the building. There'd also been the man who fascinated Sterling: Mr. Hamilton, ancient and lanky, who took flex-kneed baby steps while swinging his arms at his sides, double speed, like a goony bird attempting flight, in an attempt to stabilize himself as he traversed the distance from his old car to the building's front door, taking fifteen minutes to reach what others would have managed in a few quick strides. There were the retired teachers, lots of them, some not particularly fond of each other. Now there seemed to be no grace period, no living alone, the way so many women of Mama's generation had done when their husbands predeceased them. Old people went down the rabbit hole into assisted living. After interacting with the loonies they met there, many didn't mind tumbling deeper into the dark center of the earth, euphemistically called the Infirmary, or simply Nursing Care.

She passed the McGuffey—ah, the virtue of repurposed buildings!—then the playground, with the cluster of condominiums scattered below it. There was the church on the right, where bats swirled out at dusk.

Being glum was a curse. Papa had been that way, but never Mama. She'd have done a much better job of looking after Jonah, the family's one remaining young person. Though no one would have thought Mama had a sunny disposition, she'd been a remarkable woman in a society that retained high standards for the way women were to conduct themselves.

A woman on an electric scooter passed by, holding the handlebars the same way you'd plant your hands on a lectern. She wore a navy-blue dress, or suit—she was gone too fast to see, her hair swirling behind her.

What would Jonah have thought, if she'd said, *Yes, Sterling and I think of each other as friends, but once we took a vacation and a storm hit the shore, knocking out the power, and we ended up having sex on the floor.*

She turned right onto East High Street and continued past the endless parked cars to Second Street, wanting only to rest, not to further shock her nephew but to enjoy—what was nice, that she could conjure up?—Pavarotti singing, or being able to go to the Gardner Museum again, the stolen paintings miraculously returned. She'd have liked to sip some old-fashioned drink—maybe a chocolate soda—with Sterling at Timberlake's on the mall, where every Christmas she'd bought wonderful stocking stuffers for Mama. It was true, what Case said: she romanticized the past and was too easily charmed by things that provoked nostalgia. Case wouldn't set foot in Timberlake's. They met at C'ville Coffee, and walked through Circa afterwards to see what new furniture, rugs, dishes, and artworks appeared. His own sofa in Richmond had been special ordered from Roche Bobois. She'd nearly fainted when one of his friends let slip the price.

Why had he never remarried? He'd told her he never dated. His socializing consisted of playing poker with the firm's youngest partner (nicknamed Oxford, for the school he'd attended) the first Saturday of the month. He wore his N95 mask and went to the gym that stayed open until midnight and worked with a personal trainer on Mondays, under heat lamps set up in the man's backyard. He listened to classical music through his old sound system, which he still preferred, stretched out in his chair imported from Sweden, whose seat could be heated or cooled and conformed to his body (what *that* cost!). On Sunday morning, he usually played tennis with a former client on the clay courts of the man's club, a routine that went on until Christmas. He often celebrated holidays with his secretary and her husband the oncologist and their twin daughters, though they'd been too afraid to have him the year before.

It was difficult to believe that masks would ever disappear, let alone be collected as artifacts of a particular time, though she'd been surprised, browsing through an antiques store outside of Lexington, to see an unopened tin of Johnson's Baby Powder for sale, presumably a collectible. At Light the Way, Sterling had refused to convert oil-burning lamps, but not because they were antiques. The notion had just offended his aesthetic. They could transform their high school clarinet into a lamp base, for all he cared, but he refused to electrify the old lamps.

As she entered her townhouse, she reached up to turn on a light switch that—had this been Mama's house—would have been right there, though here it was farther in, on the opposite wall. She needed to remember to leave at least one light on. She found it strange not to have a landline, the way Mama had—that little red light blinking like a beacon.

She dimmed the kitchen's track lighting as she opened the refrigerator and found, among the few items inside, just what she wanted. She unscrewed the cap of a bottle of chardonnay. Screw caps no longer meant that a bottle of wine was cheap. Ashton had prejudiced her against so many Virginia wines that she never felt like experimenting, and you could still get a bargain on some of the California wines at Foods or at Market Street Wine, because the higher French import tax levied by Trump, the vindictive monster, wouldn't be passed on to you.

It occurred to her that her framed Vermeer reproduction should be moved where the mirror was, and the mirror hung where it could better catch the light. But she lacked the energy to make the switch. She needed a sip of golden wine, and maybe some food, though she didn't feel at all hungry.

It was dark when she awoke, nestled in Mama's silky throw, still faintly redolent of her cologne. Children's voices had stirred her, as well as distant sirens. Where were they going? Every day was filled with mysteries. Where was her brother? Was there something else she could have done to be supportive of Jonah? Would Ashton have wanted to hear from her on his birthday, or was he drinking champagne and playing games with his stepdaughter, as he'd play with the child's mother once the child was put to sleep?

That little girl now lived across the pond with a calculating mother and an old man with hair in his ears who wasn't her real father.

Monica got up, intending to call Sterling, but stopped midway to the kitchen, where she'd left her phone. She moved the footstool, climbed up, separated her feet to stabilize herself, then groped the back of the mirror, pushing up ever so slightly onto her toes to grab the picture wire and remove it from its hook. It was cumbersome, and the weight was heavier than she expected. Slowly, once she had it, she managed to move her right foot back off the stool. For a ludicrous moment, she had an image of herself as another of the town's statues, though she'd fought no wars; she'd fed carrots to horses, though she'd been too afraid to ever sit in a saddle. She wondered what any of the figures on the statues would say, in the twenty-first century, about America's having turned into a nation of joking, unreflective people (as Case always said), whose patron saints were Disney characters.

She stood with the mirror's edge pressing into her thigh, thinking of the one-sided history lessons she'd learned growing up, in the days when she'd never doubt a teacher. With her equally credulous classmates, she'd sung, "Columbus sailed the ocean blue in fourteen-hundred ninety-two." Case had been sent home from school twice in one year, first for saying that everyone had "blood on their hands" because of Vietnam, then for saying that Columbus Day should be renamed Slaughter the Indians Day. Mama had gone into the bathroom and turned on the shower to drown out her crying. Daddy had still been alive, though he'd usually felt that the best solution for dealing with his son's problems was to ignore them by going to his worktable in the basement. She'd been certain that if Case ever got through high school he'd move far away, but after graduating from law school at Yale, where had he gone but Richmond.

She'd finally managed to stand with both feet on the floor, but what to do with the mirror? She thought she'd trundle it across the floor and lean it somewhere safe, but her right hand had gone numb and her grip on the frame was precarious. The corner slipped but the mirror didn't break. As she sank to her knees, she couldn't avoid seeing herself (the mirror helped) as Narcissus, leaning forward to look at himself in the stream. But people misunderstood the myth; he didn't fall in love with himself, he only saw a beautiful face looking up that he didn't identify as his own. Should he have? How had he proceeded through life to that moment, without self-awareness? Narcissus had been aggressive, as men in myths tended to be, but he'd long ago gotten his comeuppance and become something of a joke. What was the old expression, *Hoisted by his own petard.* In limbo, like the rejected statues, hoisted up by cranes and chains to dangle in the air, on their way to permanent exile—at best, in a museum, or relocated to a Civil War battlefield, or, as her brother said, to become lawn ornaments on some sheik's Bel Air estate.

These were her thoughts as—though she didn't know it—Case was in Seattle attending mindfulness camp. In the relative silence of the woods, he was being asked to be aware of his breathing, to be conscious of his voice's volume as he spoke his "necessary words." He was there for four days, sitting on a mat rolled out next to the woman he'd met through EliteSingles, who'd left her HR job at a California university because she was convinced she could do more good by forgetting about disgruntled employees and focusing instead on the issue of childhood hunger. She'd recently affiliated herself with a new organization started by a runaway from Microsoft, a red-haired twin (nicknamed Russ, for his russet hair) who'd decided it was time to escape his brother's shadow. He had an ability to come up with ideas and get them off the ground, with the help of his lover, who'd previously dropped out of Cal Tech *and* the General Theological Seminary because he thought there was always too much talk and not enough action. This woman, too, was in Seattle, stretched out on a mat as thin as a communion wafer. Such a unique first date! Though she and Case had FaceTimed every day for weeks.

Monica checked her phone. Nothing from her brother. Nothing from Jonah. Or Sterling. What she needed to do (*thank you, Mama*) was to clear her head by taking a shower.

Yet instead, she set out again, amused at herself for being a homing pigeon, taking a different route past Fleurie to the mall. She knew the area well enough, though there were always new things to discover. She noticed that an art gallery had opened across from the restaurant, so she peered in the window, knowing in advance she wouldn't like anything. When you were alone, you only needed to please yourself. It was liberating. She wasn't the only woman who was divorced, missing her best friend on another coast. There were several people—or at least two—she could call who'd be happy to hear from her. She could even call Jeanette to see how the performances had gone, and to ask if she'd like to have lunch if the plague ever ended.

Though there was every chance Jeanette had seen her in the store and pretended otherwise.

The lights were dazzling on the Paramount's marquee. For so long, the huge building had sat empty. Case knew someone who'd worked there in the eighties, when it had yet to be renovated, painting a mural on huge canvases no one in town would see, because it was sent to St. Louis. One day the painter had gone in, turned on the generator to inflate the plastic tent he worked inside, then begun hallucinating, thinking it was snowing. Overnight, moths had hatched from the old upholstered theater seats: *My god,* he'd thought, *do moths eat canvas?* Just a little anecdote she'd heard at one of Case's command performance dinners, where the "extra man" tried to find common ground with her—that ground being Charlottesville. Everyone in Richmond was always driving to Charlottesville, though in her experience, Charlottesvillians drove to Richmond to fly out of the airport.

She walked in the direction of the Omni, past the area where the Christmas tree was put up every December.

Daddy had always cut down a tree for the holidays. There'd been—awful to remember, it had been so uncharacteristic of both of them—there'd been a real altercation one year, because the tree he'd selected was too skinny. Mama would not have a scrawny tree. Go forth, she said, and get another, and make sure that it's much bigger. Off he went, carrying his chainsaw, this time with his son at his side. It was getting dark. They were gone a long time, but finally they returned with what both considered the perfect tree, large and lush, with a wonderful, fresh-cut aroma. This tree Mama had deemed insufficient, and recruited the only one of her daughters who was at home to offer an opinion. The tree wasn't straight; the trunk went off at an angle because the poor tree had leaned so far out, trying to escape the shade. And the top: little branches bristled there, only an inch or two down, so there'd be no easy way to place a star atop it. Was there no ordinary, beautiful tree in the forest? asked the mother. He took a deep breath and replied that both trees were fine, and that if she wanted a third tree—if she was that stubborn—she should go to the forest herself. There was a moon that shone brightly, and since she had such strong opinions, she should chop down a tree and bring it home—maybe her son would help her. *Of course* the mother wasn't going to march off and fell a tree, though. Both trees were fine, he insisted, gesturing vaguely toward the window, where that night a full moon would set. The first tree had been dragged out into the yard, and could be seen lit by the spotlight over the back door. The second tree leaned against the mudroom wall, smelling of pine. The husband called them "the trees that don't live up to your expectations."

Again, the children were summoned, to "learn a lesson about the pointlessness of perfectionism."

O, whatever tree is decided upon, it will be a wonderful Christmas tree, said the daughter.

Fuck this, said the son.

No tree was brought into the den. Its stand remained empty. The question became: Would stockings be hung, because they were unrelated to the contretemps over the tree? No, unless the children wanted to go to the attic, rummage around, and bring them down, with the understanding that nothing would be put in them, because the father had ruined Christmas.

Actually, though no one knew this except the mother, the father had ruined Christmas by having dinner and a bottle of champagne at the C & O restaurant with a woman who worked with him, having told his wife he was working late. Twenty years later, she confided this to her daughter, but never did she say it to her son, because men inevitably defended other men.

It was as if a tape loop had been playing in Monica's head all day. And the doctor's nice assistant, Arjun, hadn't called back. She checked her phone. No calls at all.

In front of her, a little girl in a red parka broke away from her mother, who gave chase. A man exiting a restaurant stepped back to avoid blocking the mother's way. Then the child, who really could run fast, stumbled, extended her hands, and fell. The wailing was instantaneous, though the girl tried to resist her mother by hammering her head with her fist and screaming into her ear, as she was scooped up. It might have been the polo player's child, Monica thought. No sense in wishing that woman ill; she'd be subjected to years and years of screaming. The few people walking nearby hurried on, pretending not to notice.

Being alone had its advantages. As did being childless. Something about their relatively happy childhoods had made them all wary of marriage and parenthood. Case had married the perfect person, as far as he was concerned; he'd never marry again. Cora had stopped at one child, Jonah had been so hyperactive. Monica had never wanted to be a mother. Some people, probably including the polo player, had babies as accessories.

There was a kind of itch to the air. It was almost palpable. Everyone had suddenly begun to walk at a faster pace. Something was up; they were headed in the same direction, turning by Petit Pois, past its white outdoor tent, its perimeter lined with flower boxes.

Of course: something was happening in Lee Park, or whatever it was named today.

A little-known fact about Lee's wife was that she'd had seven children, four of them daughters, and not one of the girls ever married. You had to assume she'd done something to see to that. That seemed surprising now, but had it then? John Singer Sargent had painted a group portrait that hung in the Museum of Fine Arts in Boston called *The Daughters of Edward Darley Boit*: four sisters, and not one of them had married either.

Two police cars without sirens appeared on Market Street. A man carrying a traffic cone—no, it was a yellow bullhorn—pulled his girlfriend along by the hand, farther into the park. A woman out walking her dog scooped it up and nearly collided with the man carrying the bullhorn. She rushed away.

A small crowd had gathered inside the park, Monica saw, going up the stairs. Yet again, Lee's visage served as a magnet for all that was wrong with race relations, the past, the present, the future, Charlottesville, the United States, the world, so that his likeness must be removed and his legacy negated.

The policemen hung back, one obviously keeping an eye on a woman with disheveled hair who occupied an entire bench beside the landslide of her possessions. More police arrived from the opposite side of the park and stood silently, attentively watching the crowd—twenty people so far, maybe thirty. A bullhorn wouldn't be necessary to address them. Then she recognized one of the people: the man from Solace House, the one who guarded the door, one of many eccentrics (*eccentric* was a euphemism the South provided for people with appreciable limitations), who had a way of popping up when least needed. A young woman stood beside him. George—that was his name, George Matts—with a *girlfriend?*

A ponytailed man with a video camera mounted on his shoulder stood behind and to one side of Monica, panning. Soon—although she couldn't hear from such a distance—a woman in jeans and boots, wearing a purple jacket that kept blowing open in the wind, started a countdown. The crowd began to chant, *"Let horses run free, not to battle, Let horses run free, not to battle, Let horses run free, not to battle . . ." "LET HORSES RUN FREE,"* the woman sitting on the bench hollered, followed by a fit of choking. The videographer had pivoted to aim his camera at her. Monica ducked her head and moved away, not wanting to be caught on-camera. *"HI-YO, SILVER! AWAY!"* the woman screamed. She was standing now, pumping her fist. Did they have nothing better to do than express their support for horses, when the planet's temperature was warming so fast that droughts killed vast acres of forests as uncontained fires raged, and icebergs calved?

"Take Traveller back to the pasture, Take Traveller . . ."

The wind intensified. The woman on the bench watched some of her possessions blow away. The videographer, wearing a headset, continued filming while speaking into his mic. Two young women, laughing, arms linked, walked by in pink pussy hats—god! From the January 2017 Women's March in Washington. More police arrived, though none were running, and one was casually combing his hair. They moved quickly into a loose formation, without shields; it was devoutly to be wished there were no guns—only people shouting, their overlaid voices canceling each other out: *"Run free / Let horses / back to the / Let / Let horses run free / the pasture."*

Here came the van from CBS19 News. One man moved in the direction of the videographer. George Matts ran up to them and began talking animatedly.

"Excuse me, do you have any idea why they're worried about the horse?" a woman asked Monica.

She shook her head. Of course she didn't. How bizarre to be chanting not about Robert E. Lee, but about his horse. Were they from PETA? Would the birds that used the statue as a perch sing next, as people expressed their fervent wish that . . . what would it be, that Monsanto keep its hands off their sunflower seeds, to insure that the birds would remain healthy? Fish were poisoned by oil spills, manatees wore tire necklaces, while the president withdrew from the Paris climate agreement as easily as a card shark slipped a card out of the deck, while America's conscience was represented by a teenage girl who tried to shame Congress with facts about the grim reality of climate change. And people were upset about the subjugation of a bronze horse?

Then came an explosion, and people began to move chaotically, most too clumsy and stunned to run. The videographer ran forward, zigzagging, nearly colliding with a tall man in overalls, deftly changing course to avoid a policeman with a raised hand. The policeman dropped and raised his hand again. Looking bored, he fidgeted before raising his hand another time. The wild-haired woman on the bench pulled off her wig and stood, hand on hip, phone clamped to her ear. As the videographer made a gracefully balletic half-turn, the man screamed through the yellow bullhorn, "Cut, cut!"

"Frances McDormand!" someone exclaimed.

They were shooting a film. A box had emitted the explosion; the crowd wasn't real—or it was, but the call had gone out and word had spread, so that people jogging or pushing baby carriages, businesspeople walking to the parking garage, and students from the university had found out simultaneously that they could go to Market Street Park and be filmed as part of the crowd. ("These are nonspeaking appearances, but you *will be seen on-camera*. Remember that only those fully vaxed may participate, and there *will be* people checking, let me repeat: there will be spot checks, so do not come without proof of vaccination.")

Were they even real police cars?

They were, Monica would read in the *Daily Progress* the next day. Off-duty officers had volunteered their time, though the strong wind was unfortunate, making it difficult for the director to get the shot he wanted. Finally the wind machine cooling Traveller's haunches was turned off.

The woman who'd been sitting on the bench, with her diminishing pile of possessions, dangled her curly wig on one finger, waving the curls to get the attention of the little girl in red—the girl who'd fallen earlier—who burrowed into her mother's shoulder when she was offered the brown ugly-wiggly.

Monica was reeling. Wait until Case heard about this. He had his reservations about the police anyway—in Charlottesville *and* in Richmond—but the idea that this many policemen would show up, just to appear on-camera? That the town would allow such a thing, regardless of the university's film program and its annual film festival, with celebrities flying in on private jets for its famous Southern hospitality and a chance to network with King Juan Carlos of Spain?

"You best believe this is *some* crazy-shit place," one man said to another as they cut through the park.

Monica was pulling her jacket tightly around her, half relieved, still half terrified. For obvious reasons, she'd begun to view Charlottesville as Wonderland. It really had been the strangest day—inconclusive, mixed-up, sadness passed off as irony, frightening when not simply misery-inducing. Were other protests going to become faux protests, with information spread by social media? And, really—she hated to be judgmental, but wasn't it wrong to be staging a movie in a park near where a woman had been run over and many others injured, in an area where so much anger and resentment had been expressed about the still-standing monument to the Confederacy? Wasn't it a little like a stand-up comic riffing on mortality while standing in a graveyard? Though she supposed (Jonah had told her this) Susan Sontag had staged *Waiting for Godot* in war-torn Sarajevo. Or was that different? Did everything have to be, as her brother said so judiciously, with that self-satisfied twist of his lips as he considered the inherent pun, looked at case by case?

After a day of so much reflection and regret, did she really need to put herself down yet again by casting herself as Alice, expediently dismissing present-day Charlottesville as merely a topsy-turvy Wonderland? Was she that desperate to think of herself as young again, a girl who'd be shocked by what was about to be revealed about human nature? Everyone was late and in a hurry—no surprise; that was the nature of life. Those girls in their pussy hats had looked like adventure tourists, *arrivistes* in the magical kingdom where Patricia Kluge had once ruled as the Southern Queen and roly-poly men had huffed and puffed, trying to keep order; where it was simply expected that everyone would be swept up into a spectacle that, in a safer world—with a sound track by Nino Rota—might have drawn the attention of Fellini.

But now? Trump, the showman president, had eclipsed Fellini's imaginings to prove he was really and truly mad.

She shouldn't have done it. She shouldn't have tried to escape her family by choosing Ashton, who carried with him the mixed message of being both an outsider and a confident man with enough hubris to flout convention, turning his nose up at small-batch bourbons *and* Virginia ham, with a free spirit she'd envied until he brought his girlfriend home.

A young masked woman came toward her, hand extended. At first Monica assumed she was greeting someone behind her, but the sidewalk, now lit by streetlight, was empty. The reporter held up her microphone, saying, "We're here this evening outside Market Street Park, where a film's being shot, POV Traveller, General Robert E. Lee's horse. But it's a wrap for tonight, so if you missed your moment, tickets will be given out tomorrow to the first one hundred hopefuls, starting at four p.m., in front of CVS on the downtown mall. I'm here with one of the people who came to be an extra. Can you tell us a little about what it was like just now in Market Street Park?" she asked, flipping the microphone toward Monica's lips.

"You've made a mistake," Monica said. "I'm just out for a walk. I'm headed home."

THE BUBBLE

When George Matts learned the meaning of the word *quandary*, he knew he'd been in one.

George had been engaged to Walwyn before he was engaged to Trudy. Walwyn's former fiancé had come back, begging forgiveness and presenting her with a pearl engagement ring. Wally had eagerly returned to him, so the standoff over who was George Matts's girlfriend didn't have to continue. The two women had begun eating together again on their half-hour lunch break at Solace House, Charlottesville's newest nursing and assisted living facility.

When not fulfilling the job of greeting visitors at the door from ten to two, George worked a four-hour shift Thursdays and Fridays, assisting the gardeners, plumbers, and carpenters, as well as acting as a general handyman.

The cement urns at either side of Solace House's front door that held seasonal flowers (pansies, some of which survived even in the dead of winter; decorative cabbages whose leaves cupped winter snow) had to be moved in a wheelbarrow, with a helper on either side to steady them, as George Matts wheeled them into the building, then outside again into the courtyard. The new location would protect them from the nearby fraternity boys, who'd been seen on-camera trying to manhandle one urn down the hill, drunkenly crowding around it, hooting and laughing inaudibly. They'd staggered down the sidewalk to their frat house, probably intending to use the thing as a beer cooler.

In this location, if you were confused about why something strange happened, the likeliest answer was to look toward the nearest fraternity, then try to imagine what use the boys made of the things they stole. The urn might have been a potential prop in some sadistic initiation ritual, with a potential member being plunged, upside down, to the point of drowning, as they filled it at full blast from the neighbor's hose.

Stacey, the head nurse, walked up to George as he was rubbing his hands on his jeans in preparation for washing them. He now made it a point, after one unfortunate incident when he dirtied the hallway with mulch wedged in the deep treads of his shoes, to self-inspect the minute he stepped inside.

"George, have you checked your phone? The idea is that you respond to a text," Stacey called out as he headed toward the bathroom.

He had no idea how to keep the iPhone 11's volume audible. The sound was too soft or too loud, even when he set the volume right in the middle. The phone would start to make its sound, then go silent, like a sneeze that tickled but didn't gather force.

At the moment, he was recovering from a severely sprained ankle he'd suffered while hiking to Crabtree Falls with Trudy. This many weeks later, the ankle began to swell after an hour or so of standing, and he had to sit and elevate his foot.

A number of empty rooms remained, or were being altered before the residents moved in. Covid had further complicated things, so that only one family member a day could visit for fifteen minutes. What this translated into was that George, in his soft cast that felt like a blood pressure cuff pumped too tightly, would recruit Wally, who was now no longer his girlfriend but merely his friend, to watch the door while, for example, he advised a seventy-five-year-old man whose mother was ninety-eight (he walked with a cane; she didn't) to pull into the farthest place in the lot, so he'd have ample room. But he didn't enjoy feeling as unsteady on his feet as the residents. He'd told Stacey it was embarrassing, but she'd tried to persuade him otherwise, substituting the word *humbling*. He'd slipped off the trail after drinking most of a bottle of merlot, which he didn't even like, but Trudy had forgotten to pack his two ginger ales, and he'd been parched.

This new romantic affiliation had happened fast—his relationship with Wally ending, followed by his telling Trudy she'd always been the one, whispering in her ear that he was relieved Wally had moved on. Merely thinking of the word *moved* reminded him of his accident, his right foot slipping off the path into mud, his reaching for a branch to steady himself, his hand grasping only air, so that he rolled down the incline, landing on his side. He could have broken his hip, which had been badly bruised. That had been the first thing the ER doctor mumbled through his mask. At Solace House, some of the residents for various medical reasons could not be masked. Though Mrs. Johnson had no medical reason for not wearing one, she took hers off regularly and stuffed them in her bra. Other people's slipped down to cover their top lip, rather than their nose. Trudy said she liked it that the masks drew more attention to the residents' eyes (usually their eyes remained their best feature—though not, for example, if they were taking Seroquel), but George focused as well on their big, sad ears with lima-bean lobes, the ones they'd been taunted about as children, only larger. He could also test how good his vision was by seeing if he could locate, on the old ladies' earlobes, that tiny spot where the skin had filled in the piercing because they no longer bothered to wear earrings.

He was: Observant; Focused; Kind.

Stacey was right there in the hallway when he exited the restroom. He tried to be patient with her, because she'd gone to bat for him, she'd gotten him hired, so now he didn't have to do custodial work. She sang in the church choir with Harriet, his mother, and had brought them a casserole made from fresh, wild-caught salmon after his mother's gallbladder surgery. The previous weekend he'd helped Stacey and her brother, who was as nice as she was, lay a patio, as her husband supervised from his wheelchair. Ches's favorite thing to talk about was why laymen should never climb onto a roof.

"George, we've got to get this phone situation figured out." Stacey looked at the floor, looked up again. "I'm sure we will," she said, "but meanwhile I want to say two things. One, I have successfully located the snake you need, which will be delivered this afternoon; and two, I've gotten two strange telephone calls from that woman who visited Mrs. Johnson weeks ago, saying she might be visiting, and she might not."

"Why does it matter?" he asked.

"Between you and me? Something was off. Her voice was drifty. You know what I mean?"

"Like driftwood."

"Sort of. I might not have selected the best word. More like, she might not be quite herself. Do you remember the person I'm talking about? The one whose brother just won that big trial in Richmond against the utility company?"

"The quarter watermelon," he said.

"Exactly. The bag that dripped all over the floor. So today, if you don't mind, maybe you could stick your head in and make sure everything's okay with Mrs. Johnson, if what's-her-name does show up. Do you know what I mean?"

"Peek."

"Yes, that's . . . You can enter the room, of course. Just knock first."

Down the corridor came Ms. Dresky, her walker adorned with plastic sunflowers: *Good afternoon, it is a lovely day. Please tell me what time the train arrives, am I in the right place to pick up my mother?*

Both of them knew that it would be best if they didn't answer. In another few seconds, Ms. Dresky would forget that she'd asked.

George was polite, but he didn't like her. She was the one who'd thought a herd of cattle had run down the corridor, mistaking the mulch he'd tracked in for shit and making quite a scene.

"Do you have time to hear an amazing story?" George asked Stacey.

"I actually don't, unless— hello, Ms. Roncelle. Watch out for Ms. Dresky there! I see you're making good progress today, headed toward the lunchroom."

"Turtle speed."

"That's fine. As we all know, the turtle won the race!"

No answer. She continued, advancing the walker by inches. Finally Stacey gestured, and she and George passed her on the left, on their way back to the nurses' station. As they walked, George said, "Ms. Benforth's son, who worked for the Army Corps of Engineers? He worked in the Everglades . . ."

I don't hear the train. I wonder if I have the wrong day. Do any of you know if the train is expected shortly? Ms. Dresky asked two women with their eyes closed, sitting in their wheelchairs.

"I feel like we're in a Russian novel," Stacey said.

George, unfazed, continued: "First day he was there, her son in the Army Corps of Engineers saw a man coming ashore in a canoe with a Doberman, when a gator came up and grabbed the dog. Two guys attacked it with shovels, and the gator spit the dog out feet first, breech-birth-style."

"Breech-birth-style!" Stacey exclaimed.

When they reached the nurses' station, Stacey sank into her chair. George was excitable. If there wasn't enough going on, he'd excite himself. There was always some disaster playing out in his head. It had taken Stacey a while to understand that he loved to hear about real or potential disasters not because they were nightmarish, but because they were a way to soothe himself, by realizing those things hadn't happened to him. Her son, Sturgis, had been that way, talking almost as much as George did—as a child, of course; as he got older, his only interest was in making an end-run around her and his father, enacting how he was going to drop-kick the Three Little Pigs, or paint the sidewalk with the sticky adhesive used in mousetraps so that when Mary Poppins floated down, she'd stand forever where she landed.

Raising Sturgis had prepared her for letting anxious people have the last word, which she tried to remember when talking with George. Two call lights lit up. As George walked away, she spoke to Ashleigh, the young aide. They rose in unison, she heading down one corridor as Ashleigh loped off in the opposite direction with her habitual horse-like gait.

George was thinking that he'd have liked to track down the vandals who'd tried to steal the urn. "I could have shoved those Dekes into the urn, *then* rolled it back to their frat house," he hissed to himself. That thief would have been lucky; he'd be Sisyphus in reverse. (He knew who Sisyphus was because he'd asked the woman in the apartment across the hall from his mother's what her dog's name meant.) If he'd done that, you could bet those boys would have been so drunk, they wouldn't have noticed. And if they did? A good way of getting home without having to pay an Uber.

A call light came on as soon as he passed an open door. This could be *coincidence*.

Trudy had told him that now that the relocated urns provided someplace to hide cigarette butts in the courtyard, Ashleigh had given up vaping and gone back to Marlboro Lights. In his peripheral vision, he saw a smoke puff waft up out there, but Ashleigh wasn't outside. Someone had donated a heated patio in memory of his mother, so that in winter the snow would melt quickly. The Norfolk Island pines, their plastic pots settled into two decorative Mexican pots from T.J. Maxx, didn't much like the heat, though. Every day more brown patches appeared. He went out and trundled them to the side, just off the patio. This was *proactive*. As he was turning to leave the courtyard, he saw the Sad Girl. How could she have gotten in without his noticing? Uh-oh. But there she was, sitting silently in the opposite corner from where he'd relocated the pines, watching him. She had on a white hat and a long skirt and a jacket that looked like one of his grandmother's powder puffs. Remembering that he should not overlook the likeliest possibility, he thought she'd probably come down from upstairs.

He wished her a good day. She was there, she told him, to meditate.

He apologized for interrupting. She said that no apology was necessary. She was actually taking a break from helping a resident put together a jigsaw puzzle of Monet's water lilies. The box contained one thousand pieces, though the front-desk guard had given her a heads-up that several had disappeared. Sometimes the residents became confused and ate things they shouldn't.

With pain creeping up his leg, he envied her for taking a
time-out.

She was pretty, though he could hardly sit beside a stranger. So
he sat alone on the metal bench with the brass plaque:

In Loving Memory Idell Deiter Debbs
and her devoted Pointer, Ranger
b. Livonia, Michigan, 1931 · d. Charlottesville, Virginia 2020
Some say the world will end in fire, some say in ice.

"My mother works in the main house. Eustacia Tazewell," the
girl said.

"Oh! I know her. You've got a nice mama. Somebody came to
visit one of the residents and brought her cocker spaniel puppy,
and it threw up in the entranceway the minute she set it down,
and peed too. They sent me up because Woody's in quarantine
after playing pickleball with a guy who tested positive."

She started to speak, then stopped.

"I'm a handyman and a jack-of-all-trades," he said.

"I'm a waitress," she said.

"Whereabouts?"

"Downtown mall."

"Which restaurant do you work at?"

"If you're female, you're not supposed to be specific about
where you live or work, because men can stalk you."

"Do I seem like somebody who'd do that? Everybody here'll
vouch for me. Also, I'm engaged."

She looked at him a long time. She touched the edge of her hat. "Simpatico," she said. "Me and my friend Alia, but she switched to last shift. She's got a sort of crush on the owner, but he's still hung up on his ex. Sometimes they fool around in the kitchen before he locks up. It's a really bad time for her, because her boyfriend's gone."

"Where did he go?" he asked.

"I guess I'd have to say he went to heaven, though he might have gone in the opposite direction."

"Are you saying he died?"

"We've been waiting to see it in the *Daily Progress*. It might make the *Washington Post*, I don't know. I shouldn't speak ill of the dead, but he could be such a dick. He'd get a rubber band and pretend the little butterfly tattoo on her butt was a fly, and snap her."

"Is that right?" He realized he was echoing his mother. It was what she most often said after he'd finished telling her a story.

His conversation with the Sad Girl was followed by a long pause. When women told other women a story, they expected one in return, because women always felt they'd been through the same thing, or something similar. He'd learned that from Trudy, who wanted him to talk more like a girl. When they had sex, he called himself the Love Machine. That was because he could do it forever, because he never came.

"Her boyfriend and a teacher at the university were posting porn. The university guy's lawyer told him the FBI was going to be knocking on his door."

"Somebody at the *university*?"

"Right. But I don't know what she was doing with that guy. Now she's a total wreck. She won't answer texts. Like, she never leaves the apartment, unless Tom rounds her up and drives her to work."

"George Matts! I've looked everywhere for you. You never answer your phone. Hi, honey; I'm just having a word with George," Stacey said. "George, room twelve, please. Your snake is here and that brand-new toilet won't flush. You have a blessed afternoon, honey."

When he stood, it felt like broken glass was sifting through his leg. What if it had happened when he was alone on the Appalachian Trail? He'd been even thirstier after drinking the wine. His throat was still so dry, he couldn't stop coughing as he'd limped back to the car. The opportunity for a little affection (sex) in the woods had certainly been lost. He'd had to lean on Trudy to hobble down. He knew she didn't have a car, but coming down the trail had been the first time he'd heard she didn't know how to drive. It was his right leg, so he'd had to accelerate and brake with his left foot.

"You tell your mama George Matts says hello," he said over his shoulder. "Tell her the guy downstairs who fixed her flat tire said 'hi.'"

"You're the one? I heard about that. That was really nice of you. She picked up a nail or something?"

"Come on!" Stacey said, holding the door open.

He turned back to say one final thing: "That's how Traveller died. One battle after another, proudly did he carry General Robert E. Lee atop his back. Then one day Traveller returns to his stable, steps on a rusty nail, and gets tetanus, and that's the end of him. Lee died before his horse, but the two of them are buried in Lexington, by Lee chapel."

"Thanks for the history lesson," she said.

"George, did you make that up?" Stacey asked as he brushed past her.

"No," he said, willing to tell her even more about General Robert E. Lee, though she'd vanished by the time he reached the nurses' station.

"Somebody was flirting," Brianna said from her swivel chair behind the counter. "I'm gonna tell!"

"There's nothing to tell. I'm tried and true."

"Is that right? Well, I don't know any other men who've been engaged to two different women, all in the same week!"

Stacey was in the ladies' room, doing some quick breathing exercises. Some days it felt like she was in charge of middle school students, instead of being head nurse. She needed to insist on less talk and teasing. As it was, the staff's lunch break had been reduced from forty-five minutes to half an hour, because there were so many arguments in the last fifteen minutes. Poor George. The last thing he'd needed was to hurt his foot up on the Blue Ridge. He was a nice man. He'd been a sweet child too, though Sturgis had never liked him. She and Harriet had pretended they didn't take to each other because of the three-year age difference. A terrible thing, George's being hit by an SUV when he was sixteen, walking alongside a country road where he'd gone to pick apples. When he emerged from his coma, the doctors hadn't been sure he'd ever speak again.

At that time, the man who'd fathered George still lived with them; he had an enormous barbecue grill on which he cooked his special all-day-marinated chicken with six added spices. Then he put it in a pan and drove around the neighborhood to sell it on Saturday night, and he kept doing that while George was hospitalized, then later in rehab, where he only visited once, at Harriet's urging. (Later, she found out that when he was making his deliveries, he'd carried with him a picture of George in his hospital bed, tubes and machines everywhere, though any money he got by showing it, he kept.) When George came out of the coma, his first word had been "turtle," which they figured out was because he'd seen his mother's brown handbag on her lap as she sat there, right beside his bed. Stacey and her husband had gotten a permit and held a fundraiser in Lee Park, with Madison Duff on electric keyboard, the Porter brothers playing guitar and banjo, and Shannon Cullen singing in her beautiful soprano. Six years later, Shannon almost married Madison. If she had, she'd have been a young widow. Now she lived in a three-bedroom house in Earlysville with her banker husband from Poland, her equestrian daughter, and a Siamese cat that was a little shrill.

Blessed day: it turned out she'd been worried for no reason. Monica—Monica insisted that she call her by her first name— turned out to be very pleasant, even if she was arriving two days late. She'd brought a bag of treats for Mrs. Johnson and told Stacey she'd pass on her compliment about how well-spoken her brother Case had been on the local news after the verdict was handed down in Richmond. She also seemed genuinely fond of Dorcas Johnson, and not everyone was. Because of her feelings about the United Daughters of the Confederacy, they'd twice had to change which table she was assigned at lunch.

Then there was the other situation: Brianna had been taking a night course in creative writing at a building not far from the Preston Avenue Bodo's called WriterHouse, where she'd gotten a lot of encouragement. When Trudy said she and Wally would like it if she'd read them one of her stories, Brianna had explained that they weren't really read-aloud stories; you had to look at them. Comic books, Stacey would have called them, though she'd been informed they were graphic novels. The problem was, the novel was titled "Solace," and while none of the characters were drawn to look like the staff and residents they were modeled on, there she was, the head nurse a charging elephant, with Wally a kangaroo who cocked her head like a listening dog (Wally was, as Stacey's husband would have said, "broad in the beam") while Trudy, who saved twenty dollars every paycheck toward getting her nose fixed, was a toucan. The existence of such a book was worrisome. She'd lost sleep over it. Brianna seemed nice—and maybe she had been, before she went off to study writing—but witness what had just happened: she'd teased George when he came in from the courtyard.

Several nights before Stacey had called her friend Jeanette, who ran the creative writing program at the university, to ask if someone could *do that*. Jeanette said she could understand her concern, but since there'd probably been no nondisclosure agreement when Brianna was hired (no; who would think of such a thing?), the situation might be somewhat problematic. Jeanette said she'd contact a friend at the law school and get back to her. What was the book about? Jeanette wanted to know, and when she told her that Brianna had turned the nursing home into a jungle, and made the staff animals, Jeanette had yelped with laughter. Which had of course made her worry more that the book might be a success.

George Matts, quoted verbatim, appeared as a gorilla. He'd been drawn holding his hairy arms curved away from his sides, as if he intended to form a pair of big parentheses. The drawings seemed inherently disrespectful. In what she'd seen, the residents' aphasia made them incomprehensible, as they made ridiculous requests. Here was the problem: some of the things they said had been transcribed exactly, including the confusion that had ensued when a resident substituted the word *rodeo* for *ride*, explaining that her son was coming to pick her up for a rodeo. Silly stuff, *just like* a cartoon! She intended to wait to hear back from Jeanette and say nothing to Brianna until she learned more.

Walwyn appeared. "Stacey, can I confidence you?" she asked.

Walwyn's mother, who'd come in person to urge Solace House to hire her daughter, was nearly fifty now, and had lived since she was fourteen with Walwyn's father in West Virginia, where he and his brother co-owned a Dairy Queen. Apparently their wedding cake (they married the year Walwyn started high school) had been a homemade yellow layer cake, topped at the last minute with soft-serve chocolate-vanilla swirl, right out of the machine; in the center of the ice cream icing, the little plastic bride and groom figures stood sunken up to their waists, she'd seen, as Walwyn's mother enlarged the photograph on her phone.

"Of course. What is it, Walwyn?" (She didn't believe in using boys' nicknames for girls. She'd made that clear when Walwyn was hired.)

"Well, you know the graphic novel Brianna's working on? We were thinking it's kind of creepy she listens in on what we're saying, and, uh, Trudy said she's wearing a wire."

"She's doing what?"

"Wearing a wire. Like, secretly recording us. Because Trudy saw her in the bathroom and she pulled her top down real fast, and she was all phony casual, saying her bra was cutting into her."

"I'll see what I can find out," she said, having no idea how she would do that.

"And also? Mrs. Tazewell's daughter, Nola Mae? She might be giving us the evil eye, we're thinking. Underneath her hat, she's got pink-striped hair." Walwyn gestured to the top of her head.

"Okay, we can continue this conversation later, after I make the rounds with the afternoon medicine."

"It might be some secret signal like the Crips use or something."

"It's never good to overthink things or to rush to conclusions. It's possible Brianna might have been wearing a heart monitor— did you think of that?" (She felt lucky that any possibility had come to mind, even one so ridiculous.) "And don't tell me you haven't seen streaked hair before."

"Sometimes colors mean something."

"I think you might need to take a time-out. Take a deep breath, then return to your job. Can you do that for me?"

"She keeps pulling off the hat, then she puts it on really fast, like she's sending a signal."

"Walwyn, I have no idea why she's in the courtyard, except that it was intended as a pleasurable area, and she's waiting for her mother to get off work."

"People vape and smoke out there, and on his break Lewis comes downstairs and kicks back and does gummies and pretends they're vitamins."

"Thank you for this information. I'll—"

"And those people who flew into the World Trade Center."

"Excuse me?"

"The pilots who studied how to take off, but they didn't want to learn how to land."

"What about them?"

"They flew into the World Trade Center."

"Yes, I know. But I don't understand what you're saying."

"They were acting super strange, but nobody paid any attention."

"Ah! You're worried about your personal safety." She amended this: "Our personal safety here."

"Yeah, because Nola Mae was never downstairs before, whipping her hat on and off, and Brianna's recording everything we say. You know, there are hand signals they teach you on TikTok, to use if you don't feel safe. For example."

"If you were me, what would you do? I mean, what would you do right this minute?"

"Leave the building," Walwyn said.

This was not the answer she expected, but there it was. She did not think that either Brianna or Mrs. Tazewell's daughter Nola Mae was a spy for the CIA, or a terrorist, though. She said, "I can't talk any longer, but I'll try to be more observant."

"Also, Brianna's going to a private party at one of the vineyards where Ivanka Trump's going to be. It's a fundraiser for children, but that'll give Brianna a chance to pass on any information Donald Trump should hear."

Might Xanax help? Because this person did not at all resemble the shy young woman who'd said "Yes, ma'am" so quietly in her interview. Knitting and making cupcakes had been her hobbies.

"Please go back to work now," she said.

Instead of "Yes, ma'am," Walwyn said, "I'm very observant, but I'll tell you one thing: I'm blind when it comes to men. Bobby said that if I loaned him money so he could make the last three payments to the jewelry store, he'd put my car payments on his Visa, and for three months he said he was doing it, but he wasn't, and they repo'd my car." She began to cry.

"I'm so sorry, I'm . . . That's awful. Did this just happen?"

"And I want to say one more thing: in the bathroom—when Brianna was adjusting her bra? She had a bird tattooed on her back, with its claws down like landing gear, a really big bird of prey inked in, whatever it was, which isn't normal."

"I'll speak to a friend who may be able to help, but in the meantime, please try to focus on your job, and we'll talk about this tomorrow. Can you do that?"

She nodded.

"That's good. I appreciate it. Because the residents really do need our help. 'There's always someone worse off than you are' is an old saying, but it's good to remember."

The light had changed during what had seemed like an interminable conversation. At dusk, the solar lights came on, though the spotlights aimed down from the building lit large areas brightly. The solar lights were a nice touch, though—a good idea of George Matts's—a nod in the direction of energy conservation.

The pharmacy would be making a late-night visit, bringing antibiotics for Mrs. Sewell's UTI. There was a message from the psychiatrist's office, saying that the doctor would be in the next day to assess Dorcas ("I insist you call me Dorcas"), who'd been picking her nose until it bled. Someone from the water filtration company would also arrive. There was a request from the daughter of one resident to please call, and one from Sturgis, asking if she knew why they couldn't get HBO. Chandler's would deliver Mr. Montgomery's birthday cake the next day at 11 a.m., but they'd called to double-check the spelling of his name. *QUEST ANSWERED*, she read, in Brianna's unmistakable handwriting.

This reminded her how upsetting it had been when Sturgis defaced a book. He was about four years old, by all indications headed toward being taller and sturdier than his father. He'd started complaining that all he had were "baby books." Then she found two missing books under his bed, one with whorls of ink and cross-hatching across many pages, but *Babar*—she'd been shocked. He'd gone through the entire book and cut off Babar's trunk, page after page, with (she later found out) her manicure scissors.

"George, Harriet's going to think I'm cruel, keeping you here all this time. Why don't you stop and get her something nice on the way home, like a brownie from the bakery, or some flowers?"

"If I bought those things, it would be for my fiancée, not my mother!"

You'd think he'd spent his life reading Jane Austen novels. Love, love, love. He'd have to look farther afield than the staff if he intended to actually marry one day. But, as her own mother always said, there was someone for everyone. It was difficult to look at George standing there, grinning as if there was something to be happy about. He *did* have big teeth, and his posture was awful, with those shoulders hunched all the more as he struggled to walk in his soft cast, so she could understand why Brianna had transformed him into a gorilla.

What a strange world it had turned into. She had a repetitive dream it had taken her a long time to figure out—in fact, it had been a kaleidoscope she picked up in a gift store that made it come into focus—the shards of the dream bits and pieces of a bigger puzzle, shifting, rearranging, one last fragment moving into place. What she'd realized was that she was occupying her husband's vision, as if she could see what he'd seen in the seconds when he was falling off the roof: bits of tree streaking down oblongs of green, the flash of a red wheelbarrow, as the birds lifted off from somewhere within the nested pick-up-sticks colors. How amazing that she'd been locked in her husband's head.

She gave LaTanya, the second shift nurse, some quick information, saying that under no circumstances should Ms. Ott be given a glass of grapefruit juice, because it couldn't be taken with her medication. Also, though it seemed to have resolved itself, Mr. King had experienced eye spasms earlier in the day; the eye was bloodshot, though his blood pressure was normal, and the doctor had been called.

George had left, finally. Good. He spent too much time there. He was too helpful, and of course his being at ease with her meant that he talked all the time. She keyed in the code that would open the side door. The light came on automatically when she pushed the door open. On the way out of the parking lot, looking in the rearview mirror as she backed up, she saw George talking to Trudy . . . no, to Nola Mae, on the pathway that led to the permanently locked door near Mr. King's room.

At the second traffic light, a funny feeling came over her. What had the two of them been doing, standing there out of sight? Frightening, recurring dreams of falling, premonitions—it wasn't just Walwyn; *she* was starting to feel great anxiety.

She passed Settle Tire where she went every spring for her free tire rotation. Around the corner from the intersection was Milli Joe, where the younger staff liked to go for coffee, though they'd have done well to save their money, rather than spending it on expensive drinks with added shots of this and that, and transparent domes clamped over piles of whipped cream.

No one knew she was augmenting George's salary partly out of her paycheck, as well as from the ample supply of petty cash for all the supplies he needed to buy and sometimes for his transportation back to his mother's, if the weather was bad. Even Harriet wasn't really aware of how he'd been hired. All she knew was that George had a job, and that he had Stacey to thank for it. That part was true. Nobody needed to know. He was an enormous help. Without him, there would have been higher repair bills, no question. That little boy who'd focused his energy with so much determination on his Rubik's cube had become a man adept at problem solving, in spite of other limitations. When Stacey was being interviewed for the job at Solace House, she'd run into his neurologist—a doctor she'd met in passing during the long time Ches was in rehab, then again a year or so later, outside a little church in Keswick, for the blessing of the hounds.

She'd gone there with a friend, a *National Geographic* photographer whose wife kept horses and was about to ride in the hunt. The neurologist caught her eye and she'd smiled, raising a hand in greeting. A moment later he walked over, and she introduced the two men. How, exactly, had the conversation turned to George . . . she couldn't remember. Then they'd had a little chat, though of course he couldn't really talk about a patient. Her own uncle (now deceased) had been one of the doctors who were at the university hospital when the ambulance brought in Christopher Reeve after his horse riding accident. He'd never even mentioned it to his wife, who told him about the awful accident as she was reading the next day's *Daily Progress*. Reeve's fall from the horse had left him paralyzed. Stacey supposed doctors being tight-lipped gave you a good feeling about confidentiality, though she thought it would be naïve to believe there was any profession devoid of gossip.

"How are *you* doing, how are things with you?" the neurologist had asked.

She'd said she supposed she'd been spending too much time at home. Even Ches was urging her to go back to work.

"Have you heard about Solace House?" he'd asked. "No? An assisted-living or full-care facility, but it was started by women, and it's inclined toward slightly more alternative medicine—massage and acupressure. My sister, who's just relocated her practice here from West Linn, put me on to them. It's owned by a private company out of Seattle. There are three or four in that general area, but this will be the first one on the East Coast. Though I have to admit, they were rethinking things, until my sister spoke up for the town. She majored in archaeology at UVA. Went to graduate school in psychology."

The horn was blown and the riders rode off, the dogs, frantic to join the action, still held on strong leashes by two teenage boys dressed in beige corduroy suits.

"How nice that you're both in the same town."

"It is. I never thought that would happen. But her becoming a therapist didn't surprise me. She was always inclined that way."

She should say goodbye, she knew—several times he'd held up a hand to greet someone—but her friend was still busily photographing. Now the dogs had been released.

"I was hinting about my sister," he said.

"What do you mean?"

"I think you two would get along. I'd see her myself, if I wasn't her brother. She was extremely jealous when I was born. You know what she used to do? Apparently, I slept very soundly, and she'd stuff wads of chewing gum in my nostrils. I guess it's good she didn't have a similar plan for my mouth. Do you have siblings?"

"An older brother," she said. "What's your sister's name?"

"I was hoping you'd ask," he said, reaching for his wallet. He pulled out one of his own business cards. *Anne Jackson Johnsforth*, he wrote on the back, adding a telephone number below that.

And now, in half an hour, she'd be seated in one of Anne Jackson Johnsforth's leather club chairs, telling her that she didn't seem to be able to prevail as an authority figure to the staff, and that one person in particular was doing something that was upsetting the aides and that she, personally, worried might draw negative attention toward Solace House. What could she do about someone who'd appropriated the residents and used them, in their new guises as talking animals, to suggest that the animals had taken over the jungle—that would be Solace House—so that the beak-nosed, long-clawed, bushy-tailed residents, who were needy, cloying, ancient, and oblivious, were the ones in control?

Though, as so often happened during these sessions, she was inclined to lapse into talking about George. Now she felt there was reason to worry about him, because . . . she'd seen him talking to Ms. Tazewell's daughter, standing on a path? This was because she had ambient anxiety. So many people seemed to be acting strangely, everyone seemed so frayed. And she had an excellent job. Really, she shouldn't let herself become preoccupied with the young women's squabbles, their gossip, their litany of urban legends and superstitions. It was just so disheartening that they operated under the sway of misunderstandings and misperceptions and biblical references that didn't remotely resemble anything you'd learn reading the Bible.

Stacey found a parking place on the roof of the parking garage and took the elevator to ground level, to walk to CVS and pick up Ches's prescription. A musician with wild red hair and an electric guitar was playing music outside New Dominion bookstore, with a fishbowl at his feet. Good heavens, a goldfish swimming around! and a dish atop the bowl for tips. There was a keyboard to his left, where an Asian man stood holding a tambourine, a harmonica clamped in a holder around his neck. "Thank you kindly," the red-haired musician said. "Our next one comes from the late, great band Marah: 'Angels of Destruction!'"

Only a few people stood nearby, including a young woman holding her hand over one ear and ducking her head to talk on her phone. She had the stance of one of those crazy news reporters who went out in hurricanes to broadcast live. The other two people didn't seem to know each other, though they might just have been practicing social distancing. A girl wearing a jacket with a bull's-eye on the back swayed and smiled appreciatively—maybe the musician's girlfriend, or it might have been boyfriend; on second glance, Stacey was probably looking at a very fine-featured man. A teenager in a logo-less baseball cap leaned against a big, empty planter that Godzilla would have had trouble moving, let alone a few scrawny fraternity boys. The building where Bashir had had his restaurant was closed—a real loss to Charlottesville. So many storefronts had FOR LEASE signs in their windows. The teenager looked impassive: probably stoned, considering the twitchy finger movements of one hand as he clasped a Pepsi in the other. *"Here we go, it's just around the corner . . ."*

Youth.

She continued on, past Timberlake's where her mother had liked to meet friends. They'd sit at tables in the back after having bought stamps at the post office, trying to remember the name of the historical novel they wanted to buy at New Dominion, where a big poster was always on display in the front window of John Grisham, staring out with those amazing eyes, at the perfect level to connect with yours. The posters changed, but they were always shiny and intriguing; he either crowded the camera lens or it crowded him. Every time he published a new book, he generously went into the store off-hours to sign copies.

She went into CVS, walked to the back, and said hello to her friend the pharmacist—long ago, they'd been in the same book group at what had then been Anita's house. She'd died, and after living alone for many years, Robert Anderson, her husband, a well-known doctor, had moved out to Ivy, rather abruptly retiring. That was the opposite of what most widowers would do; they moved *into* town when they were alone. She should call on Dr. Anderson, she really should. She added a box of Junior Mints to her purchase, as well as a container of Carmex so tiny that even the occupants of a dollhouse would have wondered how its ointment could be apportioned so that everyone could have a pinhead-sized dot. She'd long ago given up on lipstick. Now lipsticks were called things like #35, but her mother's favorite color had been Revlon's "Cherries in the Snow." She could remember a time when she'd wanted to be a grown-up just so she could wear that lipstick. Lipstick seemed so alluring, until it didn't. Imagine not even having a tube in her purse (or now a *crayon*), only Kiehl's lip balm, sunk below the face masks and tissue packets, the keys, pens, and mini-notebook, the brush, the eye drops, the eyeglass wipes, the bottles of medicine, the B12 gummies, the Eucerin sunblock, and reams of CVS coupons as long as the rolls of toilet paper her first boyfriend had loved to plunk down on the aerial of his father's car, so they could watch them unfurl as he drove fast at night on back roads. Jerry Joe had been his name. She always lost her lip balm, Sturgis lost receipts (well, he didn't *take* them), and Ches inevitably lost his guitar picks—though he hadn't played since his accident. No one in her family mislaid anything; they lost it. All of them simply assumed that once something went missing, it was never to be found.

Anita had said to her once—dear Anita, always so forthcoming— "I can well imagine what it would have been like to stop after one child, but Robbie grew up Catholic in Charleston, so, you know, he never could."

Stacey ate the candy as she strolled along. It was horribly, thrillingly sweet. The musicians were gone. There was no trace of them, though she had to give them credit: they really had managed to sound calamitously chaotic and wild.

It was windier. She closed the candy box and dropped it into her purse, fingertips touching her phone. She could call George

Matts. Why not put her mind at rest? She feared that he wouldn't pick up, though—he just did not seem able to adjust his phone so he'd hear the ring—and, sure enough, that was the case. She tried once more from the car, pulling to the side after she exited the parking garage. To her relief, he answered. She didn't want to seem intrusive, as if it was her right to know his whereabouts, so she asked if a key ring that had been left at the nurses' station was his. No, it wasn't. She heard background noise, and—déjà vu—realized it was the same song she'd heard on the way to CVS, playing at earsplitting volume. "Where are you?" she asked, knowing it was none of her business.

He said he was at Entropy. "It's a new performance space in Belmont. Hey, you should come over. There's a show of Brianna's art. It's pretty strange."

"You have a good time," she said. "I have to get home."

"I might be breaking my engagement," he said.

"Oh, George," was all she could manage. She agreed with her therapist: the whole *engagement* routine might have been tongue-in-cheek on his part. Maybe she shouldn't underestimate his having a little in-joke with himself that, yes, also made him feel like one of the players.

"Okay, see you," he said. Whatever was said next, before he hung up, was drowned out by what had to be a much larger band.

It was Chinese takeout night at their house. Not exactly an incentive to rush home. Maybe she'd Google Entropy, find out how difficult it would be to stop by after her therapy session. Really, it had come to this? Planning something for the moment you left therapy as a delaying tactic, instead of going home, that you'd talk about the next time you were in therapy?

Google provided a photograph of Entropy's exterior. The brick building was wrapped in caution tape. No, she saw, as she turned the phone horizontally, the yellow tape was painted on. There was enough droop, enough crisscrossing to look convincing, but it was trompe l'oeil tape.

At her age, with the responsibilities she had, going to such a place?

She told herself that she'd drive home directly after her session with Anne ended, stir-fried beef be damned. By skipping Entropy, she wouldn't need to reveal that, yet again, she was concerned about George Matts.

It was obvious why she kept worrying: She felt sorry for Harriet, and even sorrier for George. Also, though it was painful to think, even as changed as George was after the terrible accident, he remained the Good Son, who tried hard to do his best, and who'd retained his manners throughout the long ordeal and come out the other side smiling.

The office was simply furnished, though there were boxes of Kleenex in two places and a pile of throws in case you felt cold. Until the faulty ductwork was altered, the new addition was doomed to stay cold.

Anne greeted her in a turtleneck sweater and black pants. She bought her shoes at Scarpa: expensive in proportion to how understated they were. She wore no jewelry except a gold wedding band.

What would it be like to have Anne as a sister? No wonder her brother was glad she'd moved to Charlottesville. She seemed sincere, rather than professionally sincere. Her husband had come up with the idea that she could work from home, if they sacrificed the garage. He'd had a carport constructed.

So here she was, in the therapist's office again, trying to figure out coping strategies for dealing with anxious, impressionable, often ill-informed young women with whom she had little in common, except—and this was a big exception—that they were all women. This, while seated in a converted garage with potpourri hidden somewhere, and a lighting fixture dropped so fashionably low from the ceiling, she had to shift her position several times to block out the light. They'd already agreed not to discuss the décor, which was a delaying tactic.

Anne waited for her to speak.

Stacey remained silent. How would she explain what Walwyn had told her about her friend's seeing a large bird tattoo on Brianna's back, crisscrossed with wires. *Actual* wires.

"We were talking, last time, about some concerns you felt about leaving your husband alone. Is that something we should revisit?"

"We could, but I know I have to do my job at Solace and proceed with my life, that that's best for both of us. I'm wondering if I could describe something that happened earlier today, though, that I don't think I responded to properly."

Anne nodded.

"Your shoes are lovely," Stacey said.

"Thank you," Anne replied. Legs crossed, she did not move her foot even slightly.

"I think when I leave I'm going to stop at a place in Belmont on the way home. I was invited . . . I was going to say that a friend invited me, but the friend was George. About whom I've had a lot to say already, I realize. Anyway, there's some sort of, I don't know what you'd call it, *real understanding* these girls have. I find it heartening that they're quite compassionate: they go on outings with him; Trudy's cooked him some of his favorite things as his foot is healing. They're even willing to wear a ring and not contradict him when he says they're engaged—though I understand, I can see the downside of that—but in their way, they're very respectful of him." She paused. Anne maintained eye contact. She said, "What I was about to say is that they assume I'm in on the . . . whatever you'd call it, this little pretense, that pleases him so much—though I don't know that they, or I, am doing the right thing at all."

"Why might it not be right?"

"It's condescending, isn't it? I mean, he's the only one not in on the game."

"Is that the correct word, *game?*"

"I don't really see it as a game, no. You know what I mean, though. He's made us, well, he hasn't *made us* do anything, but I guess in trying to be kind, we've been complicitous, and I'm not sure that's helpful, but if it isn't, I'm not sure how to handle it. They—the girls—tell me things I really don't want to hear, rather intimate things—it's back to my problem of not knowing how to assert my authority, because what really worries me is that I don't think I understand them."

"Can you give an example of what you don't understand?"

"I don't know. I just feel that there's some disconnect. I hear what they're saying, but it's so often based on things like superstition and astrology. They're like horses spooked by seeing a cat or something."

Anne waited.

"They haven't gotten a good education. They're empathetic, they're more tolerant than I was at their age, but they're doing their jobs thinking that Trump's a strong, effective president who has their best interests in mind. I don't know how to talk to people who think that. And I have no idea what a tattoo of an eagle, or anyway some huge bird tattooed on Brianna's back, means. And I'm told she was wearing a wire."

"Brianna who's writing the graphic novel?"

Stacey nodded. She said, "I don't know what an eagle's supposed to symbolize now, since I don't even know what the flag symbolizes anymore. And you have to read those rainbow lawn signs carefully, because they're coded: WE SUPPORT OUR POLICE actually negates BLACK LIVES MATTER."

"Go on," Anne said.

"She says Brianna's listening in on private conversations—I saw some of the pages when the girls kept them long enough to show them to me; Walwyn's exactly right. Brianna's drawing the residents as talking animals. Maybe she means it to be humorous, I don't know. But it's so insensitive: the residents are hugely exaggerated in terms of their dementia and obliviousness. One of our residents can play Chopin perfectly from memory. You can't—"

"An apologue," Anne said.

"What?"

"A satiric text in which the characters appear as animals."

"I didn't know there was a word for that."

Anne nodded. She said, "You feel justifiably protective of people in your care, who have a right to privacy and who are being disparaged."

"I do. What if she brings us all down?"

"How would she do that?"

"By making everyone look stupid and laughable."

Anne nodded. "As we've said before, this is the moment when Gabriel Byrne would say, 'Mm.'"

"You're trying to add a note of levity because you think I'm too upset. But it's my job."

"Understood. Are you concerned that someone is doing something transgressive, or is it more an issue of not being sure how to proceed?"

"I used to blunder more. I feel like that was better than the way I'm functioning now. I'm uncomfortable listening to crazy imaginings and paranoia, but they're my staff. They're trying hard. You can't imagine how difficult their jobs are sometimes. Some of them grew up in awful circumstances. I mean, *they* don't like to be afraid, but it's not like they're not used to it. Their entire lives to this point—"

"How do you feel the Effexor is working for you?"

"Does it piss you off that you have to ask a doctor to write a prescription?"

"No," Anne said.

"How do I feel it's doing?" Stacey echoed. "I want to be able to do my job, I feel perfectly equipped to do that, but something's stopping me. All of them want to take me aside. I couldn't possibly let them talk as long as they wanted and still function effectively. I feel like a stand-in for their mothers, or the mothers they wanted to have, which is so ironic because my own son wants me to vanish—at least, if I get HBO before I disappear. I think I'm the one who's not well adapted. Maybe they're right: I should worry more; I should ask more questions."

"Can you think of someone you know who's better adapted?"

"I assume everybody! My husband accepts his limitations. Sturgis is a mystery to both of us, but he's not a drug addict, he's not getting stopped for DUIs, he's not robbing banks, he just avoids us entirely, the way dogs have radar for avoiding skunks."

Anne raised her eyebrows. A little higher, and they might have reached mid-forehead.

"Oh, god," Stacey said, covering her face with her hands. "Okay, so I think of myself as a skunk. That is *so embarrassing*."

"Mm," Anne said. "Since we're nearing the end of our session—any last thoughts?"

"The whole time we were talking, I didn't say clearly enough that to avoid going home, I'm going to a place I didn't know existed, where I'm sure the only person I'll know will be George. I'll be the oldest person there, and I don't have any idea what's motivating me."

"Okay. We can pick up there next time."

Anne stood.

"Thanks," Stacey said, still embarrassed about her revealing faux pas.

"Stacey. An unprofessional warning: if it's the place I'm thinking of, the DEA has their eyes on it. Last week an altercation there was kept out of the paper. Just a word of caution."

"A fight?"

"I don't know the specifics. I wasn't there," Anne said, holding open the door. "See you next week."

STILL, SHE WENT.

She drove through a quagmire of streets, some partially closed with traffic cones, one-way, dead-end. It gave her time to rethink what she was doing, but she felt so lucky to see a car pulling away from the curb that she nosed her car in to make sure the place was hers, instead of pulling forward to parallel park.

Belmont: funky, gritty Belmont, newly fashionable. Now there were chic, expensive condos in the Woolen Mills—never mind how many times that area had flooded. From somewhere, a line intruded on her thoughts: *"God gave Noah the rainbow sign / No more water but fire next time."*

People as young as she'd expected were standing around outside Entropy by the time she'd walked the four blocks back, raising her mask at the last minute. There were two guys in bow ties she'd seen somewhere before—there were always such duos in

Charlottesville—so thin, their pants with suspenders were ludicrous. Some part of her hoped that George had come and gone. She could play armchair shrink with herself and realize that she felt frustrated in her relationship with Sturgis, so George had become, for her, the better son.

Few people were wearing masks. It would be safer if more people wore them, but there was nothing she could do about that.

She resolved to drink nothing, because cops loved to hover in Belmont near the confusing configuration of streets near Mas. The last thing she needed was to be picked up for drunk driving. So here she was, in another situation about which she was too smart not to be skeptical. Why did she find it so amazing that her therapist would be wearing four- or five-hundred-dollar shoes? There were thousand-dollar shoes. Two-thousand-dollar shoes. If she could dismiss Anne as one of those stereotypical, throw-the-assertion-back-to-the-client-and-let-them-psychoanalyze-themselves shrinks (which she wasn't), she could have been turned off by the whole process and quit, but Anne always exhibited just enough humor to remain human, even if she did wear expensive shoes. Maybe that was what you paid for magic slippers these days. Forget shopping at Belk. The whole Fashion Square Mall was nearly empty, closing to become, what? More condos. A tech company. A billionaire's new home, with a landing pad on the roof.

At a quick glance, she was the oldest person there by at least ten years. She quickly dismissed her dire scenario of one drink leading to her being pulled over and made to walk the line, after which she'd be taken to jail to be bailed out by—god, it was true:

Ches couldn't come. It would have to be Sturgis. She ordered a can of hard cider to sip, instead of a glass of wine she couldn't resist finishing.

An item was being raffled. A tall girl wearing black tights, platform shoes, and a miniskirt, her little tee draped with an enormous camouflage jacket that fell below the hem, picked a ticket out of an ice bucket. "Number forty-two!" she called, bending her knees deeply and straightening up again, because she couldn't jump in such shoes.

"I got it, I got it!" another girl hollered. People clapped her on the back and cleared the way. She was handed a stuffed lion at least the size of a golden retriever, with a zippered stomach that held pajamas printed with a jungle scene: its umbilical cord.

Inside, the building was larger than it looked. In one corner she saw a jungle motif: fake trees in pots; stars projected onto the roof-sky. *"In the jungle, the mighty jungle, the lion sleeps tonight,"* someone sang in falsetto, as another musician jumped onstage amid flashing lights, to play the last few notes on the electric keyboard. More applause, the lucky winner's hands raised above her head in triumph. She lowered her mask, smiling a big smile before dropping her arms and clapping madly for herself.

Stacey swallowed a stinging sip of cider. A drum roll. Then the second prize was announced, though the crowd was already bored and began talking over the announcer: a white angora hat, "made by nuns," was handed down to *"Num*-ber twenty-three!" by—good heavens: by Nola Mae! Her hair did indeed have a single, bright-pink stripe down the middle. Number 23, a man with a head the size of a volleyball, handed the hat to his girlfriend, who pulled it on to a ripple of applause. "Last, but not least"—hardly anyone was listening—"two tickets to a performance of a play by Mr. Samuel Beckett, at our nearby university theater. And if you already know you can't endure that, the tickets can be traded to our bartender"—a whistle; applause—"who'll take them in exchange for shaking up two delicious Super Cosmos, garnished with a leaf of lemon verbena. Okay, give it up for . . . number five! Number five: *Ladies and gentlemen, LGBTQ sisters, brothers, and non-binary citizens, including any and all personal pronouns* . . . Where, oh, where is number five?" The keyboard player pounded the electric piano. "Last call, number five!"

There was a sound from the back, by the bar. It was a baby, crying. "What's that you say, my good man, you're the winner, but you lost your ticket?" The baby was screaming so loud, it began to choke. The bartender had run out from behind the bar. All music stopped. Word began to spread:

Blood.

"*Somebody had a baby in the bathroom,*" the bartender said. "*Oh, man. Oh, wow.*"

"I'm a medical student," a young woman shouted through her mask, pushing through the crowd. "Call an ambulance!"

"I already did call an ambulance!"

"Where's the mother?"

"*Okay, everybody, chill.*"

"What's he saying? Is it the bartender's baby?"

"No, he found it."

"He found it where?"

"That's not a real baby. I saw it. It's not real, people."

"Give me your phone."

"I'm with her, she's second-year. I assure you, she'll have this situation . . ."

"Why doesn't the mother come out of the bathroom? What the fuck!"

"Don't we need a real doctor?"

"Nobody gives birth and runs off thirty seconds later. Not in the history of the world, man."

"What's he saying?"

"The woman's bleeding in the bathroom. That's why he's holding the baby."

The man who was with the second-year medical student was doing a pietà with the bartender, who'd either passed out, or nearly passed out.

"Is the baby okay, is it?"

"Sirens. Hear them?"

People were rushing out, carrying their coats rather than putting them on.

"At least half the people here called 911, *duh.*"

"What's the deal? Where did the bartender get the baby?"

"That poor baby."

"What's the matter with the bartender, did somebody shoot him?"

Stacey stood absolutely still. The conversation around her was like a brushfire. Had someone been with the woman to cut the umbilical cord? It was crazy-making, everybody speaking at once. Who was with the woman who'd just given birth, the medical student? A lot of people had run for the front door—even more, at the first sound of distant sirens—but a few women had rushed toward the bathroom. People in motion were silent; the people wondering aloud were the only ones talking. She hadn't had to say she was a nurse. At her age, she was invisible. She was there, but not there. She was already rehearsing a story with herself, noticing things but insisting on the refrain that she wasn't there. It made no sense whatsoever that she'd come to such a place, so, no, she hadn't. She'd even told George earlier that she had to go home. She could have stepped forward, but she'd assumed it was a prank—that she was the one out of sync; what had happened seemed not exactly impossible, but more likely something was happening that she had no way to assess—though, every time the baby cried, it was proof she'd been mistaken about that.

The ambulance had arrived. Number 42 could be seen from behind, running out into the street with her lion clasped under one arm. Stacey turned to see that George had drifted to her side, holding Nola Mae's hand, both of them wide-eyed. The medical school student was holding the infant. Time stopped, though people began to whisper, and for a few seconds, Lady Gaga's voice filled the room: *"In the sha-hah-dows,"* then nothing. Her voice was gone. The EMT team was moving through the room in speeded-up time. People jumped out of the way.

"Where's the mother?"

"In the bathroom. A friend of hers is in there with her."

"I saw about a dozen women go in."

"*Step back.*"

She was a nurse. This was not the reaction she'd thought she would have. She was absolutely failing to be a responsible adult, in George Matts's eyes.

"Cops!" a man shouted.

"I've got number five," a man in a tunic said. "I thought it said eight, but it's five."

People were pulling on their coats and rushing out. The bartender, who'd been helped to a barstool where he sat clutching his head, had been recruited for the evening by his boss, Tom, who'd passed on the opportunity to pinch-hit when he got the call ("What the fuck! I *own* Simpatico, why would they call me to bartend? But if you want to make some extra cash, Jonah? Be my guest"). The bartender stood upright again, without the stranger's hand weighing down his shoulder; he grabbed the edge of the bar, only to lean on a button that sent stars swirling, crazily speeded up, a seizure-inducing light show for any epileptics. The cops and the EMTs were in a huddle around the medical student, who was splattered with blood, though she seemed to have quieted the baby.

"Stand back, please. Give 'em space," a man hollered, as two men with a stretcher raced in. There was a lot of confusion as the all-male team rushed toward the bar. The medical student holding the baby really did not want to relinquish it. The baby's mother stood staring at the young woman holding the baby as if trying to see through a blinding snowstorm. The musicians were scrambling to pack up. There were many policemen inside, only a few of them masked, asking questions.

"The cord was cut," someone said.

Stacey understood. She didn't know if the woman who'd given birth had been caught by surprise—unlikely, but not impossible—or whether for some reason she'd intended to deliver her baby in the restroom; this was sad, shocking, but not unprecedented. It seemed so disturbing that people never stopped speculating, when what had happened was so obvious.

Two cops were talking to the bartender. Where was the baby's mother, did he know? "Over there," he said. He was a waiter at Simpatico, he wasn't even a real bartender. He'd almost invited his friend Alia to join him, but he'd held off because it seemed better to see her at the end of the evening.

When Sturgis had told her Ches had fallen off the roof, she'd said whatever she said, there in the ER, though she couldn't hear herself talking because she'd gone deaf. She'd heard what her son said, but as he spoke, the whole world had gone silent.

More sirens. A woman with a corgi on a leash stood in the doorway, trying to gauge whether it was okay to walk in. Two perplexed women carrying guitar cases made their way past her into the club, one with flowing white hair, the other with the hair of a bristly hedgehog and rings in her nostril. "Hey, what's the story?" she asked no one in particular.

Who are they, who are those women? I dunno, there were supposed to be a lot of acts tonight. It's a fundraiser, I think. A fundraiser for what? I don't know. I've never been here before. That lady's one of the singers?

Yeah, that would be my guess. And that's the bartender——the one who found the baby? Yeah, where you been, bro? Door locked on me. I was having a little snort outside.

The musicians were the Daring Darlings, from Nashville, none too happy that their Ford Explorer had overheated, so they'd had to cab it from the Omni. Hedgehog was pissy, asking where the manager was. "A baby was born in the bathroom," a girl in a red leather jacket said. "What?" the white-haired woman exclaimed. "What the fuck?"

It's already posted. Look, it's on Instagram. It's the baby. The baby's trending. She's a social media star. Look at all the likes! Are we sure it's a girl baby? The medical student said it was. What are they saying? The baby's on Instagram.

The next day's *Daily Progress* headline was already being redone. How was she not going to tell Ches? Though if she did, how would she explain her presence there? She looked at her watch and was amazed: little more than half an hour had passed, from the moment she entered. Complete chaos in Belmont, where Ches's first cousin Lou had once owned a vacuum repair shop and eaten two doughnuts for breakfast every day at Spudnuts. Ches probably didn't even know the area had been so transformed. What could she tell him? That she'd been worried about George, and that after her therapy, she'd driven there to see if she could give him a ride home because of his painful foot? Though none of that was a lie, she could imagine how odd it would sound.

Now more police were circulating, asking to see the manager, asking people to point out the bartender. On her way out——yes;

like a ghost, she could just float out into the night—Stacey saw the goldfish on the stage, its bowl sitting in a tangle of wires. It was an accident waiting to happen. A young woman turned toward her to ask, "Don't you work at Solace House?" *Caught*. Stacey didn't recognize her, but hers was a job in which she was highly visible, while the visitors' faces melded together. "I'm LaTanya's sister. We talked last winter when I dropped off her boots and umbrella, when it was snowing."

"I remember. She'd called a taxi, and I thought she'd walked to the corner to wait for it—"

"I told her, 'LaTanya, all you had to do was walk back to the Infirmary, and they'd have figured something out.'"

"I felt terrible when I found out she'd walked all the way home in the storm."

"Not on you. 'You didn't just go back? You know you coulda walked back there,' I told her, but I'm her baby sister, so she doesn't take my advice. This town closes up when snow starts falling."

Stacey was not going to dodge responsibility. She wasn't. There had been too many horrible slipups, with young women out on their own, never seen again. "I should have made sure she got safely into the cab," she said.

The musicians from Nashville walked past them, carrying their guitars. Hedgehog held the door open. They were gone.

"Wow. They must be pretty bummed. They came all the way from Nashville, I heard."

Stacey nodded. George Matts was walking in the front door. He was alone. Where was Nola Mae? Saying goodbye to LaTanya's sister, whose name she'd never asked, she walked toward George. She was about to ask him to please not say anything to Ches about her being there, when he said, "I'm sorry I got you into this. Don't tell my mother. Please don't tell her I was here."

"Let's not tell anyone," she said. "Let's have this be the first time in the history of the world a secret's kept. Do you think we can manage that? It would put us in the *Guinness World Records*."

"Yeah," he said. "With the man who ate the most grilled cheese sandwiches, and the person who walked the farthest distance on stilts."

He'd never lost his sense of humor. He had a sweet disposition, and he glowed when someone smiled at a witty remark. "I'll tell you another secret. Nola Mae had some pot, and I said I didn't want it, and she said she didn't want to get engaged, and she walked off."

All these women, marching off into the night.

It was on the tip of her tongue to say something, but she thought better of it. It seemed strangely like the inevitable conclusion to the evening.

"Did you ever do coke?" he asked.

The day had been full of questions: those asked, those implied, most unanswered, certainly this last question unanticipated.

"Once or twice, in a different life," she said.

They were almost outside when he said, "Wait. You've got to see Brianna's paintings. She's such a snob, she didn't even come. If they were mine, I would have been here. She told Nola Mae she was going to get five hundred copies of her book printed once she finished, then she was going to tweet it out, and get Seth Meyers's attention."

On stage, one man jostled another, who stumbled and knocked over the fishbowl. George hobbled sideways to avoid the spill, clearly making an effort not to mention his pain. It took all his concentration, she could see, but if she *had* pointed out the little tragedy of what had just happened, he would have found water for the bowl and tried to scoop up the fish, to put it back in. Then, being George, he'd have taken it home to his mother—though how he'd explain such an unwanted gift was as difficult to imagine as it was for her to think what she might say to Ches about where she'd spent the evening.

In front of them, three girls were laughing and whispering about the four paintings on display. The police were leaving. The remaining crowd began reconfiguring, already telling and revising the story of what had happened, someone filling in a detail, another person contradicting what was said. One of Sturgis's favorite singers, Alanis Morissette, was booming through the speakers: *"Well I'm here to remind you of the mess you left when you went away. . . ."* Sturgis could listen to and watch her for hours, invisible particles in her red lipstick magnetizing her to the microphone; then, in the next second, she'd be strutting across the desert in her white suit, tossing her lush hair extensions. It had to be that song, nothing else. That song, over and over.

Well, there they were, looming up in front of her, paintings much worse than the individual pages the aides had sneaked to her: ugly paintings almost interchangeable with graffiti, the one she was staring at an enormous rat with linguini-sized whiskers, addressing a group of cats, the rat saying, LET'S GO TO NEW YORK I HEAR THOSE OUTDOOR EATING PLACES ARE

GREAT AND WE CAN SCARE THE SHIT OUTA PEOPLE,
the cats huddled to talk among themselves: LET HIM GO, LET
HIM FIND OUT WHAT LIFE'S LIKE WITHOUT SOLACE.
Another mouse in the corner said: MY DAUGHTER'S COMING
TODAY TO EAT ME. The long-armed, hairy gorilla stood eating a banana—surely George must see the resemblance—saying,
COME IN LET ME OFFER SOLACE, the cat in the corner
saying, THIS IS THE WINTER SOLSTICE? Yes, it had been
much joked about that when Dorcas thought her daughter (poor
woman! her daughter lived in Alaska) was coming to take her
to a restaurant, she'd expressed that by saying her daughter was
coming to eat her. The other paintings were equally idiotic. Stacey located herself: her square jaw; the deep wrinkles creasing
her forehead; her admittedly unlovely ears enlarged into elephant
ears, as the gray beast lay on its back, hooves pointed at the sky.
A cartoon bubble extruding from its trunk had her saying to the
turtle beside her: MEAN DISPOSITION? I THOUGHT YOU
SAID MISSIONARY POSITION!

It had certainly turned into a hellish day.

"Kinda weird," George said.

She said nothing. Nothing in the painting of her had been over-
heard. It only implicitly criticized her worsening hearing and the
amount of weight she'd gained during Covid.

"You're my guardian angel. I wouldn't even know how to get
the bus from here," George said, as they walked out.

It seemed a minor miracle that they'd left Entropy behind them.
That they'd finally escaped. When Ches had been taken to the ER

after falling from the roof, there had been so much confusion, so many doctors, so many pieces of paper to hold or sign. Sturgis, all the while, had been as agitated as a carnival barker, so terrifying that he'd been ordered outside, or they'd call the police. But why was she reliving that?

"Another couple of blocks," she said. "Shall I get the car and come back for you?"

"I'm good," he said. "Brianna invited me to a wine tasting tomorrow. I'm not going, though. I don't drink anymore. What's that over there?"

"It looks like a cactus trimmed in lights."

"Cactus grow in Charlottesville?"

"It appears that they do. My friend who works for *National Geographic* did a piece once about cactus smugglers. They fly over the desert in helicopters and pull saguaros out of the ground. They don't even land, they just hover. When the cactus are uprooted, the way they're taken ends up killing half of them. It's obviously illegal. Plant landscapers buy them and sell them for thousands of dollars. One of the smugglers let my friend fly with him. Lights shone down from the helicopter; he said they lit the ground like a sports stadium, and lassoed one and flew it through the air. That seems more shocking, and much sadder, than anything Brianna was attempting in her so-called art. Though looking at it made me feel like what she'd really like would have been to remove our hearts. In spite of all those words, she'd have much preferred to pluck out our hearts."

George considered this. Several expressions passed over his face before he short-circuited. He said, "It makes me think of a song we sang in first grade. When Miss Wembly was my teacher. Do you know the rubber song?"

She didn't.

George cleared his throat a bit too loudly, then began to talk-sing: *"Just what makes that little old ant, think he'll move that rubber tree plant?"*

"Shut up, ya fuckin' drunks," a man shouted out the window of one of the houses.

George put his hand over his mouth to stifle a laugh. But what else would the man have thought? He must be used to drunks. That man was lucky, though he didn't know it, to have escaped the night's pandemonium.

It was true: It was over. They hadn't been there. It never happened. The baby was undoubtedly safe, however unwanted. She was pleased that on their way out, she'd turned back at the last moment, and on the paper provided for closed bids on the paintings she'd written—printing carefully in block letters, to make her handwriting as anonymous as possible—*FUCK YOU BRIANNA UGLY PERSON UGLY MIND*, then put the paper into the envelope, her tongue so dry she could barely lick the flap.

She beeped open the car. George got in with some effort, reaching out to lift his right leg in, gingerly settling his foot on the floor. She let her head fall back against the headrest, closing her eyes, as she wondered what her priest would think of her if he'd seen her note—he simply wouldn't have believed it, that was the answer. Then she sat upright and fumbled the key into the ignition. The car's overhead light had burned out. She'd asked Sturgis four times to replace it, but he hadn't. She didn't have time to go to the garage just to have it fixed. Also, she was proud of herself for not being a martyr and breaking her fingernails, as she had the other time.

"Do you ever think, *What if I didn't go home?*" he asked.

"We're still in secret mode?"

"Sure. We can just stay there, if you want."

"I confess, I thought that many times today, which is what led me into such a bizarre and upsetting evening," she said.

"It's got to be way better to have a husband than a mother," he said, after a long pause.

"George—you're *talking* to someone's mother."

They drove in silence for a while. Then he said, "I wasn't going to say anything, but Sturgis was outside tonight. He saw you. You'll get caught if you say you weren't there."

"What?" she said. "He was there?"

"Like I told you, I went outside to say goodbye to Nola Mae and she asked if I wanted to do some drugs, and I said no, and she walked off. He was getting out of a car with a couple friends. Guys who moved here from Alabama. They were with the Tiki Torchers, and it turned out they liked the town."

"Really!"

"One of them's still back in Alabama under house arrest for going out of state after failing to meet with his probation officer. I guess he figured, *What am I gonna say, that I'm going to Charlottesville to raise hell?* They ID'd him and put him on a Greyhound, shackled to some cop, or whatever he was. I never met him, but the other two are bad news."

"These men are Sturgis's friends?"

"Yeah. Trudy and I were walking to the mall to go to Miller's the night they were spray-painting *HERO* on the base of Lee's statue, this long after the protest."

"*Sturgis* was with them?"

"Yeah. You know, he thinks I'm a pussy. He only talks to me if you or my mother are around. I pretended not to see him, and he pretended not to see me. Trudy never met him, she was just all upset in general that vandals were defacing the statue of somebody her father kept a picture of, over their TV."

"You forgot to swear me to secrecy," she said, once she caught her breath.

"I thought we were already in secret mode."

"Oh. Right," she said. "But you're still taking a chance, thinking Sturgis's *mother* won't find some way to bring that up. My god. Not that I'm not glad you told me."

"I know you'll tell Ches, but please don't tell Sturgis I told you."

"I'm so sorry this is the way things are," she said.

"Well, you know Sturgis. He likes to stir things up. At least he finally got on the right side of things. He might have liked those Tiki Torchers the other time, but he didn't do anything but spray a bench when I saw him, and all he wrote was the f-word on the whatsit, the base of the statue."

"The plinth," she said.

She'd begun to talk silently to herself: *I'm driving the car*, she thought. *George is sitting in the passenger seat. I'm stopping for a red light.*

ANN BEATTIE

"I talked to some guys who work at Lowe's who are on call to haul Lee out of there. They're going to bring in cranes to lift the statue part off, sort of lassoing it like a cactus. Then I guess some other company's coming for the"—he paused—"the plink."

She almost spoke, but didn't. It had been a long night.

"Yeah. Because if they left that, people would be reminded of what was there. You know how his horse died?"

"You were telling Nola Mae. Didn't you say—"

"Traveller outlived his master. But it stepped on a nail in its stable and got tetanus and died. I walked all around that statue. That was one beautiful horse."

"Here we are," she said, coasting to the curb. No light shone in his mother's apartment. "George, we've got to stay friends forever, so I can drive and you can tell me what's going on in my life."

"Okay," he said. "Here's what happened. We were working late. That's what I'm telling my mother, if she even asks, which she probably won't. She doesn't like Trudy because she has a loud voice and she voted for Trump."

"Oh no," she said. "Is that true? She voted for Trump?"

"I don't let politics affect my love life," he said.

"Please, George, let's not talk about anything more, unless you have a surefire way of getting to sleep when you've been through a day like today—though if you do, I'd appreciate hearing about it."

"Two Tylenol PM," he said, "washed down with a cup of chamomile tea."

"I'll see you tomorrow," she said. "Prop up that foot. And you really should let the doctor know how much pain you're in. I'm worried that it might be infected." It was a soft cast; she could pull up under a streetlight and look at the foot. But she dismissed that idea. "The sooner any medical problem is dealt with, the better, even if it doesn't seem that way at the moment."

"What if he says there's something really wrong?"

"He'll tell you the truth," she said. "You've been through a lot worse than this, George."

"That's all foggy, though. It seems like it happened to some-body else."

None of this will ever be in that comic book, she thought, driving away. *No one can laugh at us because Brianna wouldn't have the slightest idea how to bug the car.* Such things were better left to MI5 and the Russians and to whoever became the next James Bond. Meanwhile, a rainbow flag flew from the building on the corner, and here she was, driving through the town about which it was said—more with envy than as a put-down—that it existed in a bubble. But in Lee Park, that bubble had popped—as had her own protective bubble—though the hot-air balloons, the big, inflated, gas-powered bubbles that dangled baskets in the sky, were a wonderful distraction from the present-day world. They'd still be launched to float across fields and houses and any remaining farmland, rising up, up, up. Those not faint of heart could take an aerial view of people-ants, rushing to and fro.

It wasn't easy to remain curious, as you got older. There were too many unhappy surprises. Still, if you did manage to retain even a slight sense of wonder, you could pay your money and take your chances. You could look down and think, *How vast it is. How green.*